I0721700

A SABOTAGED ESCAPADE

Triona Keane

Orla Kelly Publishing,
27 Kilbrody,
Mount Oval,
Rochestown,
Cork,
Ireland.

TABLE OF CONTENTS

For the memories that will never grow old,
this is for you Dad.

To girls like Jean and Maggie – may you always find a
friend to help you through the darkness.

CHAPTER 1

Maggie was a nervous wreck. She sat in her bosses' office butterflies of nerves threatening to engulf her and force her to throw up. She definitely felt queasy but she did her best to ignore it and decided to distract herself by taking in her surroundings. Looking around the big spacious office, she marveled at the litany of colour as opposed to the usual white-washed walls that often dominated big offices. She urgently needed her boss to agree to her proposition and she wasn't entirely sure how he would react. In her minds' eye, she had imagined all sorts of scenarios including one where he lost his temper and Maggie found herself chuckling as it was so unlikely.

Maggie chastised herself for day dreaming and brought her attention back to the present. Now, Mr. Barreton, her boss, sat before her briefing her on the days' headlines and outlining the stories that he wanted her to target. In other words, the stories he thought her capable of. They mainly concerned the latest health research or case studies on families/individuals living with health ailments. She was fresh out of college and aiming for Health Correspondent after all.

"There is alarming new evidence on the obesity epidemic suggesting that seven percent of nine year old children are obese. I would like you to conduct a little research and draft an article on it for tomorrow afternoon if that's alright?" Mr. Barreton began, an air of authority creeping into his dulcet tones.

Maggie searched desperately for an opening, even a whiff of an opportunity to speak to him about Nepal, but it just didn't seem to come. She struggled to understand why she felt as hesitant as she did, it wasn't like her. Mr. Barreton powered on full steam ahead intent on clarifying the workload for the next two days.

"No longer than 3,000 words; let's keep it concise and to the point" he continued on. His voice more business like than usual. "Any questions?"

He had that envious ability to command a situation with ease, an innate flair for managing the extraordinary. His larger than life presence dominated any room that he entered. It was this ability that drew people to him like a magnet and rendered him so successful in his field.

Maggie took matters into her own hands and seized her moment. This was her golden opportunity and she didn't intend on wasting it.

"That's fine, Mr. Barreton, I do have one quick question," she began, thinking fast, trying to choose her words carefully, assimilating her thoughts in an orderly fashion. "I want to travel to Nepal for six weeks this summer and I was hoping to use all of my annual leave together to facilitate it. Would that be okay with you?"

There. She had said it. She didn't know why she was blowing this all out of proportion. It wasn't like she was asking to take over the newspaper company. Plus, Maggie was one of the fortunate few that actually liked her boss. He was a plump man in his forties looking every inch the prime candidate for a heart attack. On his round face sat a pair of oversized spectacles framing kindly blue eyes complete with rapidly balding hairline. Maggie had always maintained a good working relationship with him. He was a fair boss and always did his best to accommodate his employees. This would be the ultimate test of his generosity.

Now, Maggie searched his face for a reaction, even the tiniest insight into his thought processes, but his expression was quite unreadable. At last, he spoke with the immortal words. "Maggie, I think that's a fantastic idea, take the six weeks and go exploring."

Maggie sat in her chair rooted to the spot, hardly daring to believe her luck. Relief washed over her and she permitted herself to relax. What she had neglected to tell him was that the trip was in fact already booked, her accommodation in the volunteer house all organised. She had one last obstacle to overcome but she was confident she could pull that one off. After Mr. Barreton had made a few pleasant enquiries, she made to leave the office.

"Thank you, Mr. Barreton, I really appreciate it." she said now, genuinely grateful for the support he had shown her.

"And Maggie, be careful out there." he said, gazing at her with a look of concern in his eyes.

"I will." Maggie managed to reply before getting up from her chair and exiting the office.

Ever since the brainwave of volunteering in Nepal had usurped her, she had been swept along on a tidal wave of excitement and anticipation. It had been a childhood dream of hers to travel out to a third world country. She wanted to go hiking in the Himalayas. She wanted to experience first-hand the culture and ritual traditions of a different world, a world far removed from her own. Humans had always fascinated her. But most of all, she wanted to help those less fortunate than herself. Maggie knew she was lucky to be born into a privileged family and she had always wanted to give something back. When she had stumbled across the brochures advertising volunteering trips in Nepal, it had been a done deal for her. A no-brainer. She had never wanted to do anything more in her life.

She'd always been an outcast, she guessed. While her best friend Jean always fit right in anywhere she went. Maggie had never had anything much in common with their peers. Charisma was not a word that could be used to describe her for she didn't have much of it. But what she did have was a steely determination and inner resolve to get what she wanted. It had taken her a long time to accept but the older she got, the more she realised it was worth its weight in gold. While girls her own age were preoccupied with the latest fashion trends and material items, she had learned to value the more important things in life like family and friends, a long time ago. She had learned these valuable lessons the hard way she supposed.

Now entranced in a state of euphoria, she quickly fished her phone out of her bag and dialed Jean's number. She was damned if she was going to travel to Nepal by herself. She decided to begin by paying Jean a few compliments, she always responded well to praise. Jean picked up after three rings

"Hello?"

"Hi Jean, how are you? Great game on Saturday, you really won that match for the team," Maggie tried. She hadn't a clue about basketball really or any sport for that matter but she knew Jean would appreciate the compliment. Desperately hoping her efforts weren't futile she tried to search her brain for something more convincing to say. At last, she found it. "That three-pointer you scored was superb," continued Maggie while silently berating herself for her poor efforts.

"Haha! Okay, you're up to something. What do you want?" replied Jean, immediately on to her best friend's lame attempt at compliments. She had never received a worse one in her life.

Maggie flinched. This was not going to plan.

Maggie and Jean were lifelong friends. Growing up in the same neighbourhood in inner-city Dublin, their mothers were good friends and so Maggie and Jean had been virtually inseparable since birth. Jean was everything Maggie was not. Standing at five foot six, Jean was the envy of many of her female counterparts with her long dark hair, brown eyes and flawless sallow skin. Maggie rarely saw her looking anything but elegant in her perfect size ten figure, covered from head to toe in the latest fashion trend. While Maggie was the strong, intelligent one, Jean was feisty. And while Jean was always the life and soul of the party, Maggie was happy to take a back seat. They had been through everything together from school trips to holidays to their troubles with men. Maggie knew she was blessed to have such a good friend in Jean.

"Well..." Maggie stammered. "I've just seen a brochure advertising volunteer trips to Nepal and I was hoping you might come with me?"

Maggie held her breath and waited.

"Nepal? Are you serious? You expect me to travel halfway across the world and stay in some dump without so much as running water?"

"Yes"

"You do?"

"Yes!" said Maggie, her voice barely above a whisper.

"And don't even get me started on those mosquitoes. Living in squalor really doesn't appeal to me." continued Jean, appearing not to hear her.

Damn it! Maggie urgently needed to sell this trip to her and sell it fast.

"My God Jean, that's not the point. The whole purpose of volunteering is that you make a difference to peoples' lives. I thought you of all people would know that?" Maggie retorted.

As soon as the words were out of her mouth, she regretted it. Maggie knew she should have held her tongue. But she was so desperate to persuade Jean to come on the trip with her.

"Don't you dare! You know how I hate to revisit my past," replied Jean, angry now, her tone cold.

"I'm sorry, I shouldn't have said that. But even you have to admit that it defeats the purpose if the volunteers stay in five-star accommodation while helping others who supposedly have nothing?" Maggie replied in her firmest voice.

Jean didn't like remembering her past. It haunted her.

Her mother had suffered terribly from clinical depression. Her father had abandoned them when she was a toddler and she had been left with her mother to provide for her. Only she didn't.

Jean could still remember that day she came home from school. She was six years old. She arrived home to find her mother fast asleep in bed. By the time six o clock arrived, she still hadn't surfaced and Jean was hungry. Not wanting to disturb her, Jean went to make scrambled egg and toast and a cup of tea. She waited for the kettle to boil. Gosh, that kettle really took forever, she remembered now. Hearing it click and the scourge of the water to signal boiling point, she went to lift it and in one fell swoop it fell out of her hand sending the scalding water flying everywhere. She had suffered second degree burns to her right leg and she had the scars to prove it. Not that she was embarrassed of them, in fact she flaunted them at any opportunity she got. She was proud of them and why shouldn't she be? Waking her mother up, they had reluctantly paid the accident and emergency a visit during which her mother had constantly barked in her ear that she was a clumsy, careless child. When her mother was like this, she had no interest in taking her to the beach, to birthday parties or any form of kid's entertainment. If she wanted to go to a birthday party, she often had to get a lift from one of her friends' parents. She had no interest in anything, in her appearance or in any of her hobbies. She lost count of the number of jobs Pamela had ploughed through. She would never forget the highs of her mother landing a job and the lows of losing them. All due to her depression. Funds had been extremely tight and they had never been able to spend lavishly. She even remembered a few eviction notices sifting through the door at one point. She had only been a child then but she knew enough to understand they had sailed very close to the wind. Jean used to worry so much about everything, about the state of their finances, about her mother and it would be a long time before she would recognise that she was very sick.

When she was twelve, her mother had slipped back into the habit of staying in bed again. Only it was worse this time. She wouldn't get out of bed at all, barely able to make it out for an hour a day. Finally, Jean had snapped and forced her mother to get the help she so desperately needed. Together, they had visited the GP who prescribed anti depressants. They had never once looked back.

"My dear Maggie, just because you're miss goody two shoes doesn't mean we all have to be," Jean replied now. "I'm sorry, but it's really not my scene. I'm not going."

"Fine!" replied Maggie with a subdued sigh.

There was no way Jean was going to travel all the way to Nepal to help a bunch of strangers in the depths of poverty manage their lives. Unlike Maggie who lived and breathed this kind of thing, Jean didn't have a caring bone in her body; not unfeeling, it just didn't come naturally to her. This really wasn't for her. She would feel awkward and inept teaching English or computers to Nepalese women and children with very limited education. And don't even get her started on children, she hated them.

What was the point anyway? Sure, wouldn't she be gone again in six weeks' time and what would they do then? No, she was not interested investing her time and efforts in something that wasn't sustainable. Not until the fundamental issues were rectified and solved. It would take more than singing 'Kumbaya' around a bonfire to appease her thank you very much. Besides, she was no fool. She knew well that their government bred large-scale corruption. Instead of education, health and transport being at the forefront of their financial agenda, their politicians were pocketing the money themselves. Foreign donors were consistently lending them $200 million over four-year intervals for crying out loud. Where was that money going? As far as she could see, Nepal would never resurface out of the depths of poverty until this was rectified. Why was it up to her to fix it?

"Oh, come on, I really don't want to go alone. Can't you please just do this one little favour for me? Please?" Maggie protested at the other end of the line, interrupting her thoughts.

"No Maggie, I've told you I don't want to go. Why are you insisting on this?" she asked.

"Because I don't want to travel by myself," replied Maggie simply.

More as a courtesy to her friend than anything else, without any real intention of travelling, Jean found herself uttering the words "What's in it for me?"

"An amazing adventure on the other side of the world, that's what. We can go hiking in the Himalayas, go shopping in nearby towns and villages and get beautiful clothes for a fraction of the price. Seriously, what's not attractive about that?" she asked.

"Anything else?" enquired Jean, her curiosity now slowly beginning to get the better of her.

"They have beautiful food."

"Really? From what I've heard, it's rice all the way. Beautiful food, my hat."

"They have beautiful clothes, gorgeous, colourful sarongs and everything," Maggie said, desperate to convert her friend.

"You already said that."

"I know, I know, but they really are beautiful."

"You're not selling this to me Maggie."

"We can visit a proper jungle… Buddhist temples… and there will be plenty Nepalese men there," ventured Maggie in a last-ditch attempt to coax her into coming on the trip.

"Fine, I'm in." Typical! The temptation of the male species had worked, thought Maggie. It was always the same. "But I'm not happy about it. You know how grumpy I get when I can't wash my hair for three whole days." moaned Jean. "And I'll have to double check with work first."

"Ah Jean, we're not exactly going to outer space. There'll be hot showers and everything, will you relax."

"Yeah, try telling that to the bush I'll be growing in that heat and humidity."

"You'll be fine," Maggie reassured her. "I'll send you all the details so you can begin your preparations. Thanks."

Maggie put down the receiver and breathed a sigh of relief. She had expected Jean to put up a fight but she hadn't been prepared for that. For a while, it really looked like she'd be going alone. Maggie had a grin from ear to ear for the rest of the day. This was really happening. She was going to Nepal.

****

Jean clicked off the phone call. Maggie was like a dog with a bone. She was so wound up it was difficult to get a normal conversation out of her. As Maggie blabbered on about Nepal, all Jean heard was a "Third-World" country which spelled disaster for her. She had no interest in going only agreeing to the trip to satisfy Maggie. Her best friend had been so excited Jean didn't have the heart to refuse.

She sighed inwardly. She was not looking forward to it. She hadn't gone three whole days without washing her hair since she was a child; that was a lifetime to her. She had better have access to hot showers. How was she going to cope? Reluctantly, Jean made her way to her study to switch on her computer. She picked up a notepad and a pen and tried not to think too much.

Jean was a fan of her home comforts. Now, if she was travelling anywhere on holidays' she stayed in nothing less than four-star hotels. She had worked her butt off to get to where she was, thank you very much and it was a far cry from her childhood days. Growing up with her single mother, their "holidays" had consisted of a week long stay in a hostel somewhere down the country. It was all her mother could afford. Her mother had dipped in and out of jobs for years and did her best to provide for them but they always seemed to be strapped for cash. Her mother had sacrificed her entire life and she would be forever indebted to her.

But she decided at a very young age that she would never end up like that and when she got her first job as a waitress at sixteen, she had worked like a Trojan and saved her pennies.

It seemed rather ludicrous now to think about her rebellious phase and how she may not have ended up where she was today. At fifteen, she began to rebel. Jean lost all interest in her school work, demanded to spend more time with her friends, and began drinking heavily. Jean smirked to herself as she reflected on this period of her life. She had given her mother a terrible time. It was with disgust that she remembered her gothic phase. She remembered dying her hair black and almost overnight her wardrobe became a wall of black. The palest of foundation became her new best friend and she even got her nose pierced. Jean thanked her lucky stars that she hadn't become a slave to the tattoo. Imagine being stuck with that for life. Naturally slim and svelte, Jean looked every inch the goth. Academically, her grades began to slip as homework and studying didn't feature on the agenda. The more her mother harassed her about it, the more disillusioned she became. Her mother made some attempts at grounding her for poor grades but to no avail. She had become rather adept at a means of escape out of the house. Influenced by her peers, she began to drink heavily and fall in the door late when her mother thought she was already home. She also had her first taste of cigarettes and quickly became hooked. Jean laughed as she cast her mind back to the first time she had dabbled with cigarettes. Jean and a few friends had arranged a trip to the local cinema and before heading into the safety of the big screen they had decided to venture out the back for a cigarette. Desperate to fit in with her circle of friends she had stubbornly maintained that she was a regular smoker. As she fumbled with the cigarette and the lighter while maintaining her all-important charisma, she would never forget the cloud of smoke that assaulted both her airways and her nostrils. Her cool exterior deserted her as she broke into fits of coughing and she succumbed to the grips of nausea. Not one to be deterred, however, Jean had proceeded to smoke several cigarettes that day. Soon she was smoking up to twenty. Overnight, Jean had gone from typical girl next door to rebellious teen. Mercifully, she did draw the line at taking drugs. She was seventeen before she finally realised the error of her ways and began to perform academically.

In the end, she saved enough money to put herself through college to study marketing. She would not stop until she landed her dream job as a marketing executive for a Dublin based five-star hotel. Only then would she shed the remnants of her working class past. One day she would be able to afford regular facials and manicures, attend the hairdressers once a week, dine in the finest restaurants, indulge in nice clothes, buy some good quality make-up and stay in some of the worlds' most exotic hotels. And she had no intention of ever going back!

Although she didn't like to mention it to Maggie, she knew volunteering in a third world country would bring back stark reminders of her past and this was part of the reason she had been reluctant to go. She wanted to distance herself as much as possible from all levels of poverty and forget that she had ever been a victim. It was selfish she knew. If anything, she should be keen to help those in need. But Jean had never been that way inclined. Damn it, she had fought hard to shed those roots a long time ago. Besides, nobody had helped them when they were struggling. Why should she feel obliged to help those in need now? She chewed the top of her pen, something she always did when she was nervous. She was fretting now. To distract herself, she switched on her laptop and checked the email Maggie had sent her with all the info. And she began to research everything about Nepal. Whether she liked it or not, this trip was inevitable.

CHAPTER 2

Across town, a man sat pushing his two young daughters on the swings in his back garden. It was a bright clear day and the sun pervaded the clouds casting its warmth on the earth below. It was the beginning of July and all the roses and chrysanthemums sat happily dispersed in a variety of destinations around the garden, their sweet aromas scintillating the air.

Noel Brady definitely wasn't as fit as he used to be. The constant pushing of the swings cost him unprecedented amounts of physical exertion and he could feel his arms beginning to resist. At forty-five, he was definitely past his sell-by date. Completely oblivious to his pain and discomfort, the two girls roared and squealed with delight as the swing soared higher and higher into the air with every push. They loved every minute, each push helping him to feel that he had aged another ten years. Was it his imagination or did the swings keep returning to him with increased frequency? He really wasn't able for this anymore.

"Higher." squealed one of the twins.

He sighed to himself. He hadn't wanted children but then it wasn't fair to deny his younger wife the privilege. He absolutely doted on his twin girls but it didn't feel natural to have such young children at his stage of life, they were only six. He felt stifled, like he was trapped in a monotonous way of life that he couldn't escape. As he was their main carer, he was the parent who got them up in the mornings, made their breakfast, dropped them to school, collected them and did their homework with them.

He was the one who attended parent teacher meetings, bought the presents at Christmas and birthdays. His life had become a horrifying blur of domesticity and he bore all the hall-marks of a house husband. He couldn't remember when or how he had ended up in such a rut. When had life become such a chore? He hated his job as a Civil Servant, documenting the statistics of people's lives. Yes, everyone was just a number, there was no room for individuality in his job. He really must be suffering a midlife crisis, he chastised himself.

He had met his wife Michelle at a Christmas party over ten years ago. She had taken a temp role in the same building while saving funds to open up her own beauty salon. A tall attractive blonde in her mid-twenties with a strong independent streak, he had been instantly attracted to her. He was ten years her senior and had been flattered that she had even noticed him, let alone display an interest in him. The first few months of their relationship had been fantastic and they spent every spare minute together like two love-struck teenagers. Ah yes, those first flushes of love were great.

It wasn't until Michelle finally launched her business, that things began to rapidly deteriorate. She became increasingly moody, volatile and gradually spent more time away from him. He now had more of a relationship with Michelle's answering machine than with Michelle herself. He felt rejected but he never said anything. As the pressures of starting a business began to take its toll, she began to demand that they get married. And so, he had felt backed into a corner. Looking back, he realised he should have finished it with her there and then. God, he was such a wimp, he thought to himself. They should never have got married.

It had been her independence that had attracted him to her in the first few months of their relationship; how ironic that it was that exact trait which would now spell the end of their marriage. Her beauty salon business was taking up all her time. Even when she arrived home in the evening, she didn't switch off. She sat in front of the television glued to her laptop, sending emails, organising meetings and making phone calls on her blackberry. He felt woefully inadequate beside her. And she was happy to drag him along to work functions that centred around promoting the business, invariably spending the evening talking to other business minded people. As far as he was concerned, most of them were snobs and they bored the hell out of him.

His insecurities plagued him day and night. His wife was now a smart and savvy business woman. It was like she had changed over night. He knew it was only a matter of time before she got bored of him and gave him his marching orders. It was better to get out of this loveless marriage before it was too late.......and leave Michelle on his terms.

He looked down at his two young children and felt a pang of guilt for what he was about to do. He was going to cause irreparable damage. They were innocent and it wasn't fair to involve them. But he had to get out. He couldn't stand being trapped anymore. He had reached his limit.

****

"Abdul, we're in the shits! Our clients are getting tired of seeing the same women here night after night. We've got to do something about it or we'll lose our clientele, they're threatening to leave."

Abdul was sitting behind his office desk as his assistant director Marco rambled on. Marco helped to oversee the day-to-day operations of the brothel, but today he was furious. He wanted Abdul to bring fresh women forward for the brothel clientele.

"Who will leave?" asked Abdul.

"The clients. They'll find somewhere else to go."

Abdul sighed and stretched his legs out as he sat back in his large office chair. A quick glance at his wrist told him it was 11pm. It was late, but obviously this meeting was important enough to warrant Marco travelling all the way from Kathmandu, landing him in his office.

Abdul was used to these impromptu visits, they were a regular occurrence, often resulting in tempers flaring. It was never a good omen. But, by now, he had learned how to manage his colleague's quick temper.

"I know, I know, what do you expect me to do about it?"

"Well, as director of this brothel, you've got to do something." his assistant director demanded.

This meeting was stressing him out, like he didn't have enough sleepless nights worrying about the brothel. Everyday presented a new challenge, a new obstacle to be overcome and he was exhausted. If there weren't problems on the financial front, there were problems with staff, he never seemed to catch a break. He had known for quite a while that his clients were unhappy with the current set-up of women. They didn't excite his clients anymore and they were frustrated.

His brothel business shouldn't be failing, of course. If anything, it should be a thriving business accounting for $150 billion a year worldwide.

Ever since the 2015 earthquake had severely disrupted social and economic structures across the country, it had been easier than ever to traffic women and force them into prostitution. It had also worked against him, however, as the tourism industry had taken a hit meaning young tourists were not as plentiful. But he had worked too hard to get here and refused to let his brothel business fail. He would do whatever it took to make it work.

"I told you our previous accountant screwed us over with our money, stole our savings." Abdul said now.

He was distracted by the large blue vein bulging out of Marco's forehead. His eyes were like slits, little dark pockets of fire dancing around in his tall dark frame. He was irate and could not sit down, almost banging his fist on the table in a temper.

"What about the money you made while smuggling drugs in to all those foreign countries?" demanded Marco.

Marco had a wife and three children at home that he needed to feed. This business could not be allowed to fail. He wasn't going to sit back and watch Abdul let the business turn to rack and ruin. Yes, he had travelled all the way from Kathmandu. Now was the time for action before their clients started leaving them. Before it was too late.

"Jesus Marco, are you a fucking idiot? I told you, I put all that money into starting up the brothel." Abdul vented, annoyed now at his colleagues' stupidity.

"You see, I don't know if I believe you. How do I know you haven't got huge savings stashed away somewhere?"

"Are you kidding me?" Abdul said, unable to believe what he was hearing. "Everything I have, I've pumped into this business. Everything."

"I thought you might have had some left over?"

"Well, I don't."

God bless Marco, he really hadn't a clue. Even though he was assistant director, he had never understood the many practicalities involved in running a brothel. All that concerned him were the numbers and he could not see beyond that. Nobody ever saw him out in the firing line. Instead, he operated from his desk in Kathmandu, mulling over spreadsheets and lived in his own little cocoon. He had no idea of the real challenges associated with running a brothel.

"So, what are you going to do about it?"

"I'm sick of this crap, I'm working night and day to get the right kind of women into the camp."

"What kind of women are you looking for?"

"Tourists mainly!"

"Is there a reason for that?"

"Yeah, it diversifies the camp and it's also more economical."

"More economical? Really?"

"Yes, it is actually, believe it or not."

"Are you certifying them pure?" Marco asked then. He had to, his clients would want to know.

"Yes, mostly."

"What does that mean?"

"It just means that sometimes we might take women a little older than 16 or 17 if we believe they are attractive enough or if we feel our clients would like them."

"Okay good. Let's catch up again next week then."

"Fine, we'll see you then."

And like two professionals at a business meeting, they shook hands before Marco left the office. Marco was at least satisfied that he would be able to feed his family for the time being. But still, he wanted to see progress on recruitment and he would not rest until he did. His livelihood depended on it.

Abdul Khamid was a bad piece of ass. A devout criminal, he was one of the most wanted men in his native Albania. He wasn't long out of school when he realised there was money to be made in the drug trade. He was desperate to make a name for himself and make his millions and to him, this was the perfect opportunity. It had been little tasks at first, like smuggling small amounts of cocaine into foreign countries. He had been well prepped; every movement, every tiny detail meticulously planned down to a fine art. He smirked as he remembered how terrified he had been. Him, terrified? The very thought was laughable. He was an arrogant gangster. But he had been wracked with nerves on that first journey. All of his senses had been on edge as he carefully watched everything happening around him, watching for any indication that someone was on to him. He slowly made his way through the airport, on high alert in case any dogs came sniffing at his suitcase or in case he was picked up at customs. As he walked through the body scan without a glitch and his hand luggage sailed through the scanner beside him, he had never experienced such elation in all his life. It had been a rush like no other.

He had earned decent sums of money continuing to smuggle drugs into countries all over the world for the next couple of years. He made a name for himself in the drugs industry and became an accomplice in his field.

It was his looks he supposed. His boyish dark-haired looks and angelic features could fool even the most cynical. His impossibly good looks especially worked with suspicious female staff. He just used his charm, his wit, feign sincerity and he would pass through the most precarious situations. Women were such fools, he mused. Show them a handsome man and they believed anything you told them.

He had moved on to far more advanced operations now of course. Drug smuggling would bore him to tears now. Oh no, he had set his sights much further afield. He had moved on to drug trafficking and women. He targeted young women in Nepal mostly. He had relocated there several years ago and opened his own brothel in the capital, Kathmandu. With his business falsely operating as a singing restaurant, he targeted Nepalese women as well as tourists.

It wasn't difficult to plunge Nepalese women into the world of trafficking and prostitution. All he had to do was promise them a job as a domestic worker, wealth and a chance at a new life and they were falling at his feet. Nepalese women were so uneducated and so undervalued, they were willing to jump at any opportunity they got to better themselves. If only they knew what they were really signing up for, he mused.

Tourists in particular were such easy prey. They stood out immediately and it was pitifully easy to lure them away from safety under false pretences. Take women hiking in the Himalayas for example. All he had to do was promise them a spin in his "top of the range Ferrari" that was conveniently parked somewhere remote and they were hooked. By the time they arrived at the car, realised it wasn't a Ferrari and that he was telling fibs, it was too late. No-one would hear their screams now. To be fair, women rarely went hiking or took part in any activity alone, but two women was not a challenge for him. Other times, he might play the lost tourist card trying to find his way back out of the Himalayas, in fact, this one worked very well. Women were overly helpful when he played this card, offering to escort him down to the entrance to the hiking trail. Once there, he'd pretend he couldn't remember where he had parked his car so invariably, they helped him to locate that too. Once at the car he'd simply hit one over the head and be ready for the next one before repeating the act. He would tie them up and bundle them into his Ferrari before speeding off to his secret hideout. Once he had the women at his destination, he would prep their veins and inject them with heroin before they came to. Some of the little darlings couldn't hack a dose of heroin and he had lost a number of them. Ooops!!

He hadn't always been this prejudiced against the female species, quite the opposite in fact. Born and reared in Albania, he had borne witness to the vicious gang-rape and murder of his mother when he was six years old. His father had owned a business when three burglars raided the house one night, looking for the key to the safe. They had tied both himself and his father up and forced them to watch as they raped his mother one by one, both of them helpless to stop it. He could still hear her shrill cries of desperation and the final scream as a bullet was shot straight at her chest. Even now, he shuddered at the memory. He had done his best over the years to wipe it completely, but of course, the human brain never forgets, never forgives.

And now his brothel was in need of some fresh meat, his customers were getting bored of the existing pieces of trash they had to offer. He needed to hunt for his prey again. He would go to the Himalayas in the next week or so to see what he could find. He would use his charm once more.......

****

And suddenly it was the night before departure. Maggie glanced in the mirror as she packed away her make-up. People always described her as a pretty twenty-year old, mainly due to her big smile she guessed. At just five foot two, Maggie was petite but elegant. A wave of short brown hair fell softly on her face and a set of bright green eyes stared back at her from the reflection in the mirror. They were her best feature, aside from her sunny smile of course. Her complexion was somewhere in the pale category, Maggie supposed, and it was a long-standing joke in her family that all she was missing was red wavy locks to complete her Irish status.

Timid though she might be, she had always been exceptionally headstrong. When she got an idea into her head, it consumed her until she became impossible to be around. As soon as she had seen the brochures, she knew she wanted to volunteer abroad. She had only ever gone abroad on sun holidays; now Maggie wanted to do something different. Never one to sit on her laurels, she was always searching for the next mission, the next challenge. Volunteering in Nepal fit the bill perfectly.

Maggie checked over her list again. She still needed insect repellent, ponchos, dry shampoo, sunglasses, sun-cream, hand sanitizer and all her shoes.

Maggie looked around her bedroom at the cream walls adorned with two old fashioned photo frames complete with childhood pictures and suddenly arrived at the harsh realisation that she was going to miss home terribly while she was gone. She glanced at her luxurious double bed with her purple bedside lamp. She had always admired her big fancy wardrobe parked neatly beside a very fashionable chest of drawers. The lush pine colour exerted a classy feel to the room and interrupted the tidal wave of boredom that otherwise threatened to engulf it. She would never make an interior designer that was for sure. Maggie wondered what kind of accommodation awaited her so far away from home. Mr. Barreton had warned her about the primitive conditions under which she would be living for the next six weeks. Five-star hotel accommodation coupled with luxuries was not to be expected.

Maggie was beginning to feel nervous, she had never done anything like this before. Would she like it? What would Nepalese people be like? Would she be safe? In her line of work, she heard about all sorts of stories splashed across newspapers every day and they were never good. Most of the time it was related to rapes, acid attacks, and murders or women ostracised from their community because of a facial disfigurement or a marital breakdown. It was one thing to write about these stories from the safety of her office, quite another to visit the country where all these terrible atrocities were currently taking place. She was incredibly fortunate that Jean was able to accompany her on the trip.

Maggie paused for a moment and turned to look out the window. It was growing dark outside. How she loved this time of year. It was mid-June and the flowers were in full bloom as the valley of summer had sprung to life. She only had to turn her attention to her own back garden to witness the soft blowing daffodils, experience the enticing aroma of lavender as the leaves cascaded on the gentle night breeze to the ground.

But roses were her absolute favourite flower. Standing tall and proud in the centre of the garden several bundles of roses greeted her and soared over her head and beyond. They stood ever so still and lent themselves to the majestic quality of the garden. Maggie sighed. It was largely in her father's honour that Maggie and her mother had worked so hard to keep the garden in top shape. It had been her fathers' pride and joy and Maggie could not source one childhood memory that did not revolve around it. Sunny days were exclusively spent in the back garden soaking up the sun. Maggie and her parents had spent many an evening here watching the sunset on the horizon, the magnificent primrose pink casting a soft night time glow across the land. In her mind's eye, Maggie could still visualise looking over at her parents in the back garden as they sat out late at night, both of their smiling faces staring back at her, bathed in the soft pink glow radiating out from the sunset. In those magical moments, she felt safe and warm in the love of two wonderful parents. She hoped it would shield her forever.

Every spare minute he had, her father spent it tending to his garden. He had been meticulous about weeds. In fact, they had been his worst nightmare and he went straight to get rid of them at first sight. If he wasn't planting seeds, he filled his evenings feeding existing flowers with water or mowing the lawn, there was always a constant stream of work to be done and Maggie usually found herself roped in to help out. Over time, she found she began to enjoy it and eventually she wanted to learn more about all the different types of flowers from lilies to chrysanthemums and lots more. She had certainly developed her love of all that bloomed from him.

She picked up the claddagh ring her dad had given her for her thirteenth birthday. It was a special token from him and she cherished it deeply. Like a good luck charm, it followed her everywhere. Twisting the ring on her finger, she wondered what he would think if he could see her now. Would he be proud of her? She hoped so.

"Maggie!"

She was interrupted from her reverie by the shrill sound of her mothers' voice. "Have you packed your insect repellent?" appearing at the doorway to the room, her mother was evidently a little flustered.

Maggie smirked as she replied. "Mum, I think it's you going on this trip, not me!"

"I know Maggie my love, I just don't want you to forget anything." Ava Adams replied now concerned for her daughter.

"I won't, I promise."

They both managed a giggle before finally locating the insect repellent and storing it in the bag. Reverting back to her list, Maggie noted that she still needed to pack her sun-cream, all her insurance paperwork, cleansing wipes and dry shampoo which was still looking at her from the top of her chest of drawers. She packed her camera in anticipation of all the adventures that awaited her. With every bit she packed, the more her excitement grew until finally in the presence of her mother, Maggie conducted a final check to ensure that she had remembered everything. Finally, satisfied with her evening's work, Maggie closed her suitcase and went downstairs to have a cup of tea with her mother.

****

Across town Jean was also getting ready for her departure. She was just fishing the last of her clothes out of her already overflowing wardrobe, when something fell out onto the floor. Jean stooped down to pick it up. It was a picture of her and three girls from school dressed to kill on one of her many nights out in her first year at college. While Jean was grinning from ear to ear suffering from a severe dose of sheer delirium, the other three girls, Carlotta, Rochelle and Alison, gathered around her pulling faces. Hair extensions ensured that her hair travelled well past shoulder length, she had been going through a phase of constantly applying hair extensions at the time. Thick black eyeliner accentuated her eyes and bright red lipstick finished off the look to perfection. This night was particularly special as it marked a major celebration. Jean could even recall the date, March 27th. Jean's band Three Dimensional had just been awarded a coveted performance slot at Glastonbury in June. All four girls were in high spirits as they partied the night away and digested this fantastic piece of news.

Three Dimensional had happened by accident. It had started out as one isolated idea and grown into this extraordinary phenomenon landing them a performance slot at Glastonbury. The band consisted of four girls,

Jean, Carlotta, Rochelle and Alison. All four had studied music together at school and Jean had wanted to major in vocals. When she learned that two of the girls, Carlotta and Rochelle, played guitar, she had suggested they get together for a jamming session. After all, it would be more fun to play together. With Jean on lead vocals, Carlotta on lead guitar and Rochelle on bass guitar, they managed to create a unique sound of their own and they knew that this was the birth of something remarkable. They had one problem though, they badly needed a drummer. After a bit of detective work, they found Alison. Alison was another girl in their music class and was quite the pro with a set of drums and so their band was officially complete.

Carlotta had been her favourite complete with exotic looks, big personality and her stunning ability to crack a joke at any given moment. Rochelle was the shy, retiring member of the band but as soon as she stepped on stage, she transformed into a totally different person. Alison identified as the band's resident rock chic with funky short hair, thick eyeliner and stud piercing in her nose. Quirky in every sense of the word, she breathed new life into their songs and performances.

In first year, Rochelle heard about a competition for a performance slot at Glastonbury. All they had to do was perform a half hour overview of their material in a popular pub in Dublin and impress four top music moguls in the industry. Easy!

All four girls waited backstage amid loudly beating hearts and sweaty palms. Ten bands were competing tonight, Three Dimensional were the final band in the line-up. All around her, band members were warming up their voices, practicing harmonies, tuning their guitars or getting into rhythm on their drums. Everybody was out to win. Suddenly, the stage manager was calling them to get ready for their performance. As they waited in the darkness, Jean tried to steady her breathing. Finally, a strong beam of light assaulted their eyes as the band exited the stage and it was time for Three Dimensional.

"And now, for the final band of the evening, an all-female rock band, please give a warm welcome to Three Dimensional."

Jean took her place at the microphone, felt the familiar rush of adrenalin kick in and her performance took over. Singing her heart out in front of four top music moguls had been the most exhilarating experience of her entire existence. Afterwards, the girls awaited the all important scores out of ten from each of the judges.

They waited with baited breath as the first judge, a tall slim man who looked in desperate need of a decent meal announced his score.

"Nine." he bellowed.

The next judge, a plainly dressed woman in her fifties wearing a ghastly pair of spectacles, allowed the tension to build before giving her score.

"Nine." shouted the woman.

The excitement began to grow, if they kept up these scores, they were well on their way to winning that performance slot. The audience began to roar with the suspense of it all, each rooting for their own favourite. It was within grasp of their fingertips now, they hardly dared believe they would win. Could they?

"Ten." roared the next judge, an elderly man in his

eighties. Dressed from head to toe in a formal suit he had looked enamoured with every band on stage that night. He was everyone's safety net, the lowest score he had given all night was nine.

Now, they were neck in neck with one other band and they needed at least eight points from the final judge to win. A young man in his thirties, he had been doling out low scores all evening. He was a low sized man of average build with a mop of dark brown hair and sallow skin. Exotic brown eyes accentuated his appeal. Dressed to kill in a pair of Levi's black denim jeans and a smart check shirt, this guy was the man of the moment. A top record industry executive, his approval could alter the course of your career. All four girls covered their ears, hardly daring to breathe. They were so close now they could almost taste it.

"Nine." he boomed.

As the audience erupted into a thunderous roar of applause, they made their way back on stage to perform one of their songs as the newly crowned winners. It was official, they were Glastonbury bound. It had been an incredible night, surpassed only by the Glastonbury gig itself. Jean could only smile at the memories, humming to herself as she finished the last of her packing.

CHAPTER 3

Maggie woke with a start when the alarm sounded. She'd been tossing and turning all night, had barely slept a wink with excitement. She hoped she'd be able to make up for lost sleep on the long flight over.

Switching on her bedside lamp, she stretched and yawned before committing to the day that lay ahead of her. This was it, the adventure began here.

She must have made for such boring company over the last few days, Maggie reflected with a smile. Ever since she found out she was travelling to Nepal, she hadn't stopped talking incessantly about the trip, invariably bending the ear of anyone who dared to listen. Her work colleagues especially, had been given quite an earful, Maggie mused.

On a more serious note, Maggie couldn't imagine that she wouldn't be affected by the trip. People always remarked that these trips changed you as a person. When you witnessed how little these people had and were subject to their infectious enthusiasm for life, you never viewed your own life in the same way.

Maggie made her way downstairs to the kitchen to find the smell of bacon wafting out the door to meet her. Her mother was obviously cooking a full Irish breakfast to see her off. It was probably her mothers' attempt to make sure she really did leave and didn't come crawling back home from Dublin Airport. She was really going to miss these little touches.

"Morning Maggie, all ready for your big day?" her mother greeted her with a cheerful smile as she walked into the kitchen.

"Morning Ma, yeah, as ready as I'll ever be. I just want to get on the plane now."

"Good. It's going to take a while to get to the airport so we'll aim to leave as soon as Jean arrives at half seven, okay?"

"Yeah perfect, don't worry, Jean's never late. You couldn't be late with that girl if you tried."

"Now Maggie, that's no way to speak of your best friend," her mother retorted with a hint of a smile forming at the corner of her mouth and they both broke into hysterics.

Maggie had arranged for Jean to travel with them to the airport. She'd better get a move on if she was going to be ready for her seven-thirty arrival at the house. Jean was the ultimate master of punctuality and had never been late in her life. It was a wonder they were friends at all sometimes.

As she sat down at the kitchen table, she glanced at her mother with affection. She was worried about her. Maggie knew it would be a long six weeks for her alone in a big empty house. Even after all these years, she still struggled to cope. She would never admit that to her, but Maggie knew. She tried to suppress a nagging sense of guilt at leaving her but what could she do. She had to get on with her life. She couldn't stop living life just to prevent her mother from feeling lonely. She would phone as often as she could though. Sometimes she desperately resented all the responsibility falling on her shoulders, sometimes the pressure was enormous. It was one of the major downsides of being an only child, Maggie reflected. She was used to it now, she supposed, but she would definitely have loved the company of a brother or sister growing up. It would have helped.

Maggie was attempting to close her suitcase when her mother called her downstairs.

"MAGGIE, Jean's here!"

Jean arrived in the door dressed in a denim pinafore, fishnet tights and heels. Red blotchy eyes betrayed her cheerful sunny smile and her attempts at light conversation. She had evidently just said a tearful goodbye to her mother.

The girls chatted amicably all the way into Dublin airport, excitedly discussing the trip that awaited them. Before they knew it, Maggie's mother was pulling into the set down area of Terminal One. As she stepped out of the car, Maggie turned her attention to the sky above her, noticing all the planes exiting the country bound for foreign lands. She wanted to remember this moment. It wasn't everyday you got to travel to such unique locations, there would be enough time to be getting on with the mundane when she got back. The trip would fly by, she wanted to enjoy it.

Maggie hugged her mother goodbye, promising to keep in regular contact throughout her travels before picking up her suitcase and making her way into the departure's hall with Jean in tow. As she wheeled her suitcase behind her, she grimaced at the weight of it, she hadn't realised that it was so heavy. She sincerely hoped it wouldn't be overweight at check-in.

After a successful check-in, the girls sat in the airport restaurant sipping coffee discussing Jeans latest drama. Maggie could only laugh to herself as she listened to her friend rant about a guy she had gone on a date with during the week and hadn't heard a word from since. Clearly, she had really liked this guy. This was just typical of Jean, she always seemed to lurch from one drama to the next, especially where men were concerned. If she wasn't complaining that a guy was too clingy, she experienced problems on the opposite end of the spectrum where the guy didn't keep in touch enough or had a wandering eye. She just couldn't seem to find middle ground. Sitting before her now, she was in full flow about her date during the week.

"So, I just don't get it. He took me out for dinner and drinks. We really gelled, we had brilliant craic and there was definitely a spark there."

"What did you talk about?"

"Everything. I told him about Three Dimensional, he plays in a band too, he's the drummer." Jean finished looking starry-eyed.

"Oh no!" said Maggie, seeing that her friend was so keen on this guy. She really dived in head first didn't she? "And what did he say at the end? How did ye leave things?" she finished.

"He said he'd call me, didn't he? I told him I was leaving today but he still hasn't called. I don't know Maggie, maybe I need a hot Nepalese man." she exclaimed in desperation.

"I wouldn't count on it. Look, maybe the date went well for you but you don't know that he feels the same. It sounds like you're more interested in him and maybe it's not reciprocated." Maggie replied.

"Yeah, I know, just it's been three days now. I was really hoping I'd hear from him. He seemed like such a great guy............"

Maggie had stopped listening. This was typical of Jean, always self-absorbed. Her favourite topic was herself and it was beginning to grate on Maggie's nerves. The nature of their friendship was founded on Maggie acting as Jeans personal counsellor. While there was no denying that Jean had been a great friend to Maggie over the years, sometimes she got sick of playing the role of counsellor. It was tiring and exhausting. It was difficult not to feel that this friendship was a little one sided at times. It would be nice if Jean could take an interest in her life from time to time. And now more than ever, she wanted to focus on enjoying their time away together, not spend it listening to Jean on an endless tirade about some guy she went on one date with.

Their friendship had been frequently tested on this front. Maggie remembered their most recent falling out which had nearly culminated in the end of their friendship. It had been a particularly ugly fight that had taken place on their last trip to sunny Spain. Jean had been dominating the whole trip from the very beginning and was frequently seen ordering everybody about. The itinerary was packed with activities of interest to Jean with no consideration for anyone else. Most of the holiday revolved around staying out all night and sunbathing at the pool by day which did not sit well with Maggie. It wasn't her style to party all night and miss the sunshine. Maggie wanted to explore the sights, catch some rays on the beach or even consider a sky dive. Even more disconcerting was the fact that most of the other girls were dissatisfied with this kind of holiday as well, but like puppets on a string they followed suit.

Everything came to a head a few days in, resulting in a vicious argument. Maggie was fed up, she was sick of Jean and her self-centred ways. She thought the world revolved around her and Maggie had enough. She was no longer prepared to be used as a shoulder to cry when it suited Jean.

In a fit of anger, it had all come pouring out of her.

"Jean, I'm sick of you bossing us all around. There's six of us here together on this trip in case you hadn't noticed and we don't want to go partying all night, every night. What a waste, we could do that back home."

"Ugh, you're such a whinge Maggie, I've never known anyone quite like you for moaning. If you want to go home just leave. Go on then, go running back to mommy where you belong."

"How dare you say that? You of all people, you should know better. That's the lowest of the low."

"Oh, grow up Maggie!"

Maggie had to stifle a sigh of relief as the announcement came to board their flight. A massive scramble for the departure gates ensued and people quickly began to form a queue in an orderly fashion. Maggie and Jean drained the last of their coffee and made their way to their gate for the first leg of their journey.

****

Noel Brady sat staring out his sitting room window, his very old fashioned phone held firmly in his hand. What he was about to do could change his life forever. He knew the road he was about to travel would be a long and difficult one filled with hurt, anger and tears. Tears, hurt and anger that he could never rectify, at least not in this lifetime. He had a lot to answer for and he had to shoulder his share of responsibility for the events that had unfolded more than twenty years ago. But damn it, he had had his reasons! It was now or never, he had to take a gamble on this one.

He turned his attention back to the phone, tentatively he dialed his former lover Pamela's number. He held his breath and waited. After four rings, a familiar voice spoke into the phone.

"Hello?"

"Pamela, how are you? It's Noel here."

"What do you want?"

In an instant her voice turned icy cold and Noel's heart sank. It was obvious she was still livid with him and he could tell from her tone that she wasn't going to grant him what he wanted. He sighed inwardly. Why did life always seem to conspire against him? He really wasn't a bad man. Some might say he was a bit of a commitment phobe, but he wasn't. That just wasn't true. Well, he was damned if this bitch of a woman was going to stand in the way.

"Please don't hang up. Look, I know you're still mad at me from all those years ago, but please, I want to talk to Jean?" he ventured.

"Oh now you want to talk, now that it suits you and your schedule. What's wrong Noel? Did your whore of a mistress leave you? Is that why you're trying to come running back to us?" spat Pamela, venom flying from every pore of her being.

Noel faltered over what to say next, he was taken aback at Pamela's attitude towards him. Since when had she become so bitter and hard as nails? It really wasn't like her.

"No... it's not like that at all." Noel tried, searching his uncooperating brain for the right words to say next. "I want to make amends before it's too late. I've realised the error of my ways, but you have to understand my side of the story too."

"What's that then? That you couldn't raise a child for a few months while your partner was sick?"

"It was a hell of a lot longer than that Pamela, you know that as well as I do." he retorted, the anger beginning to rise in him. He had been determined not to turn this phone call into an argument, so much for that.

"Or was it that you decided you weren't cut out for children at all? Except when they are grown up and all the hard work is done." continued Pamela, seemingly ignoring his previous comment.

"Oh, give me a break. I did my best, I held us together for as long as I could but I just couldn't keep going anymore. Enough was enough. And you refused to get help. What would you have done?"

"Jean was only a toddler, how could you do that to her? She did nothing to deserve any of this."

"Oh, for goodness' sake, we're going around in circles here. Can I please just speak with Jean or at least get her phone number?"

"Well, she's not here at the minute. She's gone volunteering in Nepal." declared Pamela with a clear air of triumph. Noel pinched himself

"Nepal? What is she doing out there?"

"I told you, she's gone volunteering with Maggie."

"Well, when will she be back?"

"In about five or six weeks."

"Can I contact her then?"

"I'll think about it." replied Pamela and promptly hung up.

He could remember the day she was born as if it were yesterday. She was so small. She had been perfect, soft gentle skin and pink rosy cheeks. He savoured every little detail, imprinting it in his mind's eye. The first time he held her in his arms, she had looked up at him and smiled with her baby blue eyes. He vowed to stick by her through thick and thin. God, he was such a wimp he thought to himself. But how was he to know that circumstances would take such a disastrous turn for the worse. How was he to know that Jean's mother Pamela would develop post natal depression and become a never-ending blubbering mess. He was sick and tired of being judged by society for being the father that abandoned his daughter. Had anyone ever thought of how tough it had been for him? There were days he came home from work and Pamela hadn't even got out of bed. He tried to encourage her to visit the doctor and discuss how she was feeling but she had refused, insisting there was nothing wrong with her. In the end, he had no choice but to send Jean to crèche, the woman wasn't capable of looking after herself, not to mind a young baby. He had juggled working full time, all the housework and taking care of a new young baby. It was exhausting but he didn't mind at first because he believed it was just a phase and Pamela would eventually come out of it. But after ten months there was still no improvement and his patience was wearing thin. He was sick of arriving home to find Pamela perched on the couch reading a book with nothing done around the house. He was fast approaching burn out and he didn't know how much longer he could keep it up.

At the end of the day he wasn't married to her, he didn't owe her anything. They had only been going out six months when Pamela discovered she was pregnant. It had been a happy accident but now it was turning his life into a living nightmare. Pamela was no longer the woman he had fallen in love with, was merely a shadow of her former self. While he loved Jean dearly, he was asphyxiating with the claustrophobia.

When Jean was just over a year old, Noel had gone out to do the weekly shopping on a Saturday morning. He decided to leave Jean in the care of Pamela on this occasion because he was in a bit of a hurry, something he rarely did. He arrived back armed with the weeks' shopping, to find Jean sitting in front of the television watching Barney videos. Instantly, the smell assaulted his nostrils and upon inspection, he discovered she was soiled right through.

"Pamela!" he called out urgently.

There was no response. He was furious now, he was really walking on a thin line. Immediately, he swept Jean up in his arms and made his way to the bedroom to find Pamela fast asleep. Evidently, she had just put Jean in front of the television and gone straight back to bed. This was the final straw and something in him snapped that day. He was a devoted family man and he did his best to be sympathetic towards Pamela, but this was a step too far. If he couldn't even leave Jean alone with her while he had to run errands, what hope did he have? He couldn't help someone who didn't want to be helped. This was a toxic environment and he could stand it no longer.

"Pamela, wake up." he shouted, shaking her awake.

Slowly, she opened her eyes and fixed her sleepy gaze on him.

"What is it? What's wrong? I'm tired."

"I came home to find Jean soiled through, that's what's wrong. When were you going to change her exactly?" he barked and waited for a reply.

"I didn't know she was soiled. If I had known, of course I would have changed her." Pamela protested, awake now.

"Well of course you didn't know, you just dumped her in front of the television watching Barney videos. She's a child Pamela, she needs someone to play with her, she needs stimulation. Either you get your act together and start taking care of our daughter or I'm out of here."

"But you know I haven't been feeling well, I'm not able to care for her. I need you, I can't bond with my own baby girl" she pleaded with him bursting into hysterics. She was sitting up in bed now and trying to drag both him and Jean closer to her.

He looked down at her unkempt appearance, heard the desperation in her voice and saw the pleading in her eyes but he felt nothing. She had a responsibility towards their daughter, plain and simple. She was a mother now, he didn't want to hear her pathetic excuses.

"You get your act together or we're finished" he demanded and he turned and left the room.

Now, Noel decided to take matters into his own hands. He couldn't waste another six weeks and face the possibility that Pamela might stand in his way again. He would have to find Jean himself. He had sabotaged his relationship with her enough, he didn't want to waste another minute.

CHAPTER 4

As Maggie disembarked the plane sweltering heat of intense proportions enveloped her. In an instant, Maggie felt her clothes drown in a bucket of sweat and stick to her body. This would take some getting used to, she thought to herself. Besides, it wasn't the intense heat she resented, it was the resulting lethargy that inevitably took hold.

As they made their way into the arrivals hall, both girls looked around for a rep from the volunteering organisation "INTEC". It had been agreed before they left home that one of the reps would meet them in the arrivals hall at the airport and escort them to the volunteer house. After a few moments, a small dark skinned woman with exotic looks and long dark hair approached them. Around her neck, she wore her identification badge.

"Maggie? Jean? Yeah?"

"Yes, that's us." Maggie replied gratefully.

Maggie's shyness often bordered on crippling and she never liked first meetings with people. It always took her a long time to adjust to personality traits and get to know people before she could begin to feel comfortable. Prior to reaching that point, however, she struggled with conversation and could never really find the right words to say. Jean was by far more boisterous, more daring and more adventurous. She was pure, wholesome and strait-laced by comparison. It was either a great irony or a happy coincidence that they had become the best of friends. Maggie was a natural leader, however, and Jean was happy to sit back and let her take the lead in such circumstances as they found themselves in now.

"Great. My name is Sanou, I'm one of the volunteer coordinators with INTEC. I'll just show you to the car and you can put your luggage in. I must just pick up some more people and we will be ready to go then." she informed them in her strong Nepalese accent.

She escorted them out to what could only be described as a very old truck. There was no such thing as a boot, their luggage had to be attached to the back of the vehicle with a rope. Reluctantly, the girls parted with their luggage and climbed into the truck for their next journey. Several moments later, Sanou arrived flanked by two more girls from The Netherlands, both destined for adventure. One of them was tall and slim with long strawberry blonde hair while the other girl was smaller in height and displayed a more rounded figure. Bleached blonde hair was tied back off her face in a ponytail accentuating her bright blue eyes. Their luggage had to go on the roof of the vehicle as they were completely out of space. With everyone squashed into the truck, the driver who introduced himself as Raoul took off for the volunteer house. A decent proficiency in English as demonstrated by both girls enabled them to converse with ease and the four of them spent the entire trip babbling with excitement as the vehicle rattled on edging ever closer to their final destination.

As they travelled, Maggie was astounded by the scenes that met her eyes. At one point, they passed a vast open space of scorched earth, the corner lit ablaze by a burning fire-food was being cooked. Through a kaleidoscope of colour, she could see a group of Nepalese men and women dancing around the fire in celebration. Evidently a Nepalese tradition of some kind. As they made their way further into the centre of the town, Maggie was struck by the noise, the pollution in the air, the erratic driving and the sheer volume of people that lined the streets. Roaring engines, frantically beeping horns and the loud cries of a foreign tongue surrounded her now, intensifying as they grew closer to the city. Her attention was caught by the natives wearing masks over their nose and mouth to protect themselves from the pollutants circulating in the air. All around them, motorbikes whizzed past, cars veered up on their inside or outside and darted past. It was then Maggie realised there wasn't a traffic light to be seen. It was like they were travelling over a series of hump backed bridges such was the condition of the roads they travelled.

As she peered out the window, she was confronted by shanty towns and slum villages lying destitute in the suburbs of the city. Maggie had never seen such poverty in all her life. Most of the natives appeared to be living in little huts. The doors lay open and women congregated out front dressed in bright sari like garments. Washing hung out to dry from windows or clothes lines. Young children ran around playing hopscotch in their bare feet, some of them dressed in light shimmery dresses, others in plain shorts and t-shirts. They greeted the tourists walking the streets, engaging them in conversation, they were all too aware of the privileges and advantages of the outside world. They passed schools which to Maggie's naked eye appeared to resemble nothing but run down dilapidated buildings. In most cases, some of the windows lay broken into smithereens and the paint was peeling badly. Wild overgrown gardens did little to boost their decrepit look. Was this really where they educated their children? Did anyone even care? They passed Buddhist temples which announced their presence in the form of perfectly erected buildings and cheerful colours against the backdrop of a gloomy slum area. Some of them were shaped like domes, while others took the form of a Cathedral but each building was exquisite, defined by its own unique ornamentation. It surprised Maggie to learn that eighty percent of the Nepalese population were Buddhist worshippers and not Hindus as she had initially thought. She couldn't wait for her opportunity to explore this land of obvious spirituality and diversity further, she had a feeling she was going to love it here.

After what seemed like an eternity of twists and turns on bumpy roads, Raoul eventually pulled up close to a laneway that permitted them to enter the volunteer house.

"Oh my goodness, we're here." cried Jean in relief.

The driver had pulled up outside a narrow laneway that veered downwards into the middle of a slum area. Muddy paths dribbled all the way down to a gated entrance behind which stood a vast pale white building. They collected their luggage and dragged it behind them down a small hill to the house. It quickly became apparent that they would have been better off lifting their suitcases rather than wheeling them along as the mud was beginning to cover them in a nice coat of paint. Maggie winced at the sight of peeling paint and parts of the scaffolding looked like it could collapse at any minute. In fact, she wondered how the building was standing at all if truth be told. Ensconced in the brick walls allowing the infiltration of light, were small windows laden with filth and grime. The words 'run down' and 'shabby' came to mind. Nevertheless this would be her home for the next six weeks. Five-star accommodation indeed she thought to herself.

"Seriously Maggie, you're expecting me to stay here. Look at the place, it's a dump."

Somewhere in the distance, Maggie could hear her friend speaking but she wasn't interested in her petty moaning and protestations. She was like a spoiled child sometimes.

****

Volunteer coordinators prepared you for a culture shock before departure as best they could but nothing could prepare you for this. Maggie had been here mere hours and already she could sense the devastating poverty, the difference in their way of life and cultural norms.

They entered immediately into a communal space. To their left loomed a large bright window shaped into a semicircle and a worn couch was perched underneath running the length of this half of the room. A number of bean bags were located in the centre of the floor which was punctuated by a dull grey carpet, presumably for relaxation purposes as the volunteers took a break from their programmes. Off to the right lay the main staircase and the route to all the volunteer dorms. Veering straight ahead lurked the Volunteer Coordinator's office space. There were two computers in this room which were available to volunteers for instant access to the internet and emails, a much needed necessity for any home sick volunteers. Not that anybody here was showing any signs of missing home.

All around her, the volunteers chatted away amicably in foreign tongues or in English, depending who they were talking to. As always, English was the Universal language of choice. The place was a hive of activity. Volunteers were either enjoying some time out, arriving down the stairs from their dorms or arriving back from their project sites. Some of the Nepalese helpers were trying to rally a few more volunteers, ready to take them to their new place of work. Behind her, more people were arriving in their droves from distant lands, also about to begin this exciting adventure into the unknown. It was a lively place.

Maggie was amazed at the multitude of nationalities here – Spanish, German, Swiss, Dutch, Italian and English. The list was endless. Of course, the Spanish were instantly recognisable with their loud voices, brass behaviour and they flocked together like sheep.

"First of all, girls," said Sanou, addressing the four of them, "you can take your bags upstairs. We will introduce you to everyone later. Your room is on the third floor." she finished, indicating the stairs.

Naturally, Jean looked around for a lift. It was the simple things, Maggie mused.

"Is there no lift?" insisted Jean. "What kind of building doesn't have a lift?"

A lift, Maggie thought, the girl was actually looking for a lift?

"Are you for real? I don't think we're going to find one here Jean." Maggie responded, half serious half smirking to herself.

It was so typical and yet so ironic of Jean to expect things like lifts in a third world country. Maggie wondered if there was any brain inside that head sometimes. Jean had become so accustomed to a rich and affluent lifestyle, she had forgotten her roots. Wasn't she born into poverty? And the irony was that Jean was actually the more practical one of the two.

Amid another torrent of moaning and grumbling from Jean, the girls dragged and hauled their suitcases up three flights of stairs. Maggie had never felt so relieved to reach the top of a staircase. Their room was basic with two bunk beds and two large trolleys to place their clothes and accessories. A big window stood in the corner of the room where all the sights of the busy streets of Kathmandu could be seen. They were sharing the room with the two Dutch girls that had travelled out with them.

Maggie and Jean dumped their suitcases before being summoned to the roof for a tour. The roof they discovered was washing central. As all the new volunteers gathered around, Sanou explained to them:

"If you want to wash your clothes you will need to fill the bucket here with cold water." she said, pointing to a red bucket. "You should all have brought your own supply of soap or washing detergent. There is a clothes line behind me where you will be able to hang your clothes to dry."

Maggie glanced over at Jean again and she could see a clear look of incredulity on her face. Evidently, she had not expected to have to manually wash her own clothes, she had expected washing machines. Had she not read any of the information Maggie had sent her? What would she expect next? Hand dryers? Gas cooking? Full range of electricity?

The girls spent much of that night chatting to other volunteers and getting to know them. They swapped stories over a plate of Nepalese cuisine, boiled rice with chicken tofu. Maggie loved getting to know the other volunteers and learning about their reasons for coming to Nepal. For most, it was their first experience of volunteering while others were seasoned travellers. Everybody seemed so friendly and genuine and Maggie felt like she had arrived home. This was where she belonged, this was what she wanted to do with her life.

Later that evening they met all the other volunteer coordinators in the house. There were five of them in total. Shamar was the head man commanding a strong presence and overseeing the smooth operation of the day-to-day running of the house. Raoul was the charismatic one of the bunch responsible for organising trips away for all the volunteers at the weekends. Thanks to him, volunteers were offered amazing trips up the country to the jungle and an overnight stay in Pokhara. Saoul was the head woman with a strong personality charged with coordinating everyday volunteer activities. Finally, two young Indian girls identified themselves with responsibility for getting everybody to their project site on their first day and thereafter. Maggie noticed that, although friendly, they were very timid and complete introverts.

Shamar spoke at length about personal safety.

"No one should leave the volunteer house alone after dark. If you must go out after dark, please go out in a group."

Maggie was listening intently as he spoke. He had a thick Nepalese accent so it required severe levels of concentration to understand him, but Maggie persevered nonetheless.

"Lots of women are abducted in various places across the country so it is especially important to stay safe as a woman. If you plan to go hiking, travel in a group and never leave anyone by themselves." he continued.

Maggie felt a lump form in her throat. One of the things she had been most nervous about was her safety. Women went missing here all the time, never to be found again. Now, listening to Shamar harp on about it again her fears were re-ignited. Would she be safe travelling to her project site every day? What about the weekend trips to other parts of Nepal that Raoul was planning? Would those parts of Nepal be more or less safe for them to visit? And she knew for a fact that she and Jean wanted to go hiking in the Himalayas at some point over the six weeks, would they be putting themselves in extra danger by embarking on the hiking expedition? So many questions went round and around in Maggie's head. At times like these, she really wished she wasn't such a worrier. Jean certainly wasn't going to be the responsible one.

Eventually, Maggie managed to persuade herself to put her worries to the back of her mind, she was going to relax and enjoy the trip. She was halfway across the world, this was a once in a lifetime opportunity for both of them. They were only going to be here once and she was determined to make the most of it.

Maggie got into the top bunk of her bed that night (Jean had chosen the bottom bed) her mind much more at ease. As she tossed and turned, sleep seemingly evading her at every turn, Maggie longed for her father. The loss of her father had been devastating, and even after all these years, it still had the capacity to thwart her emotions. Just when she thought she was cruising along, pangs of grief came banging on her door in great tidal waves when she was least expecting it. And this was one of those moments. He would be so proud of her now, she thought, helping others in need. She missed him terribly. How she longed to hear his voice, to see his face light up when she arrived home after her day at school. The ache in her heart, the constant yearning for his presence, his love and affection never went away. As far as she was concerned, the void left by his absence had never been truly filled.

It had been fourteen years now. Of course, she still missed him terribly. There wasn't a day went by that she didn't think about him, didn't yearn for him to come back into her life. The ache in her heart would never go away, forever broken to smithereens by a loving kind and gentle father who had been right at the epicentre of her existence, but now passed on from this life.

She could recall with perfect precision the day he had died. It started out like any other day on a wet November morning. The rain clattered on the windows and fell to the ground in sheets. As Maggie peeped out her curtain window all that was visible on the horizon was a bank of grey cloud. She was fourteen and in second year at school. As the family gathered at the breakfast table, Maggie and her mother chatted amicably about the days' events while her father looked on in silence. With hindsight, Maggie realised that he had barely even acknowledged her. The sound of the kettle boiling on the hearth, of radio presenters greeting the world in the early hours and the smell of burning toast were all familiar to Maggie. This was a house full of love, warmth and affection, thus, her fathers' behaviour was peculiar. As she studied him more closely noting his unkempt appearance, his unshaven face and unruly hair, she realised with a jolt that he seemed to have lost interest in everything that was important to him.

In many respects, over the past few weeks he had reverted to a mere shell of his former self. As Maggie attempted to make conversation with him, it was as if he didn't want to acknowledge her. All she got were responses of the monosyllabic variety.

"How are you this morning, Dad?" enquired Maggie.

"Fine." growled her father.

Maggie had felt rather let down at the lack of enquiry into her own life. It was most unusual of her father to behave this way. On any given morning, he greeted her with a warm smile, poured her tea, made her toast and wanted to know about everything that was happening in her life so this marked a clear departure from the man she knew. But what was the matter with him? Had something happened at work? Was he experiencing difficulties with friends or family? Like a sinking boat, Maggie was at a loss for answers, she didn't know what was wrong!!

While Maggie's sharp instincts clearly indicated that something was amiss, she pushed it to the back of her mind, hoping it was just a bad mood that would pass. Not for one second did she anticipate events taking such a sombre turn for the worse. Little did she realise that her father was actually plotting his own death and destruction.

Maggie made her way to school that morning as normal. She groaned as she saw that she had double math's class first thing. As the teacher droned on about theorems and probability, Maggie was dreaming of all the reasons why she would never make a mathematician when, suddenly, the announcement came over the intercom summoning her to the principals' office immediately. Maggie gingerly got up from her chair, desperately trying to ignore the stares from all her classmates and made her way to the principals' office. As soon as she arrived at the door, Maggie's instincts instantly told her the news wasn't good. She would never forget the sight that greeted her as long as she lived. Her mother looked a deathly shade of white and coupled with her bloodshot eyes she could easily have resembled something straight out of a horror film. The principal, Mrs. O Connor, sat opposite her looking equally aghast. Evidently, she too had been floored by the news. Gradually, Mrs. O Connor managed to compose herself and informed her that her father had died, he had been found by her mother when she returned from doing the grocery shopping. In her wildest dreams, Maggie had never imagined this, it wasn't real. They were just a normal family sharing a life together, how could this have happened to them. Neither Maggie or her mother had had any real indication that this was on the cards, she had considered it simply a bad mood that would pass.

Maggie stood in the office too stunned to speak, frozen to the spot in her disbelief. Her father had been so precious to her, the cornerstone of her world, and in one split second all that had been wiped away. Twenty-four hours ago, Maggie had a happy family, now it stood on the brink of destruction by this one selfish act. This was like a dagger to her heart, pulling on the heartstrings. Maggie began to shiver with the cold and felt on the verge of collapsing into convulsions with the shock. Tears began to flow but very quickly her emotions escalated into debilitating anger. How could her father leave them like this? Did she matter to him at all? Was she not enough of a reason for him to continue living? Had he considered HER feelings when he decided to take his own life? Pulling a stunt like this was so out of character, in that moment Maggie felt like she didn't know him at all. And suddenly, she was overcome by a crippling rush of hatred for the man she had once adored. When she thought of him now, all she could see was his selfish existence.

The funeral passed by in a blur of chatter, tears and reminiscence but all Maggie could feel was complete shock and numbness. Mourners turned out in their droves to offer their condolences and Maggie found it utterly bizarre that they appeared to be more upset than her. Utterly captivated in her own little bubble, she could not think, she could not feel or sense anything. She did not cry once. As if she were a robot, she engaged herself in automatic mode and was just attempting to get through those awful funeral days.

Before she knew it, Maggie found herself facing her first day back at school. Arriving in the door of the classroom, her heart sank as she noticed the plethora of whispering that erupted around her. Taking great strides towards her seat, awkward sympathetic faces stared back at her, unsure of what to say. Maggie had hated that. She did not want people to pussyfoot around her, she did not want people's sympathy and she definitely didn't want to be that kid in school that everyone avoided. Maggie was utterly relieved when Jean arrived over to talk to her and it completely took her mind off the tension surrounding her. It was in moments like these that Maggie thanked her lucky stars for her best friend. Jean had been a beacon of light throughout the darkness over the past few days. She had stayed over the day of the funeral and chatting with her until the early hours, offering words of comfort. Jean had also assisted Maggie's mother with the funeral arrangements, something Maggie had felt unable to do. Maggie had felt too numb, too raw to acknowledge what had happened, let alone contemplate funeral arrangements.

As the scars slowly began to heal, Maggie began to experience an overriding sense of guilt. If only she hadn't so blatantly dismissed her fathers' poor mood. If only she had voiced her concerns to her mother perhaps her father would be alive today. There were so many 'what-if's' in the equation and Maggie found herself fluctuating between red hot fury and guilt at missing the cues. It was exhausting experiencing this myriad of emotions going round and around in her head. It took her a very long time to understand that it had nothing to do with her, that it was her fathers' decision to take his own life, his mind was made up, nothing she could have done would have stopped him. For many years she had carried around the guilt, the shame and the suffering.

With thoughts of her dad firmly on her mind, Maggie lulled herself into a gentle sleep and put all her worries to the back of her mind. All the volunteers were going to be together twenty-four seven for the next couple of weeks and travelling in large groups, what were the chances of anything happening to her? Right?

****

Michelle Brady sat opposite her husband Noel completely shocked at what she was hearing. She could see his mouth moving to form words but she might as well have been deaf because she couldn't hear him. Or rather she didn't want to. Once he had uttered the first few words, she had zoned out, completely shocked and dumbfounded.

"Michelle, I've been thinking... I need to find Jean. I need to know how she's doing." pleaded Noel, a look of complete desperation and hopelessness in his eyes.

Michelle had not been expecting this. She knew he had a daughter that he had lost contact with a long time ago but she hadn't expected this. He rarely mentioned her. He didn't even send her a card on her birthday, well, that was because he didn't have a postal address for her. But why now? Why after all these years did he need to find Jean? He had his own family now, he had forged a new life for himself with her and the children. Weren't they enough? Why was he so intent on digging up the remnants of the past?

There was a long pause, before Michelle finally spoke:

"Why is it so important to you all of a sudden? I thought that was all in the past. I don't understand. You don't even send her cards on her birthday!" she tried.

"Because I carry the guilt with me every single day. I shouldn't have given Pamela such a deadly ultimatum. I should have tried harder – for Jeans sake."

"You know you did everything you could. Who was to know she would just up and leave while you were at work? You couldn't possibly have foreseen that." she argued.

"I know, and I did try to find her initially but Pamela had orchestrated everything in such a way that I'd never find them. They may as well have disappeared off the face of the earth. And then it just became too much hard work." Noel admitted.

"Look, it was Pamela's choice to prevent you from having any contact with her, you are not to blame for that."

"Yes well, the little cow hasn't completely won. I sourced her phone number a month back so it's only a matter of time before I source Jeans number. She has no right to stop all contact between us."

Michelle smiled to herself, he was like a little boy who had lost his favourite toy. It was exactly what she had found so devastatingly attractive about him when they first met. He could make a statement or get an idea into his head and have absolutely no idea of the consequences. She felt certain he thought this was as simple as organising a coffee or a lunch with Jean and everything would miraculously work itself out. He had no consideration how Jean might have felt about her abandonment all those years ago. In her head, he had abandoned her, there was no doubt about that. Michelle was sure that Pamela had fed her a whole concoction of lies growing up and injected her poisonous venom into the poor girl. Jean had only heard one side of the story and she had no reason to dispute it.

Noel was going to have to fight a long hard battle if he was ever going to repair his relationship with her. While Pamela might have been the one to sabotage it, it was Noel that was going to have to pick up the pieces. Michelle stole a glance at her husband and felt a rush of affection towards him. She couldn't help but notice that he had aged enormously in the last few months. His eyes now boasted big dark circles and lines had begun to appear in places she had never known before. He looked stressed, anxious and exhausted. He had no idea what lay ahead.

Noel remembered that fateful day only too well. It had started out like any other day. He had been a man of routine and had left the house for work that morning at quarter past eight as he always did. He had kissed Pamela goodbye and played with Jean for a while before leaving the house. She had been a ray of sunshine and was capable of brightening up even the darkest day. How he had doted on her. Little did he realise that would be the last time he would see his daughter.

Noel pulled into the driveway after work that evening to find the house in darkness. He was immediately overcome with a sense of unease as Pamela had not mentioned that she was going anywhere. And it wasn't like Pamela to just nip out, he thought, not in her current state. Something wasn't right. He tried to suppress an ominous feeling in his gut that was accelerating at the rate of knots but failed miserably. Fearing that Pamela and Jean may have been robbed or worse he quickly turned on all the lights shouting out loud as he went.

"Pamela!" he shouted, running into the living room but finding nothing except a pile of magazines and a coffee cup. The house looked exactly as he had left it that morning, even a little tidier. Maybe Pamela had listened to him after all.

"Pamela!" he shouted again as he flew up the stairs wondering what on earth had happened. No response. Finally, he made it to the bedroom and found it empty. Panicking now, he started pulling out drawers and went to open the wardrobe. All of Pamela's stuff was gone, so was her roll along suitcase. She had left him. And it hit him like a dagger in the heart.

****

Yes electricity, that was the next curse to befall them. On their first night, the electricity was conveniently cut off. They were informed that this would be a regular occurrence, electricity would be cut off for about three hours several times a week. This astounded Maggie, was this country really so poor that they couldn't get something as basic as electricity right? But then again, they didn't have access to clean running water in most areas.

Maggie woke early on her first morning. Silently, she rose from her bed and made her way out onto the balcony. She was greeted by a dull grey overcast sky but the heat closed in around them and felt hot and sticky. Thank God they had the luxury of hot showers she exclaimed to herself enjoying the momentary solitude before the day began. Jean was still snoring like a trouper and evidently had no intention of surfacing anytime soon. Maggie contemplated throwing a bucket of cold water over her face.

An exciting day with a packed itinerary awaited them. In the morning they were due to be shown around the various project sites to help them to make the right volunteer choices for them. Jean had happily spent the evening bending the ear of anyone who would listen that she had no special volunteering talent.

"I'm actually not really made of this stuff, I just came to support a friend. Could you imagine me helping out in the orphanages? I think it's the children who would be looking after me, not the other way around." she exclaimed to an eruption of laughter. Was there anywhere she went that she wasn't the centre of attention, Maggie wondered?

Eventually, after much persuasion, Jean decided to make the excruciating decision to get out of bed and face the day.

"Gosh, why do we have to get up so early? I thought we were volunteering!" Jean cried.

"We are. But that doesn't mean we get to stay in bed all day."

"But why so early? They don't need us this early, that should be against the law." moaned Jean. She really wasn't a morning person.

"Come on now, hit the showers or we'll miss breakfast." insisted Maggie whacking her over the head with a towel. That ought to lull her out of her slumber.

"Alright alright, miss bossy boots."

After feasting on a breakfast of cereal which resembled something akin to cornflakes, fruit and a blackberry smoothie, all the volunteers were presented with the structure their day would take. Sanou, one of their volunteer coordinators began to speak in her thick Nepalese accent that was a quick reminder of just how far away they were from home.

"Good morning all, you are very welcome to Nepal. We are delighted to have you all here at the Intec camp and I hope you will enjoy your time here with us," she began, her loud voice booming around the room. "Today, we are going to show you all around the various project sites so that you can select a project that best fits what you want to do. I would ask you all to start thinking about what you want to get out of your time here with us."

A chorus of applause went sailing around the room as they hung on Sanou's every word, all the volunteers delighted that their travelling was over and the day could begin.

"Finally, I just wanted to let you know that monkeys are a serious issue here. On our way to some of the project sites, we will be passing through areas where there are lots of monkeys."

"Monkeys." laughed Jean.

"It's no laughing matter." Sanou replied.

Maggie shot a scornful look at Jean and for a moment she looked like a chastised schoolgirl.

"If you get bitten by a monkey out here, you will be infected with rabies." Sanou continued. "Please do not make eye contact with them, take any photographs or have any fresh fruit in your hand when passing through these areas." Sanou instructed.

"What, Why?" asked Jean, adeptly tuning into the conversation now. She had been too busy talking to the other volunteers, the cute Spanish male volunteers especially, while Sanou was speaking and had missed the entire speech. Maggie groaned. She was such an embarrassment sometimes.

"Because you could be bitten by a monkey. And if you are bitten by a monkey, you will most likely get rabies." Sanou repeated patiently. God Bless her, she had the patience of a Saint, Maggie thought.

Sanou then proceeded to outline a rough schedule for all volunteers over the coming weeks. Depending on their program, they could be volunteering as early as 7.30am in the Orphanages. All other volunteer programmes began at 9.30am, including teaching in the primary schools, helping to design a classroom or helping out in local nursing homes. Afternoons were all about the education of Nepalese women and children. The opportunity was there to teach them English and computers, something the local population was extremely grateful for. While Sunday until Thursday was considered a working day, Friday and Saturday were counted as days off. The programmes and experience on offer varied and there was something for everyone.

Breakfast was between 7am and 8am ("oh no!" said Jean) lunch was between 1pm and 2pm and dinner was served at the grand hour of 7pm. Outside of that, time was their own to spend. Although, it was expected they would put some time into preparing for their individual projects. They might have to come up with new ideas, or design posters that would explain simple grammatical terms better. The more time and effort they put in, the more they got out of it.

Lunch was the major event of the day and divided opinion. Some of the volunteers were satisfied with chicken tofu and rice, others were not. Naturally Jean thought she was back home in Ireland again and was expecting something that resembled restaurant quality pasta carbonara. She was bitterly disappointed with the menu option, tentatively lifting the lid for fear she might be infected with some fatal disease and refused to eat it. Instead, she indulged in the fresh fruit on offer to satisfy her appetite. Maggie sighed in exasperation, far away in Nepal they might be but some things never changed.

Maggie was looking forward to going hiking at the weekend. Nothing cleared the head like a good hike and the views were supposed to be spectacular. She might as well put those hiking boots to some use she thought. She hadn't spent forty euro on them for nothing.

****

Abdul was at home downing the last of his stiff brandy when he noticed his mobile phone burst to life. Picking up his phone to see who was calling him, he smiled as he recognised the number. He felt sure this was good news.

"To what do I owe the pleasure?" volunteered Abdul before the man had a chance to speak.

"I don't have long so just listen. Two Irish women, alone, late-teens/early twenties, going hiking in the Himalayas will be travelling down by bus tomorrow." said the voice at the other end of the phone.

"Excellent! Where can we find them?" he asked.

"They are booked into the Himalayan Inn Hotel but you're better off working out a strategy with your team to capture them before they get to the hotel." said the voice.

"Okay, give me all the details." Abdul instructed as he picked up a pen from his nearby coffee table and stood up to fetch a notepad from the far side of the room.

"They will be on the 5pm bus from Kathmandu and will be getting off at the main bus stop at the Himalayan resort by the supermarket. They should arrive at about 8pm. They will need to get a tuk-tuk a short distance to the hotel from there."

"Are they suitable for what I'm looking for?"

"Yes. Both good looking, one in particular is tall with sallow skin. Both young, fresh and clean living, I think they'll be a catch with your clients."

"Fantastic!" replied Abdul, sighing with relief.

He supposed he wasn't short on young females to capture really. Authoritarian father figures made recluses of most Nepalese women meaning they largely confined themselves to their own homes and rarely walked the streets, alone at least. No, he had begun to explore alternative options a long time ago. He needed to expand his ethnic mix. He thought of it like jellybeans, all different flavours for all different people.

Every day, young females arrived on Himalayan soil from all four corners of the globe desperate for that once in a lifetime experience, each of them as clueless as the last. From all walks of life, they stood out like sore thumbs with their map in hand and big lopsided vacant expressions. Most of them were only seventeen or eighteen, unbelievably vulnerable and naive, making for easy prey. Some of them might as well have been shouting their address from the rooftops. It was then he realised, his greatest opportunity lay right on his doorstep. He would have been a fool not to take advantage of the situation. Yes, he smirked to himself, mentally giving himself a pat on the back, that had been a smart move.

Invariably, they ranged from Supermodel stunning with big puppy dog eyes and plump lips to just plain average looking. His was a unique taste in that he found himself more attracted to blonde, blue-eyed women. All the women here were a roaring concoction of jet black hair and brown eyes so the novelty was lost on him. But that was just his preference.

His repertoire boasted kidnappings of up to six women such was the extent of his capabilities and he was thrilled to have a challenge. Yes, he was happy to have some more potential candidates, he would certainly give them a once in a lifetime experience on the other side of the world.

Back on the phone, the voice continued on ."But they're smart, you might want to up your game a little bit."

"Alright, good work. I'll get my team on the case." he said.

"I've got to go, I can't talk for much longer. Make sure you're there. Bye."

Abdul hung up the phone, very pleased with himself. He had been waiting for this moment, his next opportunity. This would get his clients off his back, at least for a while. In his head he was already beginning to plot a strategy to capture them. And capture them he would.

An hour later, Abdul sat behind his large desk and stared up at the faces in front of him. Three fine young men, Sajit, Babu and Kamal stood before him. They had worked on several projects with him in the past and had proven their individual capabilities.

Tall and handsome, Sajit endorsed the brains of the group. Passionate and compelling, he had the energy and enthusiasm to lead the group in their endeavours. Built with a small and stocky frame, Babu was the practical one. When everyone ran out of ideas, he was bursting at the seams with loads of fresh ones. He could make anything happen with limited resources, whether it involved using a handkerchief to halt blood loss from a wound or using any tools at his disposal to get himself out of sticky situations. He possessed quick wit and intellect which earned him a significant reputation among his peers as an accomplished gunman and attacker. His courage and bravery were renowned among his friends and ensured he was a force to be reckoned with. Fighting with Babu was like falling deep into the throes of a fearless destiny. It was a stroke of fate that allowed Babu to join this team and Abdul was sure he would be a most valued addition. With his 20/20 vision and pitch perfect hearing, Kamal was the observant member of the group. Of average height and build, Kamal could hear far away sounds before anyone else and he could see well into the night. His overriding distinguishing feature, however, was the ability to run like the wind. An accomplished athlete, he could sprint at a pace akin to an Olympic professional and this meant that he was often left sprinting after anyone that tried to get away. Invariably he caught them, they were no match for him. His specific skill set often resulted in heavy night time duty on red alert for any enemies or trespassers.

And Anoushka, the sole female. He made a point of having a female on any team that he assembled, that was one of his main strategies and it worked for him every time. It was important for empathy, call it a woman's touch. Anoushka, herself a young woman in her early thirties with long dark hair and large brown eyes would be in a prime position to earn their trust. She wore spectacles on her nose and the centre of her forehead was dotted by a pink star.

Yes, Abdul was more than happy with the team he had carefully assembled. Their individual capabilities complemented each other perfectly and together would provide all the necessary skills and resources to make this mission a success.

"I have assembled you all here today to carry out a very specific task." he began. "Two girls, two Irish tourists, both late teens/early twenties. I want you to capture them and bring them here to this house." he said.

"But sir –" protested Anoushka.

"Silence, Anoushka!" commanded Abdul, his tone silencing even the strongest of characters.

Anoushka bit her tongue and restrained herself from protesting any further. She had grown up overshadowed by her three brothers. Smarter and more intelligent than the three of them combined, she had been denied access to education past the age of ten. Her parents had claimed it was too expensive to send her to school and university, but she was no dim wit. She knew it was because she was a woman. Money was not a problem when it came to her brothers' education, but it was for hers. Her father did not value her as an equal contributor to society, preferring her to stay at home and help her mother with the housework, as traditionally most Nepalese girls were expected to do. She spent her childhood and most of her teenage years watching her brothers' get up for school every morning and get their education. How she would have loved to have been just like them. Slowly, the resentment began to eat away inside her until she arrived at a distorted sense of reality. She began to view her female counterparts as weak imbeciles for putting up with such adverse treatment. Why was she the only one being so vocal about it and standing up for a woman's right to an education? From where she stood, her female counterparts were all too pathetic to fight their corner. What a disgrace to femininity. A brainless oaf she would never be. Without realising it, her resentment of women had turned to hatred and so she no longer felt any sense of loyalty. Her blood had turned cold and she experienced no empathy for their plight. She knew exactly how to charm them and win their trust though which helped her to excel at her job.

When her father approached her about marrying the son of one of his friends at fifteen, it had been the final straw. She had been disgusted at her father's treatment, that he could sit there and expect her to marry this random man whom she had never met. It was beyond incredulous. The older she got, the less she could tolerate his absolute disregard for her feelings or opinions. She had finally snapped and decided to do something about it. She had run away from the family home without really knowing where she was going. But she didn't care, anywhere was better than home. She needed to find somewhere she could be useful. She was damned if she was going to devote her life to a loveless marriage, raising children and condemning her days to the dreary drudgery of housework, knitting and sewing. She was far too intelligent for that.

"They will be arriving at the Himalayan resort by bus about 8pm tomorrow night. Both girls are white, one is tall with dark brown hair and slightly sallow skin. The other girl is about 5 foot 2, with pale skin, and shoulder length brown hair. I don't care how you do it, bring them to me. Any questions?" Abdul was saying, bringing her back to the present moment.

"No, Sir." replied Sajit, eager to get moving on this mission.

It was show time.

CHAPTER 5

It was their first Friday in Nepal and the weekend beckoned along with an opportunity to explore the country. Maggie and Jean had made plans for hiking in the Himalayas and would stay overnight. With the help of Raoul, they had booked into decent accommodation close by. He had also given them very clear directions, sent them on the safest routes and given them tips to stay safe. Ever since herself and Jean had voiced their plans, he had insisted on helping them. Every evening over the last few days, the three of them had sat together and spent hours poring over various websites, making phone calls and pricing hotels in the safest areas. Dining out in Nepal was a precarious experience and knowing that both Jean and Maggie had only landed, he advised them of the best restaurants and the foods that should be given a wide berth.

"If you are eating out or shopping in a supermarket, do not order or buy chicken or fresh fruit as it will be contaminated and could make you ill. Stick to vegetarian options."

"What about the food in the volunteer house? We often get chicken served in those meals? And there's fresh fruit available every day? I love my fresh fruit in the mornings so I've been making myself ill for the last couple of days apparently. Come to think of it, I have noticed that my stomach has been acting rather odd.......would that be why?" volunteered Jean, while patting her stomach at the same time.

"Would you stop?" Maggie said, turning towards her friend now.

"What? If it's not the food here then what else is it?" she asked.

"Your imagination perhaps?"

"Hey -"

"Jean, will you shut up. You're no more sick than the man on the moon. Raoul here is only trying to help us. Seriously." Maggie said, escalating into a state of embarrassment. She really didn't understand Jean sometimes. She could be so rude and insensitive, she didn't know when to keep her mouth shut.

"No, that would not be why." Raoul continued, answering Jean's question and making light of the situation. "The volunteer house serves only fresh food and ingredients cooked in a clean, hygienic kitchen. The problem with restaurants or cafes is that you don't know what hygiene standards they adhere to. There are no governing food safety regulations so hand washing practices and general hygiene standards are poor. Add to that poor sanitation and you've got a recipe for disaster." Raoul finished in his soft Nepalese accent.

Raoul had extensive knowledge of the Himalayas and he even assisted them in figuring out their bus route to their destination. He had been so kind, so helpful. It would have been much more difficult to plan a trip like this by themselves.

"Well girls, I hope you have a great time, please bring me back some pictures." Raoul said now with a smile as they were gathering their bags at the front of the volunteer house.

"Thanks Raoul." Maggie replied in return.

Ever since she had arrived in Nepal, she had been overwhelmed by the utter humanity shown to her by the natives. Raoul was only one of them. Now, she just had to detach Jean from the house, she was yapping like a madwoman to one of the Spanish volunteers. Seemed quite appropriate actually, they had quite a lot in common.

Eventually, the girls bid their farewells and made their way into the centre of Kathmandu where they would catch the bus to their accommodation. The air was hot and humid but not particularly sunny. Casting her eye up to the sky, she marveled at how similar it was to home. Big grey watery clouds, dull and overcast with the sun making giant leaps to burst through but failing miserably. Yep, with the exception of the sweltering heat, she may as well be at home. But one look around reminded her of just how far away she really was.

It began with her ears. The noise on the busy streets of Kathmandu made Dublin sound like a silent movie. All around her, throngs of people spoke in a heavy Nepalese tongue at the top of their voices, while on the roads, the noisy engines of the tuk-tuks fought over the din to make themselves heard. Not that they had to try hard such was the noise that emanated from them. Other road users also added to the heightened noise levels flying past on their motor bikes and cars bouncing along the dented roads hardly daring to stop unless obliged to. The incessant sound of horns alerted Maggie to angry drivers – a particular regular occurrence in this part of the world since there were no rules to be obeyed on Nepalese roads. As she walked along the streets with Jean in tow, she could overhear the loud voices of angry drivers as they babbled away at each other in their native tongue. It frightened her to think of the volume of road accidents and deaths that must occur here.

As she stepped out on to the road briefly to avoid two oncoming middle aged women, Maggie noticed the dirt gathered in the sidewalks. Two deep crevices running alongside the pavement revealed the woefully inadequate drainage systems in operation, with dirt and grime clogging every available space. Fumes, dust and pollutants streaked the air and it seemed to Maggie that a constant cyclical wheel of particles floated in front of her as she walked. The air was never quite clear. She was struck by the large volume of natives wearing masks over their nose and mouth as well, clearly to protect themselves from the harmful effects of pollution.

The streets were lined with old shabby buildings, most of them littered with rust and run down. Oceans of colour met the stray wanderer's eye however, in the form of large posters painted over windows or colourful sarongs on display outside shop windows. The native women dressed in a beautiful array of bright vibrant colours, immediately catching the eye.

Maggie and Jean made it to their bus stop, the excitement of their impending adventure growing by the minute. Loud screeching brakes and a heavy bang alerted them that their bus had arrived. A small fragile looking vehicle with enough seats to accommodate about twenty people, Maggie feared it would turn on its head with the weight of everyone on board. They quickly paid their fare, Jean staring half stupid at the bus driver as he charged them fifteen Nepalese rupees, the equivalent of twenty cent. Of course, forgetting where she was, Jean was about to launch into a whole spiel about how she was not a child and that she was older than she looked. A timely dig in the ribs from Maggie put a stop to that.

They gingerly took their seats before the bus roared into action and whisked them away in the direction of the mountainous Himalayas. Four hours of a bus journey would bring them to their destination and neither of them were looking forward to it. Jean was not a good traveller and about half an hour into their journey she began to complain of nausea. Fortunately for her (and Maggie) she was fully stocked with Motilium which quickly put her at ease. Maggie enjoyed space and solitude while travelling, preferring to just relax and use the opportunity to let her mind wander. Jean, on the other hand, preferred to pass the time by talking incessantly. Today, she was talking about the mosquitoes. She had had the misfortune of being bitten by mosquitoes on her first night while Maggie had remained bite free.

"So my insect repellent spray is useless. I sprayed that stuff all around the room, all over my bed sheets and everything. I practically choked myself in the stuff. And I still got bitten." Jean moaned.

"They must like you, don't know what I'm doing wrong." chided Maggie, smirking from ear to ear, unable to resist a dig at her grumbling pal.

After four hours enduring Jean's non stop idle chit chat (she was very self centred) their bus finally screeched to a halt at the main bus stop in the Himalayan Resort.

"We're here!" she cried. She practically ran off the bus so desperate was she to get a minute's peace from Jeans' incessant chatter.

"Maggie wait." Jean shouted after her, but it fell on deaf ears, before she finally scrambled to her feet and dismounted the bus.

They stretched their legs with delight, glad to see the end of their long bus journey. She would have to do it all again in a few days' time but for now, she wanted to relish the moment. Maggie breathed in the air and exhaled slowly. After several days in the overcrowded capital city, it was a welcome relief to find herself in this most glorious part of the world. How lucky was she?

An endless ocean of colours, trees and mountains surrounded them, punctuated by the sinking sun which bathed the landscape in a slowly wilting orange glow. Chrysanthemums, bluebells, daffodils, roses and a whole host of other flowers that Maggie didn't recognise embellished the surrounding greenery to perfection. It was an absolutely magnificent sight to behold. This was nature at its finest.

It was a disgruntled Jean that joined Maggie moments later, she wasn't the best of travellers.

"So, Raoul said that we need to get a tuk-tuk to the hotel." Maggie informed her friend. She took a moment to observe her surroundings. The bus had evidently dropped them off in the middle of the town. All around them loomed clothes shops, tea shops, small corner shops, phone shops pretending to sell SIM Cards that would 'definitely work on your mobile phone' when in reality all they did was cost ten euro for a one minute dodgy phone-call. And of course, the obligatory souvenir shops. They were everywhere.

They had definitely left the rat race city life of Kathmandu behind. Unlike the capital where strong odours assaulted her nostrils, noise levels of dizzying heights assailed her ears and she was barely able to see two hundred yards ahead with the throngs of people, there was an air of calm to be found here. The ferocity on the road wasn't quite as intense, buses, cars, taxis and motor bikes sailed past them confident they would reach their destination but not feeling the need to break speed limits. Not that there were any in this country. A mixture of tourists and natives lined the streets, the tourists invariably standing out considerably taking their time exploring the sights, lingering in some of the little quaint tea shops or emerging from the various clothes shops laden down with their cheaper than cheap purchases.

"Ugh really, another one of those things, do we have to?" said Jean's whining voice in her ear. "I've had enough of them already this week to last me a life time. Can't we just get a taxi or something?"

"No Jean, there are perfectly good and cheap tuk-tuks that will get you from A to B." Maggie responded.

"God, you're such a cheapskate, it would probably only cost like five euro." she began in protest but faltered as Maggie shot her a venomous look. Admitting defeat and resigning herself to the fact that she was fighting a losing battle, she decided to play the part of helpful friend again. "So, where do we get one from?"

"That's what I'm just trying to figure out. According to Raoul, we should barely have to walk two hundred yards, on this side of the street. And he said there should be a supermarket opposite the tuk-tuk stop. Do you see a supermarket?" she asked, scanning the streets as they walked.

Maggie resented feeling so vulnerable, it made her uncomfortable. It was the control freak in her. Unfamiliar territory gave her the creeps.

"Well, that depends, are we talking about Supervalu or Tesco's?" Jean asked, her voice laced with sarcasm.

"Hahaha, very funny Jean. No seriously, do you see anything that looks remotely like a supermarket? You're the one with good eyesight." she said, giving her friend a playful dig in the arm.

"There," said Jean, indicating a shop across the road that could potentially be classed as a supermarket. Big, bright and spacious, it dominated a considerable amount of space. Large colourful signage alerted passers by to its presence. It was the display of some dodgy looking fruit and vegetables outside, however, that essentially confirmed its status. "That looks something like a supermarket, what do you think?"

"Technically yes, let's see if there's a tuk-tuk sign here then." Maggie said, as they made to cross the road and began searching for any evidence this might be a tuk-tuk stop.

Out of nowhere, a young woman, about early thirties, approached them. She was dressed from head to toe in a bright green sarong. She wore her long dark hair loosely back in a ponytail which draped over her shoulder. Her dark brown skin made Jean look anaemic beside her, let alone Maggie. In the centre of her forehead, she wore a pink star and when she spoke it was with broken English and a heavy Nepali accent. Instinctively, Maggie took a step back, not suspicious exactly, but cautious nonetheless.

"Are you lost?" she asked, edging closer to them. "Can I help you?"

Maggie was about to reply when Jean got there before her. "We are looking to get a tuk-tuk to the Himalayan Inn Hotel" she volunteered, carefully pronouncing her words, so that the woman would be able to understand her.

"Ah yes!" the woman exclaimed in delight. "Tuk-tuk, yes." Maggie and Jean stared at her for a moment expecting her to continue. When she didn't, it was Maggie who intervened.

"Is this the correct tuk-tuk stop do you know?" Maggie asked, again pronouncing her words with utmost clarity.

Why was it always her? She was getting rather fed up with it. As far as she could see, Jean was making absolutely no effort to help find their way. That wasn't fair. Maggie was doing all the navigating, making all the enquiries and ensuring they were on the right bus/tuk-tuk to their destination while Jean waited in the wing like a helpless child. Maggie was aware that Jean hadn't been all that interested in the trip from the outset, in her heart she knew that. but it was almost as if because it was Maggie's idea, she was happy to let her do all the work. It was starting to grate on her nerves.

"Ah yes, yes – dat will take you to hotel. One here very very soon." the woman said.

"Great, thank you." Maggie replied, giving her a warm smile.

"Your names?" she asked, beginning to show a little interest in their endeavours.

"I'm Maggie," she volunteered "and this is my friend Jean."

"Very nice." she replied. "Where from?"

"Ireland." ventured Jean, proud as always of her heritage.

"Lovely meet you, have nice trip." she said, before making her exit.

The woman disappeared into a shop nearby and Jean and Maggie continued to wait for their tuk-tuk that would whisk them off to their hotel.

"Come on tuk-tuk." Jean groaned. "I'm tired."

Moments later, a tuk-tuk catapulted to a halt right in front of them leaving a shroud of dust in its wake. They were very fragile little vehicles really running on wheels, light as a feather, almost in danger of over turning at the slightest gust of wind. They had a gaping hole at the back through which passengers could mount or dismount the vehicle.

They scrambled aboard to find two young men already ensconced. The man opposite Jean was dark and handsome, his head barely managing to avoid bursting through the roof. Jean couldn't stop ogling him and Maggie had to nudge her a few times to bring her back to reality. It could be dangerous for women to overtly ogle men in this part of the world. Opposite Maggie sat a man of average build staring straight ahead, barely even blinking. He didn't appear to be connected to his surroundings at all. They were just about to depart when the woman from a few moments earlier came dashing towards them. She was running from the shop frantically shouting something in Nepali and waving her two arms like a lunatic. She was indicating for someone to hold the tuk-tuk for her.

"Wait!" cried Maggie, shouting at the driver. "There's someone coming."

The woman quickly climbed aboard and took a seat beside one of the men. The driver directed the vehicle out of its parking spot into the traffic. They took off at lightning speed and Maggie felt an impending sense of excitement. They were almost there. Raoul had told them it should take no more than ten minutes. All she wanted was to have a hot shower and relax. She was exhausted. Tomorrow they would explore the Himalayas.

Beside her, Jean was still ogling the man opposite her. She was making some brief attempts at conversation, but he didn't respond. He probably hadn't a word of English. Thank God he wasn't indulging her, otherwise, it would have been painful for everyone.

They had been driving for about five minutes, when suddenly Maggie's reverie was interrupted by the mutterings of those around her. The two men and the woman appeared to be conversing with each other, as though they knew one another. That was odd, Maggie had assumed they were strangers and they certainly hadn't acknowledged each other until that point. She couldn't make out what they were saying but they appeared to be making a request to the driver. Maggie wondered if they knew him too. What intrigued her the most, however, was that the woman appeared to have the inside track in this conversation. Suddenly, the tuk-tuk came to a stop. They couldn't be at the hotel yet, they had only been on the road for five minutes. Raoul had told them it would take a good ten minutes. Why were they stopped? Something was amiss.

"Why are we stopped?" quipped Jean, looking around her, going to the edge of the tuk-tuk and peering out. "Where are we?" she asked, her head rotating on its' axis, all senses heightened, her earlier adoration for the man opposite momentarily forgotten.

Maggie was about to address the woman in English and make some attempt to find out what was happening. She might be able to get a bit of information from her. She was just about to open her mouth when she received the most unmerciful blow to the head from the man that had been sitting opposite. All she remembered before succumbing to unconsciousness was Jean receiving the same blow to her head from the man that she had only moments earlier been practically proclaiming her undying love for. The woman appeared to be looking on.

****

Noel Brady stood pacing up and down his living room floor, his phone balancing precariously on the back of his palm. How he had not dropped it yet remained a mystery. He had been tossing and turning all night trying to decide if he should ring Jean now or wait until she returned from Nepal. The idea of intruding when she was a young woman living life to the full did not appeal to him. This side of his brain chastised him for even contemplating such a wretched and little thought out plan. He should at least wait until she returned from Nepal. "Leave the poor girl alone" his subconscious screamed.

The other side of his brain possessed a guilty conscience for all the birthdays, Christmases and other significant events he had missed while she was growing up. While he fully accepted that his relationship with her would be strained and fraught with tension for some time, he didn't want to waste another minute.

He was getting older day by day and the older he got the clearer his priorities in life became. One of those priorities included attempting to re-establish his relationship with his daughter. There was every chance that she would blank him and refuse to even meet up with him, but at least he would have tried. If he never tried, he would never know and would be forced to spend his life wondering.

Looking down at his phone, he dialed her number. Asking Michelle to source Jean's number and email address from her beauty salon, which she had frequented twice in the last eighteen months had been a stroke of genius, he commended himself. Of course, he felt a stab of guilt at the blatant breach of confidentiality but he had no choice, Pamela was refusing to pass on her number. What was he supposed to do? Their last telephone conversation had been an ugly one to say the least. As he had predicted, the phone went straight to voicemail so he simply left a short message.

"Hi Jean, this is your father, Noel Brady calling. Can you please give me a call when you get this message? Thanks." Noel dictated, speaking into the phone. He had never been all that comfortable leaving voice messages, he was especially unhappy at being forced into leaving one on this occasion, however, given the circumstances. He didn't really know why he felt so deflated, the girl was in Nepal enjoying the time of her life. Answering the phone to her estranged father was hardly going to trump her list of priorities.

He confessed himself disappointed nevertheless. He would have loved to have spoken to her, gauged her reaction to his phone call and learn all about her trip to Nepal. Over the last few weeks, his thoughts had often strayed to Jean and her trip. He wondered where she was now or what she was doing. He felt certain that she would be enjoying one adventurous escapade after another. What adventure would befall her today he wondered?

Suddenly desperate to contact her, he began to think of all the alternative methods of reaching her and the different options open to him - letter, email, skype. If speaking to her over the phone was not going to be an option, he wanted to communicate with her some other way. He decided to steer clear of the facebook route as he didn't think that was appropriate. Allowing his brain to wander, he imagined himself boarding a flight to Nepal to visit Jean. Fat chance of that.

Sighing to himself, he placed his phone on the coffee table and walked over to the corner of the room to switch on his computer. She would have access to email, he would reach her that way. Chuckling to himself, he sat down at his computer and began to type.

****

Maggie stirred moments later to find her hands and feet tied, lying helpless and motionless. Looking around her, she saw Jean was in the same predicament. They were in some blacked out vehicle now, cruising along at rapid speed to God knew where. Instantly she recognised every single one of her captors, they had all been in that tuk-tuk. Even the man that had been driving the tuk-tuk now commanded the suave blacked out van that bore them hence. This was bizarre. What was going on?

Then she saw the woman that only moments earlier had been lending them a helping hand. And then it hit her like a brick wall, this seizure had been planned; every meticulous movement meditated to the most minute detail. That woman was supposed to find them...and the tuk-tuk that picked them up was ordained to be the exact one her captors were in. And the common denominator in all of this was the young woman who now sat watching over them, enjoying their slow registration of the events of the last hour. She had facilitated all of this. Maggie felt a rush of hatred for her so fierce it threatened to incapacitate her. It was completely out of character for her to allow such a negative emotion to open her pores and seep into her wounds but this one she just couldn't suffuse. Not this time.

They drove a short distance before Maggie felt the touch of the breaks beneath her and the van slowed to a halt. Maggie was on red hot alert, every movement made passing like a sensuous rhythm through her body and the faintest sound exploding in her ears. If only she weren't blindfolded, she thought disparagingly to herself. She was certain that she would have enjoyed spikes to her vision as well.

She heard a loud clicking noise at the back of the van and suddenly, both Jean and Maggie's ties around the ankles were loosened. Next, they were roughly hauled from the back of the van. Maggie was pushed and shoved up a winding pathway, her arms locked behind her and more than once, she made loud protestations over such violent manhandling. But every time she protested, she was shoved forward another inch.

"Just keep walking little lady and shut that filthy mouth of yours." she heard Kamal instruct into her ear.

They must have arrived at the front door of some house as Maggie heard the sound of a doorbell ringing and footsteps scrambling to answer it. A man with an unfamiliar voice spoke.

"Bring them in." he commanded.

And she was being manhandled again by one of the men, passing through corridors or halls, she didn't know which. A sharp right turn seemed to indicate that she was being led into a room of some kind and she heard the sound of a door click behind her. She was led to the centre of the room before a gentle shove catapulted her to the floor. A moment later, she heard the gentle thud of Jean landing beside her.

Maggie breathed a sigh of relief as her blindfold was removed and it took a couple of seconds before she was able to focus her vision. Looking around her, she felt lost in such a massive room and couldn't dissuade an over riding feeling that it could swallow her whole. Instantly she could tell she was in a mansion as evidenced by the marble stone floor and the exquisite furniture that decorated the room. The ceiling rose to extensively high proportions and a beautiful crystal chandelier dangled down from its centre. Off to her right stood a large piano, so vast, it threatened to engulf the room. A sofa stood adjacent to the piano set decorated in hand crafted material with vibrant black and red colours. Three cushions sat interspersed across the space of the couch and her attention was caught by a particular embellishment. On all three cushions was a large black X with a white dot. Every indication pointed to this being a symbol of some kind. Where were they? Floor to ceiling windows cast beams of light into the room giving it the impression of being bright and airy.

Off to the left, two armchairs stood with their back to her. She could vaguely make out the top of someone's head sitting in one of them. As they all scrambled into the room, he rose to greet them.

"Jean and Maggie," began Abdul with a smile. "I thought you'd never arrive." looking from one girl to the other as he surveyed them.

Maggie disliked him instantly, despising everything about him. The silk smooth lilt in his voice, the assertion of power, the charisma and the uber confident demeanour. Moreover, his jet black hair and ill fitting jaw line did not lend itself easily to an attractive look. But there was something more about this man that was troubling her. From the moment she cast her eyes on him, her first perception was sleaziness personified. He was so unbelievably smooth and sleek. It made her skin crawl. She was lucky she had managed to avoid shuddering in front of him.

"What do you want with us?" demanded Jean. She looked quite a sight, her hair was tossed in every direction, her cheeks were hotly flushed and there were marks around her eyes where she had been blindfolded. Maggie was sure she must look the same.

"Please, just let us go." Maggie interjected in a weak attempt at a plea bargain.

"Feisty, aren't we?" responded Abdul in a mock voice, the depths of a smirk beginning to caress his face. "I like that."

Abdul had seen it all before, the horror, the confusion and the vulnerability. Anytime he had ordered women abducted for his brothel, they arrived to him in his mansion in their most vulnerable state, completely at his mercy, begging for their lives and willing to do anything in exchange for their freedom. It was an enthralling and liberating experience to wield that kind of power over another and he had become addicted to it, feasting on their weakness. It was his life blood, like a soothing balm to his wounded soul. Compassion and empathy were not words that featured in his vocabulary, he had a business to run and he would do whatever it took to serve his customers.

He stepped forward towards both girls, dressed immaculately in his suave dark suit, with gleaming white shirt and black tie, walking around them in a circle, peering in close at intervals, sniffing their hair and stroking their faces. Advancing right up to Maggie, he hovered over her, his lips inches from hers, his breath close, and lingered there for a few moments. Instinctively reacting to the blatant invasion of her personal space, Maggie jolted backwards and their eyes met for a moment as he registered her displeasure. Maggie wasn't sure if she was imagining it or not, but she thought she could detect a certain sense of satisfaction at her obvious discomfort. Then he turned away, laughing and jeering with the others. What a coward, thought Maggie, he was just relishing exerting his power over two defenceless females. She would love to see him against a man of his own strength and physicality.

"Why, this one refuses me." he was joking with the others, indicating Maggie. "Such pretty meat, oh, my clients will be very pleased with you." he chanted. Turning to face them directly, his brown eyes shrank until they became mere dots in their sockets and he fixed the girls with a stare, so fierce, it brought shivers to their spines.

And suddenly Maggie snapped. She had been hovering on the edge for quite some time, just barely managing to contain her emotions. She didn't want to give anyone in this room the satisfaction of losing her temper, that would only feed right into their hands. But this was the final straw, her emotions had come flooding to the surface and burst at the seams until she lost all control.

"You twisted pervert. You let us go. NOW" she shrieked, fear clearly transparent in her voice.

"Oh, but that would only spoil the fun, I know just what I'm going to do with you." he retorted coolly, as if abducting young women was part of his day job.

"What do you want from us?" cried Jean, in an equally distressed state and spurred on by Maggie's outburst. "We're of no use to you."

"Oh, but you are." replied Abdul, seemingly trying to decide whether he should elaborate further or not before continuing. "My clients have particular tastes and need constant entertainment which I supply. It gets tedious. Every once in a while, you have to change things up a bit, bring in some fresh meat."

"Change things up?" questioned Maggie, hardly daring to believe it, but knowing exactly what he was going to say.

"Yes." cried Abdul, an evasive look in his eyes. "I can't expect loyalty from my clients if I don't present them with some new toys to play with."

"This has nothing to do with us." cried Maggie.

"Oh, but it has!" replied Abdul, his face alive now.

Maggie took a moment to process the implications of Abduls words, before realising with a jolt their significance. They were being primed for prostitution.

"You won't get away with this." Jean shouted.

"Oh really? Just try me!" he said in a threatening tone, making her quake in her boots.

But it was too late. A nod was exchanged between Abdul and his accomplices before both Jean and Maggie were hit hard over the head. The last thing Maggie saw before succumbing to unconsciousness was Kamal's evil face leering over her, his features twisted into an evil grin.

CHAPTER 6

Pamela Sayers had been enjoying a restful afternoon nap when the doorbell rang. Who could that be? She wasn't expecting anyone. Two of her sisters were living in Australia and her brother was down the country with his wife and children. A booze fuelled evening had been enjoyed by her and a few friends the previous night so she had decided to take a nap this afternoon. For a fleeting moment she contemplated not answering the door, hoping that, whoever it was, they might leave her alone. She preferred to be dressed and not in her pyjamas when she had visitors. But another emboldened rapture on the door told her, whoever it was, they were not going anywhere.

Reluctantly, she pushed the bedsheets aside and scrambled to her feet. She picked her robe up off the bed and tied it around her, checked her hair in the dressing mirror attempting to fix it with her hands and walked out of the room. Her head was still throbbing even though it was the afternoon now, she really needed to take some paracetamol, she thought to herself. She was really regretting overdoing it on the booze last night.

Arriving downstairs, she made her way to the front door, swung it open and almost did a double take to make sure she wasn't seeing things. Two uniformed gardai stood on her doorstep, one female, one male. The female, well in her thirties, was tall and slightly stocky for a woman, she wore her light brown hair back in a tight bun away from her pale skin with minimal make-up, denoting an all round look of severity. It was further accentuated by brown eyes that stood out like flints in their sockets. Pretty apt considering she was a guard, Pamela thought. She looked stressed, tired and anxious. The male guard was definitely an alpha male type with a toned physique and chiselled jawline. He wore his hair in spikes almost like a teenager, with lashings of BrylCreem. His sallow sunkissed skin looked like it had seen many a sunny day. He couldn't have been more than thirty, Pamela thought. She could tell by their expressions that they were not looking forward to this visit. Her heart caught in her mouth as she clocked Saoirse, the volunteer coordinator that had organised Maggie and Jean's trip, lurking behind them. Flawless make-up, perfectly quaffed hair and trés chic clothes couldn't disguise her exhaustion. Her bright green eyes normally dazzling with passion and enthusiasm, now just hung in their sockets like loose cannons. Similar to the female guard, she too looked tired, stressed and anxious.

One look at their stern faces said it all, call it mothers' instinct, God knows she didn't have much of it, but she just knew. Something was terribly wrong. And it concerned her darling Jean. Why else would two guards show up at her house? Accompanied by Saoirse? After a moments' pause, the female guard took the lead.

"Excuse me, Ms. Sayers?" she began. "I'm sorry for disturbing you. I'm Detective Sergeant Sharon Collins and this is my colleague Detective Sergeant Mark Roche. And this is Saoirse McGowan from the Volunteering Agency." she said flashing her badge and indicating Saoirse behind them. "May we come in please?"

"Is everything okay?" she asked, completely shaken by the presence of the gardai at her front door.

"May we talk inside please?" the Detective asked again.

Pamela stood motionless for a few more moments lost in her own thoughts and jumping to her own conclusions as to what this unexpected visit might be about.

"Of course." she said finally with a voice that she did not recognise as her own.

As if on automatic, she opened the door wide and directed them into her small but comfortable living room that bordered on overcrowded when more than four people graced it with their presence. Along one wall stood a two seater leather sofa, which faced directly opposite the television in the corner. Perpendicular to the sofa resided two single leather chairs facing both the television and a large opaque window at the opposite end of the room. In the centre perched a small coffee table. A rose tinted coat of paint licked the walls and perfectly embroidered curtains that matched the rose tinted walls finished the room's look. It was her and Jean's humble abode, their hideout, there was no need for anything more extravagant.

"What is this about?" Pamela asked as they took their seats, eager to get to the point and uncover the reason for their presence. "Is everything okay? Is Jean, okay?" Pamela knew she was waffling now but she couldn't help herself. She was desperate for answers.

Sharon took her seat on the comfortable leather sofa before she began. "I'm sure you must be wondering why we are all here." She paused before continuing. "I'm afraid we have received word that Jean and her friend Maggie never returned to their volunteer house last night."

"Oh God, no!" Pamela exclaimed.

The words were out of her mouth before she could stop herself. Pamela took her seat beside Sharon, her mind a whirlwind of thoughts and emotions. Not her Jean. She may not have been the best mother, she knew that, but they were very close, she was the only thing she had left in her life. The way she was feeling right at that very minute, she would have traded her right arm to have Jean back home, safe and well. How could anyone even think of taking her away?

All of her regrets came tumbling back to haunt her, those bright summer days when Jean was a child and she should have taken her to the beach, but instead lay in bed crippled with depression. It had never lifted. All of those adventures they should have had like any other mother and daughter but never did. It devastated her now to think that she had denied Jean a proper childhood and the guilt would never stop eating at her, rotting her to the core. It was no thanks to her that Jean had turned out the way she did. She certainly couldn't take the credit for it.

And now the guards were here informing her that her daughter was in grave danger and she had never felt more helpless in all her life. And what was it they were telling her? She really was trying to focus amidst a brain full of fog, but so far, her efforts were proving futile. Her brain was so frantic it was difficult to absorb all the information that was being directed at her.

"Ms. Sayers, we can assure you that the police are doing everything they can to find them." the guard continued. Again, she paused before continuing. "Is there anyone else we should contact? Jean's father perhaps?" She broached the subject delicately, not wanting to distress the woman even further.

"Well, yes, Jean's father is Noel Brady, but we're not on very good terms right now."

"Have you got a number for him?"

"Yes, I do." Pamela replied, reaching for her mobile phone on the coffee table. Absent-mindedly scrolling down through her list of contacts, she found Noel's number and gave it to Sharon.

"Okay, let me just give Noel a call. You wait here." she instructed Pamela.

Moments later she returned to the sitting room. "He's on his way." she confirmed.

Ten minutes later they heard the roar of an engine, as Noel's car pulled into the driveway and he parked outside Pamela's house. He practically exited the vehicle as it was still in motion, he was so desperate to make his way inside.

Pamela jumped to her feet and went out to the front door to let him in. It was like twenty years had not elapsed since they had last cast eyes on one another. She stood at the door, drinking him in. The lucky beggar hadn't aged a day. He still carried the same shaggy haircut from his youth, still carried those boyish good looks. Both were hesitant to speak at first, unsure of how to conduct themselves after all these years. There was no time for lingering or dwelling on the past, however, as Jean was at the forefront of both their minds.

While they may not have been on the best of terms recently, Pamela was grateful to have him here now, assisting her through this crisis. She could find solace in the fact that there was someone else who cared for Jean as much as she did and that meant a lot. Noel would never know the consolation that his presence gave her as they both came together, united in their grief.

"What's wrong?" he demanded, catching sight of her haggard face. "It's Jean, isn't it? The sergeant wouldn't tell me over the phone."

He brushed past her into the living room where they all stood to greet him. Not in the mood for small talk and pleasantries, Noel cut across them sharply.

"Will someone please tell me what exactly is going on here?"

"It's about Jean." Sharon volunteered "I'm afraid we have received word from the Volunteer House that Jean and her friend Maggie never returned last night." she said, her voice an air of calm. She was the right person for this job.

A simple 'Noooo' was all he could manage as he collapsed down onto the couch.

A surge of emotions coursed through him at once, threatening to consume him whole. Chills began running up and down his spine at the rate of knots, the hair on the back of his neck began to stand up and hot prickly flushes involuntarily perfused his face. His darling Jean couldn't really be missing, could she? Not his estranged daughter who he was only beginning to reacquaint himself with after all these years. What a cruel stab of fate it would be if she were to be taken from him now, didn't he deserve a second chance?

In the background, he could see that Sharon was still speaking but he was so wrapped up in his own grief he couldn't even focus. She was saying something about 'drug trafficking and prostitution'. At this, his attention peaked and he was drawn back into the conversation.

Beside him, Pamela gasped. The very thought of her darling Jean being taken in to drug trafficking and prostitution was inconceivable. Of all the concerns she might have had as a parent, this was her worst nightmare come to fruition. There were obviously gangs of men searching for women, vulnerable female tourists, to be precise, and for whatever reason, they had decided to target her Jean. The level of evil made her skin crawl. How could anyone be so callous, snatching women like they were a piece of meat and serving them on a plate in some rundown brothel somewhere.

And she knew about these kinds of places. Maggie and Jean could be anywhere, trying to find them would be like trying to strike gold in the lottery. Oh God, what was she going to do? The house would seem so big and empty without her. Why did they have to target her daughter? Why her Jean?

"What? Did you just say drug trafficking and prostitution?" she heard Noel ask the female guard now.

"Yes, I'm afraid so, Mr. Brady. We believe the girls may have been the target of drug traffickers and brothel owners. It's too early to say for certain of course, but there are several of them running in the Himalayan resort. It is very common for tourists, particularly young women, to fall victim to kidnappings or abductions for these purposes." she said.

"You mean you think they were abducted from the volunteer house?" he asked, not entirely sure he had his facts right. It wasn't like he had been in direct contact with Jean after all.

"No, Mr. Brady, the girls had organised to go hiking in the Himalayas for the weekend, their weekend being a

Friday and Saturday. They were booked in to stay at the Himalayan Inn Hotel."

"And what happened then?" he ventured, almost too afraid to ask.

"Well, when they failed to show up at the Volunteer House late Saturday night, the alarm was raised by the staff. That prompted a missing persons' case and a full police investigation." she reported.

Sharon felt a stab of empathy. She made visits like this all the time, usually to tell parents that their son or daughter was dead, but it never got any easier. The devastation, the pain, the grief, the loss and the sheer incapacitation of loved ones as they grappled with their despair. She felt like a monster a lot of the time delivering her ill-fated news. And yet somehow this was worse. In some ways, the girls would almost be better off dead if they had been taken into prostitution. It would be a much better fate than a drug riddled life with an open body. She shuddered at the thought. She could sense them fumbling in the dark for some beacon of hope, could almost hear their world shattering. Their life as they knew it was thrown to the floor and broken into smithereens.

"We are in close contact with the police in Nepal who will keep us informed of any developments." she continued now.

"And I am in regular contact with Intec and staff at the Volunteer House who are cooperating fully with police procedure." Saoirse volunteered.

"Well, you're clearly not doing enough if you haven't found them yet." Noel said, suddenly on his feet pacing the floor, furious. "I mean, my daughter is out there somewhere all alone and what are you doing about it?"

"Mr. Brady, I understand you're upset but I can assure you, we are doing everything in our power to locate your daughter. Police and forensic experts are in the Himalayan Resort as we speak tracking credit cards, phonecalls, hotel bookings, sightings of your daughter over the last three days."

"Three days??" cried Noel.

"Yes." replied Sharon.

"Wait a minute..." said Noel "isn't Nepal six hours ahead of us? How is this news only reaching us now? On Sunday afternoon?"

Sharon swallowed hard before she spoke.

"Mr. Brady, we believe they were abducted on Friday evening because our records show that they never booked in to their hotel." she said carefully, before continuing. "But as the Volunteer House didn't know or inform us they were missing until last night, when they failed to return, we did not launch an investigation until then."

The guards frowned and stole a glance at each other, their bodies tensing profusely. They shuffled in their seats in a lame attempt to disguise their obvious discomfort but Pamela wasn't fooled. The dejected look in their eyes was not lost on her nor the sight of their despondent bodies that seemed to weigh heavily on them. Perhaps she was just imagining it but Pamela got the impression there was something they weren't telling them, almost like they didn't expect to find the girls alive. She swallowed her pride and put it down to a severe case of paranoia.

"Brilliant." spat Noel, still pacing up and down the room. "So they didn't even make it to their hotel."

"Our colleagues in Nepal inform us that they have likely been taken to a brothel hideout somewhere remote in the

Himalayan region. That doesn't narrow it down much for us of course, but as previously stated, the abduction of tourists is very common in this area, especially young women."

"That's not going to do much good if she's already dead." Noel cried, before collapsing onto the couch. "Where is she?"

The guards were waffling and he knew it. Of course they would tell them they were contacting this person, that person and had big fat arse teams working on the case. But who was actually out there chasing these sons of bitches who had taken his daughter? As far as he could see, these so-called 'detectives' earned huge salaries and went home to their families at the end of the day. The cynical side of his brain wondered if they really cared about finding Jean. How could they really understand what he was experiencing? This wasn't their reality, it was his and Pamela's.

"Mr. Brady, please, I understand you're upset and that this is very difficult for you, but rest assured that every possible precaution is being taken to locate your daughter."

"Really? Is that so?" he said, before he realised the words were out of his mouth.

"Yes. We have also contacted the Nepalese Embassy here in Dublin who are liaising with the Irish Ambassador in Nepal." Sharon continued on, deciding against indulging Noel's sarcastic remark. "We understand they will place increasing pressure on Nepalese authorities to find your daughter."

"And?" enquired Noel desperately.

"Well, the Irish Embassy has agreed to fly both of you out to Nepal. They will put you up in a hotel close to police headquarters for five nights so you can help with the investigation. Is this something you would like me to arrange?"

Pamela's eyes widened in surprise. She was bursting at the seams with longing to see her daughter. She had wanted to comfort her, console her, fling her arms around her ever since she had been reported missing. Now that she was met with the offer to fly to Nepal, it was an offer she could not refuse. Glancing over at Noel, their eyes met and they both knew they didn't have to think twice about this.

They would take the gardai up on their offer.

"Really? They would do that for us?" she found herself asking the guards now.

"Yes of course." the younger Detective answered. "They will provide consular assistance and look after you throughout your stay." he concluded with a smile.

"Well, thank you. Everyone has been so kind and so helpful." Pamela replied with a trace of a smile.

"We'll take you up on it." agreed Noel.

So, Nepalese police seemed to suspect the girls had been taken into prostitution. Noel knew he could not compete on any level with this breed of criminals. Even if he were to pursue them, he had absolutely no contacts, no skills in self defence or weapon training. He wasn't a member of the CIA or any equivalent with a unique set of skills at his disposal.

He wasn't a violent man. He hadn't encountered any incidents in the past mandating martial arts training, he had no doubt that it would have been of benefit to him now. His inadequacies would only be highlighted if he were to pursue them. His instincts were firing off impulses to his brain, screaming at him to do something practical.

The logical side fought against his impulses, both sides competing for his thoughts. Eventually, with resignation, he decided he had better take Sharon's advice and let the police do their job.

"Great, I'm delighted to hear it." exclaimed Sharon, although she hadn't really expected any different.

"When do we fly out?" asked Noel.

"It will be sometime later this evening. We will aim to get you both over there as soon as possible."

"Should we start packing?" Pamela asked.

"Yes. If you want to start packing now and get your passports together, we will be in touch with arrangements for your flights." Sharon said before moving towards the door out of the sitting room.

Taking their cue from Sharon, Saoirse and the other guard Mark rose from the couch and made to leave. Reaching the door, Sharon turned back to face both Pamela and Noel and spoke in her most reassuring voice.

"We wish you the very best of luck."

After the guards left, Noel stayed around for a while to chat to Pamela, both of them preoccupied with concern for Jean.

For a fleeting moment, Noel was reminded of the woman he had fallen in love with all those years ago. It was her devil may care attitude, her steely determination and gutsy behaviour that had first incensed him, biting on him until he just had to have her. All of those traits were being awoken in Pamela now as they spoke, having lied dormant all these years. He allowed a momentary wave of nostalgia to unfold as he reflected on how different things could have been – if only she had not succumbed to the blackness of depression. They could have been blissfully happy together and he wouldn't have found himself in these circumstances, with an estranged daughter whose childhood he had not been a part of. They would get to that later, right now they had more pressing matters to deal with.

"Oh Pamela, why did they have to go hiking in the Himalayas? Why couldn't they just stay at the Volunteer House?" he asked.

"They're on the other side of the world Noel, it's what people do." she retorted. He really was so clueless sometimes Pamela thought to herself. Just because he had been born devoid of any sense of adventure, he thought everyone else should be the same. It was one of his biggest shortcomings. Maggie and Jean were on the other side of the world, when were they ever going to travel there again? It seemed perfectly logical they would want to make the most of it.

But it was impossible to explain this to Noel or articulate it in any way that made sense. He just wouldn't understand.

"Alright! alright!" he protested. "You've made your point."

"I'm going to ring Ava." she said as she made her way out into the hallway.

There was just something about this that gave him a sense of foreboding. Instinctively he knew he was preparing himself for the worst. And he was powerless to save them. As a father, that was what hurt him the most. It had already been three days for pity's sake, his window of opportunity was narrowing by the minute.

He shook his head from side to side as if this would stop these difficult thoughts assaulting his inner psyche, plaguing his inner demon. He cursed himself and his defeatist attitude, if the girls were to be found, he had to believe they were alive. They had to be.

****

Alone in her big house, Ava Adams stood filling the washing machine. Not that she had much to fill it with really, Maggie was normally the biggest culprit and she was away. You'd swear she was high maintenance the way she carried on sometimes, bless her. Ava smiled as she remembered the flurry of excitement that morning as the girls prepared for their departure. She hoped it was living up to their expectations. Twisting the clock to a deep wash and hearing the familiar roar as it began pounding the clothes into oblivion, she felt a stab of loneliness. The house was quiet, too quiet. It was so unusual not to hear Maggie coming in through the door or see her curled up on the couch watching some documentary. She was always trying to educate herself and she loved learning new things. Still, Maggie would be back soon and she was looking forward to it.

She heard the sound of the telephone going over the whirr of the washing machine and she went out to retrieve it.

"Ava, it's Pamela." she heard the voice on the other end of the line say.

"Pamela hi, how are you?"

She knew Pamela Sayers well. As mothers to two best friends, they had been subject to frequent interactions over the years concerning their daughters. And this was one such interaction.

"Can you talk?"

"Yes, of course. Is everything alright?" She didn't like the tone in Pamela's voice and she instantly knew something was amiss.

"Listen, the guards have ...."

Ava thought she must be hearing things. Surely that couldn't be right.

"What? The guards?" she interrupted.

"Yes, they've just been over with us. The girls have gone missing in Nepal. Ava, they think they've been abducted." she shrieked.

"Oh God!" Ava gasped as her hand flew up to her mouth. Her head began to spin much like the machine that was currently washing her clothes. "Are they okay? Are they hurt? Are they injured?" realising how ridiculous that sounded after the words escaped her.

"We don't know. Look, the guards have only just left, so they're probably on their way over to you as we speak. I wanted to give you the heads up."

"But...." Ava struggled to form her thoughts. She had so many questions, so many answers she needed to find. "What happened?"

"We don't know yet. I'm sure the guards will fill you in but they visited the Himalayan resort at the weekend to go hiking, remember they were talking about that? The guards think they were abducted there."

"Abducted? By who?"

"We don't know Ava, we don't have all the answers." Pamela replied feeling like a broken record.

"Have you tried contacting them on their phones? I mean, this could all just be a misunderstanding."

"What, do you think I'm stupid? Obviously, the first thing I did was try Jean's number. But their phones have probably been taken off them."

"Do we know who's taken them or what they want with them?" she asked.

Pamela hesitated a moment, unsure whether to divulge this information or not. It was probably best not to alarm her too much until the guards arrived.

"No, we're not sure yet." she lied.

"I just can't believe it." Ava said as she made her way into the sitting room and took a seat on the couch. She could feel the blood leaving her extremities and her skin cool into a milky white from the shock.

Then she was up, pacing the length and breadth of her sitting room, the staged pictures on the wall a mindless blur. She was pounding the carpet furiously burrowing little holes as she went. It was fast becoming threadbare and Ava, caught up in her thoughts, didn't even notice. Her Maggie was stranded somewhere over the other side of the world and she was in grave danger. Her head was spinning with the volume of scenarios flashing before her. Was she hurt? Was she cold or hungry? Was she all alone? She just wanted to hold her daughter tight and reassure her everything would be alright. But everything wasn't alright, her world was falling apart. She didn't even know if she would ever see her daughter again.

"Ava, are you there?" she heard Pamela's voice say through the receiver. Remembering she was on the phone she came out of her reverie.

"Yes, I'm here." she stammered. "Oh my God. What the hell are we going to do?"

"I don't know. The Irish embassy have agreed to fly us over to Nepal to assist in the investigation. Myself and Noel are going to fly over later today." She winced. It felt utterly bizarre to be alluding to 'myself and Noel'. "You should come as well." she finished.

"You're going over there?" Ava asked now, her voice becoming higher with every passing minute.

"Yes, the Embassy organised it. It's a start I guess. Are you going to come with us?" she asked again.

"Oh, I couldn't do that." Ava replied, her tone stiffening.

"Why not?"

"I'd be too scared." she replied, the tone of her voice soaring ever higher and sounding more and more unlike her.

"Too scared to find Maggie?" Pamela asked incredulously. She couldn't believe this of sweet Ava who adored her only daughter.

"No, I just don't think I could do it." Ava replied more firmly.

"Are you sure? You could travel with us."

"I said, no!" Ava said then in a tone that suggested her word was final and the subject closed.

"Okay." Pamela relented, finding her reaction strange but internally knowing it was for good reason. Ava Adams was a great mother. She had never known a mother and daughter to be so close. In fact, if she was honest with herself, she often resented their closeness. She longed for the same bond with Jean but it had never seemed to materialise. If Ava wasn't prepared to travel to Nepal, there was a damn good reason for it and Pamela trusted that.

"Will you let me know if you find anything?" Ava asked after a moment's pause.

"Of course." Pamela said gently.

"You know I'll be here thinking of her day and night, until she is home safe with me, don't you?"

"Ava, you're a good mother." was all she could say as she suspected there was another reason why Ava wouldn't travel but wasn't yet ready to reveal.

"Thanks Pamela." Ava hoarsely replied, relieved that she didn't have to explain herself. Pamela might have made a lot of mistakes in her life but one of her redeeming qualities was to not intrude too much. She never asked too many questions. It wasn't that she wasn't interested in other people's lives but she intuitively knew when she was overstepping the mark. And yet she understood. Ironically, perhaps it was mother's intuition, Ava felt understood rather than judged as a mother.

"Okay, I'm going to get my stuff together. You'll be the first to know if I find anything, alright?"

"Thank you." she said again. "Please bring them home."

"I will." replied Pamela with a steely resolve and for a moment, they were united over the fate of their respective daughters.

"And Pamela, stay safe."

"I will."

Ava hung up the phone, the whirr of the washing machine still tumbling, still in sync with her thoughts, her busy mind. Maggie, her Maggie, was missing on the other side of the world. She knew she should be travelling over with Noel and Pamela and they needed support just as much as she did but she couldn't face it. It was too much.

Ava had never forgotten the catalyst that had fuelled her anxiety, altering the course of her life forever. At nineteen, she had the world at her feet, no worries or cares to concern her. Life was good. As impossible as it might seem, she used to be fun once. It was 1981. She had planned a girls' weekend away to London. One of their mutual friends had recently moved there to study musical theatre and was starring in her first major production. It offered the perfect excuse to round up the crew and come watch their fellow comrade in action live on stage. Much like her own daughter Maggie now, all the organisation fell to her. But she had loved it – booking their flights, their accommodation and planning the perfect weekend itinerary. It was so difficult to recall that side of her now. A time when she used to be fun, used to be so full of adventure.

Like typical young girls breaking free from their cage, they squealed with delight as they boarded their Aer Lingus Flight EI164 to London Heathrow. Everything was going fine, nothing seemed in any way out of the ordinary. The flight took off smoothly, the air hostess brought them drinks and refreshments and they were cruising along nicely. Sitting in front of her she noticed a middle-aged man smartly dressed in a suit, his obvious tan glowing outside the seams. Through the gaps in the seat, she saw he was reading a lot of information about the three secrets of Fatima. But she thought no more of it as she had never been to Portugal and anyway, she was far too busy laughing wildly with the girls.

They were only about five minutes from landing in London Heathrow when the man in front of her suddenly rose from his seat and went to the toilet. He emerged to scenes of chaos as suddenly it became clear that he had doused himself in petrol. Screams of terror could be heard throughout the plane and Ava herself turned stone cold.

From what she could see he didn't appear to have a weapon like a knife or a gun, but he did have two empty vials in his hand which he claimed were cyanide. He screamed at the nearest air hostess demanding access to the cockpit immediately. When she refused, he stormed his way through anyway. Another wave of terror rippled through the aircraft. What would happen now? All around them, the cabin crew scrambled desperately to reassure the passengers amid sobs, screams and wails. Then each and every one of them felt the aircraft soar higher into the air. They weren't landing in Heathrow. But where were they going?

After what seemed like an eternity, they landed safely in France but that was not the end of their ordeal. They were held in captivity by the man who had hijacked the plane for several more hours while the French special armed forces tried to appease the situation. After five of the longest hours of her life, Ava was allowed out of captivity. But her friends were not. She had to spend a further five hours in the depths of uncertainty as to whether her friends would make it out alive or not. It was a very complicated hostage negotiation.

She had never been so relieved to see the hijacker, in his expensive black suit, marched off the plane in a pair of handcuffs and manhandled into a waiting police car. Shortly afterwards the remaining passengers and crew emerged at the top of the steps, ready to disembark. Miraculously, there were no fatalities, no injuries. All passengers and crew were taken for food and refreshments before boarding another flight to London Heathrow, where they would finally reach their destination. They did make their mutual friends theatre show but all in all, it was a very low-key weekend, shortened by events, and not the wild one that had been anticipated.

It was the invisible scars that would live on for Ava. After landing back in Dublin Airport, she refused to ever get on a plane again, much to the frustration of her friends and family. Even when she had Maggie, she refused. Maggie's father would have loved a family trip to Disneyland Paris, desperate to give her the perfect childhood. But Ava had never been able to even consider it. After her ordeal, she had been left with severe Post Traumatic Stress and it had never really left her. Something inside her had died that day, some level of naivete that had never been allowed to renew. Her friends had been traumatised too of course but somehow, in time, they had managed to get back on a plane again and put their fears behind them. But not Ava. For Ava it was different, a mental block that she couldn't seem to get past. She had never really spoken about it. At the time she had been offered counselling supports but she had refused. Even today she didn't like talking about it. Her friends had joined support groups that the passengers and crew had set up but she refused to attend those as well. It just triggered too much trauma for her. She hadn't even told Pamela about the hijacking. They hadn't been friends at the time and she didn't see the point. Although she suspected Pamela more than likely knew and was just being tactful. You could find out just about anything these days, even a full list of passengers on a hijacked flight. If anyone ever asked her why she never left Ireland, she just said she didn't like the sun. That normally satisfied people. How she wished she could look at an aircraft and feel excited again and not relive the trauma.

But now, even for her own darling daughter Maggie she couldn't overcome her fears and anxieties. What kind of a mother was she? Her daughter was in grave danger, needed her, and yet she was still crippled by her demons. It was debilitating. But it was such a huge flight… Ava knew there was no way she could do it. Even for Maggie. But it didn't mean she loved her daughter any less.

Now as she thought about what she stood to lose, all she had to keep her company were the memories. She had always wanted a daughter and it was the happiest day of her life when she gave birth to Maggie. She could still hear the shouts of the hospital staff as they announced her arrival, 'It's a girl!' She had been ecstatic with her bundle of joy. She wanted to provide her with a brother or sister but unfortunately nature had other ideas. It didn't matter though, loving this little girl, being her mother and nurturing her every need was enough. It filled her days with endless happiness and she considered herself lucky. She didn't want for anything. She remembered with fondness the time Maggie had cycled a full marathon around her kitchen floor on a tricycle, the harmonica ensconced in her mouth playing every sound she could find. She cycled and played for hours, only stopping when the hunger pangs came. She was only three. It was a wonder she didn't have to be hospitalised with a migraine, Ava thought.

It had been tough on them both after Maggie's father died. She had started to depend on her a lot more and she knew Maggie found that suffocating. As an only child, the weight of responsibility had fallen on Maggie's young shoulders and for a few years she had served in what could almost be defined as a caretaker capacity. It had forced

Maggie to grow beyond her years and Ava still felt terrible about it. It had taken a long time and hard graft to shake herself out of it and build her own life. But she had. Ava had joined the local tidy towns and never looked back. She was out every Saturday morning sweeping the streets, picking nettles and scrubbing benches until they were spotless. She loved every minute of it, even picking up the cans of Budweiser off the side of the road. She met lots of new people, individuals her own age and they were always off gallivanting somewhere. Gradually she had come to rely on Maggie less and less.

As she watched her blossom into the kind, caring woman she was today, nothing gave her greater pleasure. She didn't think it was possible to feel this much pride, but she did. Like many a mother and daughter, they were very close. More like best friends, they did everything together. They went to the theatre, cinema, spa days, for dinner and vacationed across the country. Just about everything. Those teenage years when Maggie didn't want anyone to know she existed seemed a lifetime ago now. At her worst, she grew moody and asked her to stop with the interrogation. If it wasn't that, she was on edge if Ava parked within a one-mile radius of the coolest party in town. God forbid her popularity stakes would have taken a nosedive if anyone saw her being dropped off by her mother. Teenagers. Like there weren't other mothers around doing the exact same thing. She would trade them all in now though if it meant finding her daughter alive. She desperately hoped Maggie would be returned home safely, she would pray infinitely if it was needed. It would be a bleak life indeed if she were to go without her.

As the drum continued to spin on its axis guaranteeing the clothes a thorough wash, Ava heard the doorbell ring. That must be the guards, she thought. Hopefully they were coming to tell her it was all a big mistake and the girls were safe and well in the volunteer house. Was that too much to hope for?

CHAPTER 7

Jean woke feeling groggy, dazed and confused. For a moment, she had no recollection of what had happened, but then like a tidal wave it all came flooding back. She had been cast in her very own horror movie, only it was her reality. In the next instant, a searing pain at the back of her head reminded her of where she had been hit. Her brown hair hung limp and lifeless on her shoulders and scratch marks littered her face, neck and arms. Her clothes hung on her slim frame a wrinkled mess looking in urgent need of a proper iron and her white trousers were stained black from lying on the floor. A cloth tied tight around her upper arm, a needle injection mark into her vein, a smattering of blood trickling down her arm and cotton wool lying on the floor informed her she had been injected with something. No!! She had never touched drugs in her life and she certainly did not plan on starting now. Her hands were bound in cuffs that latched onto chains stemming from the middle of the floor as were her ankles. She felt woozy and the panic began to rise in her like bile, threatening to overflow. Where the hell was she? What was going to happen to her?

She lay on the ground for a couple of minutes before taking in her surroundings. She appeared to be in some dark and dreary abandoned warehouse. Various odours assaulted her nostrils all at once – urine, faeces, sweaty BO, and the smell of despair. The air was rife with it. She was holed up in a small room with a large hole in the centre, which she could only presume were for excretion purposes. The thought disgusted her so much that she almost retched with her own vomit. A small window with iron bars was planted high up in the wall to her left, attempting to cast a miniscule amount of daylight into the room. Underneath the window, a battered, uncomfortable looking bed dominated the room. Each of the surrounding four walls was adorned with graffiti in various tongues and boasted some magnificent artwork. One word she did recognise was 'Namaste', which was Nepalese for 'hello'. During her short time here, she had immersed herself in the language and this was one of the few phrases she had picked up. It was far from a pleasant cultural experience she was receiving now. There was no door, instead, iron gates loomed big and large in front of her. She appeared to be in the dungeons, in some kind of cell. It was only then she realised Maggie was gone.

She leapt to her feet, as best as she could, with her hands and feet in cuffs, and staggered to the large iron gates that entrapped her. Peering out, she searched for any signs of life, listening intently for any sign that Maggie was in the cell next to her. Anything that might indicate Maggie was still alive – the sound of her deep slumber, the sound of her cries, the sound of her struggling to break free of the cuffs that bound her. Nothing. All that greeted her was silence.

Then she heard it, the sound of a lamp being switched on bathing the dungeons in a balmy light. She squinted her eyes against the brightness, her pupils rapidly contracting to cope with the extra infiltration of light. Then she saw him, there was no mistaking him: it was Kamal. Their eyes met and his large brown eyes bore into hers with an intensity so fierce it unnerved her. Those features would forever be imprinted in her mind. The cold stare, his gaze fixed steadily on hers, hardly blinking, the strong jawline and dark features of a man who had spent a lifetime worshipping sunny weather, his skin unblemished. He was sitting calmly at a table and chair poring over some documents as he lingered by her cell, evidently charged with preventing her escape. Jean bet that massaged his ego nicely, made him feel important. The whole thing made her stomach turn. She let out a yelp as she caught sight of a revolver dangling by his side. Had he shot Maggie? Was he going to finish her off too? Feeling utterly defenceless and not knowing what else to do, she began to scream and rant at him:

"Where is Maggie? What have you done with her? Where is my friend?" she yelled, all of her pent up anger and rage reaching fever pitch and bursting to the fore. She grabbed hold of the wrought iron bars and began to shake them violently creating as much of a commotion as possible. "Let me out of here. Let me go." she shrieked, her voice a quivering wreck. She could contain herself no longer. She began to shake involuntarily, almost teetering on the precipice of an epileptic fit. Thankfully she didn't suffer from epilepsy. But her hands were starting to shake and beads of cold sweat were breaking out across her forehead and spilling down her temples. She knew she was losing control but she didn't care.

Kamal turned his head to look at her before clearing his throat to speak. He had to dissuade her from making so much noise, it was irritating.

"Be quiet, little girl. Don't you know that nobody can hear you? Don't waste your energy. There's no one coming to help you." he drawled, as if he were bored.

"I don't know what you've done with Maggie, but I sure as hell am going to find out. You won't get away with this. Where is she? You tell me now or else I'll -" she spat, sounding more confident than she felt. She began to clatter more fiercely at the gates, drowning the place in noise.

"Or else what? You'll hit me?" Kamal said over the noise. "Unless you're Houdini, you're not in any fit state for a martial arts display." he taunted.

"I'm not afraid of you." she screamed determined not to let fear betray her. She was terrified to her core but she was not going to give these men the satisfaction of showing it.

Jean took a few deep breaths to steady herself. She had to hold it together. Plan A was clearly not working, she admitted as she stopped clattering at the gates giving way to a still silence. It was time to resort to Plan B. She needed to strip him of his masculinity, strip him entirely of any sense of importance. Men hated that. And she knew exactly how to do it.

"You think you're going to get some award or something from Abdul for keeping me here? He doesn't give a toss about you. He would kill you in an instant if circumstances necessitated it. He's got no loyalty to you! How does that make you feel?" she asked.

"Nice try but you're still not getting out of here."

"And you know, it seems to me like he's leaving you to do his dirty work, sending you down here to keep watch. Does he ever send Babu or Sajit or even Anoushka down here? I think it's fair to say that he favours them, wouldn't you? They're much more competent than you, aren't they?" she teased, trying to draw him out.

Kamal didn't say anything.

"You're not that bright are you? Compared to say…… Sajit or Babu?" she said, deliberately trying to antagonise him. "They've got brains, right?"

"Shut up." Kamal replied.

"Ouch, have I touched a nerve?"

"I said shut up." he bellowed.

"I mean, you can run like the wind, sure, but what else can you do?" she continued, on a roll now.

"You're still not getting out of here so shut up you dumb bitch." he spat, rising out of his chair and putting his face right at the iron gates to meet hers.

He shouldn't have fallen for it. He knew exactly what she was trying to do. She was trying to push his buttons, playing to his weaknesses like some psychological game of cat and mouse. It wouldn't work.

"I will get out of here, one way or another, you sick son of a bitch." he heard her say. "And when I do, I'm coming back for Maggie." she said, attempting to sound like she would follow through her convictions.

"Good luck." he retorted.

Kamal yawned. Empty threats, that's all they were. He had acquired enough experience over the years to know when women posed a serious threat and when they didn't. Looking at the young woman before him, hair frazzled, puffy red cheeks glowing and hearing her crazy rants, he knew he could relax. He had been sitting here for hours at Abdul's command before she came round. Now, she was simply ensconced in a new environment and she was frightened. Her enthusiasm and desire to escape would soon wear thin and fatigue would set in. He picked up his cigarette box and promptly lit up. As he exhaled, he deliberately sent the cloud of smoke billowing straight into her face, making her cough and splutter and he laughed at her obvious distress. No, this woman wasn't smart enough to escape from the vault. He thought about getting a coffee.

Abdul had taken extra precaution with these women. It wasn't enough to lock them up in the vault, he wanted one of his team there too. Stupid eejit, thought Kamal. What did he want extra protection for? Neither one of them were leaving this rundown warehouse without their notice. And even if by some miraculous intervention, they did manage to escape, he would be able to catch up with them before they could get very far. Still, Kamal was not one to disobey orders. Thanks to his days competing in cross-country athletics as a child and into his teens, he had become an accomplished athlete. He knew it sounded corny, but he loved the thrill of the chase. That jolt when you realise a wanted target is running away at rapid speed. The resulting adrenaline pumping through your veins and mobilising you into action as you take off to capture your prey. Yes, he was an adrenaline junkie, that was for sure. Come to think of it, he would quite enjoy it if she were to make a run for it. She would be no match for him. He would sit with this one a little while longer.

Just then, they both heard a door opening above them and the sound of footsteps fast approaching the dungeons. Listening intently, Jean tried to decipher how many people were approaching – it could be two, could be three, it was difficult to tell. Her breath caught in her chest at the sight of Abdul, closely followed by Sajit and Babu.

"Someone's awake." he taunted, looking at Jean, before turning to face Sajit and Babu. "Bring the girl." he barked at his accomplices.

Sajit and Babu manhandled her out of the cell, unlocking the chains binding her hands and feet, and dragged her up a flight of stairs which brought them into a big wide open space, like a big hut. It was grubby, dark, dreary, depressing. They were the only words she could use to describe it. Glancing around she noticed a large chair set in the middle of the room, reminding her of the kind of chair you'd see at the dentist. The chair came complete with chains for strapping the victim in tight. Her eye was immediately drawn to a switch on the wall nearby. Electrocution. She knew it. At the far corner of the room stood a table laid with a bowl of acid, several pliers and scalpels, and some filthy cloth which looked like it had been used by a car mechanic. It was obvious this was a torture chamber. She braced herself for the worst. She was going to die in this room. It's amazing how accepting one becomes when confronted with death, she thought idly to herself. It's almost like everything else in life doesn't matter and a certain peace and serenity envelops the person. That was exactly how Jean felt at that moment. She wouldn't go without a fight of course, that wasn't her style, but inevitably she knew she would be overpowered. Her thoughts strayed to Maggie, whom she hoped had not met the same fate. She closed her eyes, expecting to be led towards the chair where she would meet her fate.

But then Sajit and Babu began leading her to a door at the other end of the room, a door leading out of the warehouse. She was stumbling intermittently as she walked, still feeling woozy from the concoction of drugs and concussion.

"Keep moving." dictated Sajit into her ear, taking her arm and twisting it violently. She let out a roar of pain at his deliberate act of malice and steadied herself before continuing on her journey.

They marched her out of the warehouse across a deserted barn. Jean looked up at the balmy night sky as she walked, not one star to be seen twinkling at her, no birds flying high. The air was heavy and humid, making her sweat. Even at night, temperatures rarely dropped drastically, unlike back home when the arctic freeze appeared once darkness fell.

Her feet glided over the hard ground, nothing more than scorched earth, devoid of any form of plantation or vegetation, devoid of any signs of life. There was an ominous, eerie feel about it which was unnerving.

One man walked past them, a man of about forty, looking dishevelled, unkempt and unshaven, his shaggy mane of jet black hair unbrushed. He was fastening his belt as he went. Making his way towards the exit, he exchanged a knowing nod with Abdul, as if saluting him or acknowledging his presence. Then it struck her, the nature of Abdul's business – a brothel. It was one thing hearing him speak about it, quite another to actually witness it with her own eyes.

Looming large against the night sky, a grand marquee announced its presence. Mere yards from where they stood, men were queuing in an orderly fashion awaiting their turn. Guarding the entrance and inspecting the tickets, a man was beckoning them forward in single file like schoolchildren. He wore large black rimmed spectacles and a permanent frown between his eyes.

Inside the marquee, twenty-four cubicles, twelve on each side, ran down left and right. A long hallway ran down the middle and each cubicle was separated by a sliver of filthy curtain. Jean had long since lost all sense of time, preferring to focus on the here and now.

In one fluid movement, before Babu and Sajit had even noticed, she managed to wrench herself free of their vice like grip and flung back the nearest curtain. She stumbled backwards to the ground, reeling in horror as she took in the scene before her. On a small, shabby bed was a young girl with big hollow bloodshot eyes, her skin pasty and clammy, complete with matted down hair. She was clearly a tourist, bearing no obvious hallmarks of Nepalese descent, her pale white skin and blonde hair betraying her origins. She was barely dressed in bra and knickers but she didn't even seem to notice. Evidently, she was much further into the realms of heroin addiction than Jean was. Sitting astride her was a man at least twice her age, holding her limp body to his, straddling her every available orifice, like the girl was a piece of meat. It chilled her to the bone to watch how callously he caressed every inch of her, no bodypart left untouched. She knew the exact same fate lay in store for her.

"Maggie." she cried bitterly more to herself than to her captors, wondering what had become of her. She couldn't bear the thought of her friend lying here in one of these cubicles, a mere shadow of her former self, suffering degradation of the highest proportions at the hands of these evil monsters, night after night. It was inconceivable.

Then she felt the familiar vice like grip of her captors closing in around her, jolting her back to reality and her current predicament.

"Noooooooooooo." she screamed, as Sajit and Babu scrambled to take her back under their grip. Dancing around like a pariah, she managed to avoid their grip for a few moments. Something inside her had snapped and she started roaring at the men before her "What have you done with Maggie? Where is she? Is she here behind one of these curtains?" she demanded.

In a momentary lapse of concentration, they had managed to catch hold of her arm again, and proceeded to drag her with them.

"Oh no, don't worry, your friend is in excellent hands. Very pretty girl, so she is. We were so impressed with her we decided to put her up for sale. I'm sure she'll make a lot of cash for the business." drawled Sajit in his thick Nepalese accent which he polished off with a wry grin. Ordinarily, she found his accent difficult to understand, but she was so frazzled right now, she could hear every word perfectly, her mind doing somersaults. He was speaking slowly, lingering over his words, knowing that it was distressing her.

"You're selling her off? Where? Who are you selling her to?" she retorted, doing her utmost to remain calm, get to the point and glean some information from him.

"Oh, I don't know. We capture the women and bring them to Abdul, that is our job. It's up to him what he does after that." he said lightly. Then he turned deliberately towards her, fixing his gaze, scanning her up and down, drinking her in, before adding, "Although, come to think of it, you're not half bad yourself. Pity we didn't put you forward as well." he finished.

"How do I find her?" she pleaded.

"Find her?" he asked laughing at her. "You will never find her." he added, still laughing and looking to Babu for support. Now, there was a pair of them in it, both of them jeering at her.

She started shaking her arms violently again, trying to wrench herself free of their iron grip once more, but they were prepared for her. They were not going to relinquish their position.

"You liar. Where is she? Tell me where she is, you bastards. I know you can tell me where she is?" she shrieked at the top of her lungs.

Hearing her cries, Abdul whipped his head around to see what all the commotion was about. He pointed a finger directly at her and made eye contact with Sajit and Babu, before saying "Control her, will you?" When Jean continued to scream and rant, he cast an order that sent her into a spasm of terror.

"Drug her." he ordered, his voice ricocheting off the marquee surroundings. He intended to destroy her, condemning her to spend her days as a drug ridden prostitute. She couldn't let him. She had so much she wanted to do, so many plans for her future. Abdul moved swiftly towards her, his mouth carved into a sneer, like he was enjoying this whole debacle.

"You will never see your friend again. If you want to live you will have to shut up and stop your screaming." he said, slapping her hard across the face. She winced with the pain as it stung bitterly. "Besides, even if I wanted to, I couldn't tell you where she is. We sold her to the Sheikh last night."

"You're lying." Jean spat. "Where is she?"

"You'll see. Don't you worry, we'll take good care of her." he said before turning to Sajit. "Drug her."

And then he turned to walk back out of the marquee.

****

Jean stirred in a haze of confusion. She desperately wanted to escape but she was confronted by a number of obstacles that would only result in their demise. First of all, she couldn't leave Maggie here alone. But she was disadvantaged by the fact that she had no idea where she was. Even if she was lucky enough to escape and find help, she would never be able to identify a location. She was at a loss as to what to do. She had never felt more alone in her life. How was she going to escape? How would she save Maggie? The thought of her out there somewhere being ensnared by a big monster of a Sheikh quite frankly was revolting.

As her best friend, it was her duty, her obligation to find her. People often got the wrong impression of her judging her shallow existence and lack of substance. She was no fool and knew exactly what peoples' perceptions were. Just because she wore the latest fashion trend and stayed in five-star resorts, people assumed she had nothing to say for herself. But they were wrong. When it came to her best friend and people she cared about, she was as loyal as they came. Over the years Maggie and Jean had been through thick and thin. This wasn't even a question. It was a statement. She simply had to find her friend.

Jean sat up and tried to ward off the effects of the drugs. Recognising her surroundings, she realised she was back in her prison cell. She wasn't sure why they had brought her back here. Had she caused too much of a fuss? Glancing through the bars, Sajit sat with his legs outstretched. It must have been his turn to keep guard.

"Think Jean! Think!" she coaxed herself, trying to stir up some sliver of motivation.

It was essential that she find a way to wield power over these men – and Anoushka. She would never trust a woman again for as long as she lived. It galled her every time she thought of the way Anoushka had approached them, feigning innocence and niceties, playing the part of a poor Nepalese woman like a true professional. To think that they had felt pity for her and the whole time she had been plotting their destruction. This beast of a woman who could bestow a fate worse than death.

Jean tried to keep her spirits up but it was difficult. Eventually she sat down in the cell and waited for death to take her. Surely death had to be better than this. In her hour of darkness, she felt only despair. No light beckoned in the distance and she saw no reason for hope. She was never going to get out of here. The only person she was kidding was herself if she thought there was any possibility of escape. Of course there wasn't. She was so fond of trying to fend off her captors, they could almost predict her every move and defend it with practiced ease. She was tired, running scarce of ideas that might work or help her to overthrow her enemies. Her brain was already slowing to a snails' pace as the effects of the drugs gnawed at her insides. By the day, by the hour even, her inner resolve was ebbing away as she reverted to a mere shadow of her former self. It had only been two days now but she was beginning to lose her appetite, which was probably a good thing considering she was barely being fed anyway. What could she do? There was no way out. She was trapped out here, stuck in this eternal nightmare with no prospects of anyone ever finding her or Maggie.

Looking into her captor's face, she was reminded that this was no game. It was her reality. Witnessing Sajit's smug face, sitting down in his chair, his long limbs perforating the tiny space, as she stood helpless in her prison cell, it was all she could do not to roar the place down. How could he sit there so relaxed and uncaring, while she was stuck deep in the throes of a horrendous nightmare. It beggared belief.

The sound of a mobile phone ringing interrupted the silence and Sajit took his mobile out of his pocket. Speaking rapidly in Nepali, muttering a few words, he was only a bare minute on the phone. Finally, he clicked off and looked at her.

"Your first client." he boasted, as if he expected her to be delighted. "The boss wants you out at the marquee in fifteen minutes."

Jean's blood ran cold. This was it. Her services would become available in the brothel now and she would begin the descent into prostitution.

"Noooooooooooo." she screamed. "I won't go. You tell him I'm not going." She was desperate now, pleading and bargaining to be released from her predicament.

"Afraid I can't do that. We have to follow orders." Sajit retorted simply.

Suddenly, the fog in her brain seemed to lift and she decided to try another tactic.

"And what if you go against them?"

"I won't be doing that."

"What's the matter Sajit, are you scared?"

"No."

"Yes, you are. I can see it. Come on Sajit, what's the worst that will happen if you disobey orders?"

"Oh, you have no idea."

"So, what? You're just going to be a coward and do everything he says?"

"I have to."

"You have to allow him to do this to innocent young girls. Really Sajit, is that the best you can come up with?"

Sajit was growing increasingly agitated and could not be swayed from his mission. She was hitting a nerve. "Damn it, woman! I'm a dead man if I don't do as he says. Don't you understand that? Now get your ass out of that cell." he demanded.

"No I won't!" Jean demanded, stomping her feet to the floor. "If you want to take me over to that marquee, you're going to have to drag me kicking and screaming."

This was it. Once she went down this road there could be no way back. The path from which there was no return. Fear gripped her like a knife, gnawed at her insides and spat them back out. The physical manifestations of her fear were incapacitating and she began to perspire heavily with the futility of her efforts. She was just a young girl lost and alone in a foreign country far away from home.

Jean's efforts to prolong the inevitable proved futile. Sajit had never looked so menacing as he loomed large above her now, yanking her out of the prison cell that had become her little cave. It was only now she understood why Abdul had selected him for his team. As he manhandled her up the stairs, she felt the full force of his strength. Their footsteps seemed to follow a rhythmic pattern of their own making, his resembling a sense of urgency. Hers trying to slow it all down, delaying a terrifying fate.

In spite of her many vicious attempts to wrench herself free, she was no match for him. She found herself quitting. What was the point, she thought to herself? His dominance and force were far superior.

Time seemed to stand still. It was as though she was lost in a trance willing this journey to take as long as possible so that she could prolong the inevitable.

They arrived into a room at the top of the stairs and she cast an observant look around her. As though she were seeing everything for the first time. She took in the vast expanse of walls, the grotty small windows that weren't nearly big enough and did not permit enough light. Her pupils must have dilated to enormous proportions such was the darkness of the room. If you could call it that, it resembled a cell more than anything else.

The constant tugging on her arm was the only reminder of her predicament. They passed through the torture room, and Jean dreaded to think what they might inflict upon her if she refused to see her first client. The consequences could be dire. For a moment, her reckless brain convinced her that this was where Sajit was bringing her. Starved to little more than a bird's diet and a severe lack of fluids had brought her to a state of sheer delirium. Any minute now, she expected to start seeing things. Things that were only figments of her imagination.

As they stepped out into the night, she devoured the sensation of warm and balmy air on her face. The darkness was fast approaching and Jean drank in the fresh air in large gulps now. She had never been so grateful for something so trivial in her life, but days spent cooped up in a tiny prison cell had given her a new appreciation for such things. All of her surroundings amazed her in a way that they had never done before. Onwards they marched across the barn, every step forward, one step closer to her doom.

After what seemed like an eternity to Jean, they finally reached the marquee. Abdul was there ready to meet them. He greeted her now like an old friend, stroking her hair and caressing her arm. She jumped backwards in revulsion. Whatever about her 'client', she was damned if she was going to allow this pervert to molest her. In wild fury she spat at Abdul.

"What do you think you're doing? Don't touch me you sick pervert." she retorted.

"Making sure the product I'm about to offer one of my finest clients is tasty and warm." Abdul responded.

"I'm not your product." she snarled.

"Oh, but you are."

"You make me sick. You tell me where the hell Maggie is or I'm not going in there." she indicated the cubicles.

Abdul merely stepped forward, right up to her until he was mere inches from her face. He clearly intended to invade her personal space. Her threats didn't faze him in the slightest.

"Where do you think you are going to go, young lady?" Abdul enquired. "There isn't a town to be seen for miles around here."

"I don't care. Anywhere has got to be better than here." she responded.

"Don't make a fuss now, your client awaits you." Abdul said, gesturing a cubicle down to the left.

"Although, you might just freshen up a little first." he finished giving her filthy clothes and unruly hair a disapproving look.

"No, I won't do it." she screamed. With all the breath she had in her body, she yelled at the top of her voice. She was determined to embarrass him now, not that a scene in his marquee would cause him concern. It was probably all too common. "You tell me where my friend is."

Abdul smirked to himself. His face twisted into a frown as he feigned concern. "Oh dear, looks like we'll have to drug you some more." he responded. In the same instant, he turned to face Sajit who was restraining her but staying rather quiet throughout this conversation. "Get me a syringe and fetch Kamal. We're going to have to hold this one down." he said, taking her arms from Sajit, not that they were much use anyway as her hands were still tied.

"You can't make me go in there." Jean shouted.

"Yes I can and I will. If you want to live you will do exactly as I say." he demanded.

"Screw you. I'm not taking orders from you."

"Oh, you will." he said menacingly.

"It seems pretty pathetic to me that you need to drug women to control them." she ranted, unable to stop herself. "Do your wives not give you any? Is that it?"

"Alright, shut your filthy mouth right now or I'll hit you so damn hard you won't be able to talk for a week. Do you understand me?" Abdul said, glaring at her with intense anger in the pupils of his eyes. Jean took it to be a warning sign that she was on dangerous territory. The usually calm and slick Abdul was disintegrating into someone who was on the brink of losing control. It was rather disconcerting and the air stood rife between them.

It was almost a relief to them both when Sajit returned with Kamal lagging behind. The three of them scooped her up, kicking and screaming, and carried her into one of the empty cubicles.

"No, I don't want it." she screamed as she saw Sajit load a syringe full of heroin. She made every attempt possible to manoeuvre all four limbs but both Kamal and Abdul maintained a firm grip. Jean barely noticed the grittiness of the cubicle with its filthy curtains and loud spring beds so intent was she to avoid another injection. With every muscle in her body, she made a final attempt to wrench both arms out of the vice like grips of her captors but it was no good. She began to panic now. Her breathing started to come hard and fast and she could feel the heat flood her cheeks. She hated needles. It seemed ironic, she wished that was her only fear now.

Kamal and Abdul held her down while Sajit tied the raggedy piece of cloth supposed to resemble a tourniquet to her arm and injected the heroin straight into her veins. The heroin pulsed through her until she reached a state of complete euphoria and elation. It was happiness like she had never felt before. All she knew was that she felt nothing but sheer joy. Her head was soaring over the clouds and nothing could stop her now. She felt invincible. And then her pulse quickened to a dizzying speed. She could feel her heart working overtime to send blood all over her body. Her heart was racing so fast now, she was sure it must be visible in her neck. Not that Jean was concerned. She was enjoying the sensation. Her body seemed to take on new strength. She could feel the muscles in her limbs flexing and extending, energised and emboldened by the lethal substance now coursing through her veins. Jean was so enthralled and consumed by these new sensations she forgot Sajit, Abdul and Kamal were sitting there watching her. Watching her succumb to the evil grips of addiction. Lying there sprawled out on the bed, she blinked ferociously. Abdul stood there with a frown on his face, clearly concerned that she was going to make another attempt to escape. Eventually, they released her, satisfied that she was drugged enough.

After what seemed like an eternity, Abdul spoke.

"Now, stay there and don't move or you're dead." he commanded before making his exit.

With Abdul having made his exit, Sajit and Kamal decided to exploit her vulnerability, armed with the knowledge that she was about to entertain her first client.

"This guy is an eager beaver. He likes his girls young, hot and sexy. Isn't that right, Sajit?" Kamal enquired of his fellow accomplice.

"That's right." Sajit replied as he took out a deck of cards from his jacket pocket and engaged in a game of poker with Kamal. "He also likes his girls to be…. very daring and adventurous." he continued, dropping his voice an octave lower. Suddenly, he turned to face Jean. "He also likes to be dominated. Can you handle that?"

Jean answered with a protest to shut his mouth but Kamal got there before her. He rose from his chair, strode over to her bed and opened a few buttons in her shirt. "Ooooohhh this guy will be very happy with you." he rejoiced, rubbing his hands together with glee. There was a wild wretched look in his eyes that made her uncomfortable. She didn't like it. Kamal wasn't finished with her. He put his hand inside her shirt and caressed her breasts. "There you go honey, you're ready for him now." And then without warning, he planted his lips on hers and he was kissing her full on the mouth. She drank back the disgust she felt in the pit of her stomach and just waited for this moment to pass. But Kamal was slapping her in the face now. "Kiss me back bitch."

Her whole body shuddered at the thought, but finding Maggie and saving her own life were top on her list of priorities. It was imperative that she do whatever was necessary to stay alive, no matter what the personal cost to herself. So, she kissed him back all the while distracting herself with thoughts of saving Maggie. Finally, Kamal broke apart from her before exclaiming. "Damn it, you are one sexy mama."

Whatever her thoughts about Sajit and Kamal's complete disregard for women, she knew there was worse to come. She should have known, should have known they would poke fun at her expense. As she cursed her own naivety, Sajit and Kamal continued to laugh and jeer at her as they enjoyed a game of poker. Minutes seemed like hours as she waited for the degradation she knew was to come. She became convinced this was a tactic deliberately employed by her captors as a means of exerting their power. And then it arrived.

Abdul entered the cubicle followed by a man in his fifties. Short, plump and unattractive, it was not difficult to see why he found himself here. With a simple gesture, Abdul motioned for Sajit and Kamal to leave before stepping outside himself.

Now, Jean was alone with this man, this stranger. As they locked eyes, Jean could visibly see the man drinking her in, admiring her body, scanning her up and down. She likened it to an X-Ray as her body came under scrutiny. On closer inspection she noticed his bald receded hairline, chiselled jawline and weather beaten skin. He stood before her dressed in his best Khaki pants and a turquoise coloured shirt that looked like it had seen better days. His oversized mouth moved in large circular motions indicating that he was chewing on a piece of gum. His relaxed demeanour and casual approach told her he was a regular. And then he spoke in soft dulcet tones that made his voice sound like it came straight out of a musical.

"Hiya baby." he said with an air of quiet confidence. "They sure as hell put an expensive price on you tonight. I hope you're worth it."

"Is that the best you can come up with?" Jean said as she fixed him with a cold hard stare.

"It's getting pretty hot in here, isn't, it? Let's get undressed shall, we?"

"Piss off." she hissed.

Then he seemed to remember that her hands were bound. "Oh I'm sorry, I forgot. We need to take that rope off your hands. You won't be much good to me without those." he said. In one fluid movement, he cut the ropes free and she felt a momentary wave of relief as they fell to the ground. Glancing down at her wrists now, she noticed big red ligature marks where the ropes had been. They were tied so tight they had dug deep into her flesh, and they were slowly beginning to throb with the pain. Then she heard it.

A loud bang rang out like a gunshot and ricocheted off the wall. In the next instant, the marquee descended into chaos as people scrambled to their feet and started running in their droves. Jean did not stay to find out what had happened, but instead took her opportunity and ran. It could have been a client shooting one of the girls or, apparently police raids on these brothels were quite common. She hoped it might be the latter but she didn't hear any sirens or see any sign of police. So, she just ran, carefully avoiding the evil clutches of the man who just moments earlier had been her client.

"Wait" he shouted after her but he was way too unfit to run more than a few steps after her.

Jean kept on running.

Jean ran like the wind as fast as her two legs could carry her. Glancing behind, all she saw were scenes of chaos as the girls tried desperately to escape, their captors hot on their heels. Then she saw him. Kamal. He was rapidly gaining on her, his limbs slicing through the night. He was fast, so bloody fast. Turning around, all she could see in front of her was a wide open stretch of land, nowhere to hide. Nowhere to run for help. To her left and right, she could see the desperate efforts of three other girls, obviously fleeing the same brothel, each one of them fighting their way to freedom. Unfortunately, Maggie did not run astride them. She could see the desperation in their eyes and the horror they had been subjected to, that much was evident. In this moment of unison, they all moved as one.

With a renewed burst of energy, she gave herself another injection of speed and upped her pace. She was glad of her fitness levels now acquired through many years playing basketball.

But Kamal was still behind them. What was she going to do? If they didn't find somewhere to lose him soon, he would catch up to them and drag them back to the compound. He was close now. So very close.

Then the unexpected happened. Kamal fell over flat on his face, clutching his leg in his hand as if he had done himself a serious injury. Free from his pursuit, they carried on unable to believe their luck.

Jean kept going.

She had no plan, no clue where she was heading. All her intentions focused towards finding road, land and civilisation. Anything that would get her out of here and transport her back to safety. The darkness of the night seemed to close in on her as she continued to run without any sign of light.

After some time, it loomed large before her. Into the distance she could see bright yellow and orange lights illuminating the night sky, indicating that she was approaching a town or village. She was a slight distance away from it yet. With everything she had, she veered towards it.

She felt enormous relief at the sign of life which now lay within her grasp. She wasn't one to lament or take stock of her small fortunes but right at that moment she had never been so grateful to get away from those creeps and enter into the outside world. For the last few days, she had been carefully locked away, somewhere she would never have been found. This was her one opportunity and she intended to use it. She was sassy, she was fierce. She could do this. Without meaning to sound conceited, it was one of the traits she loved most about herself. Maggie and herself were complete opposites in that respect.

Eventually, Jean entered the small village with the girls following in her wake. Each one of them looked just as dishevelled as she did with their hair matted down onto their face coupled with their hot and sweaty complexions. Jean decided the first thing she needed to do was to find something that resembled a police station. These guys needed to be reported for drug trafficking and prostitution. She also needed to report Maggie missing so they could begin a search. And she needed medical attention to flush the last toxic remains of heroin out of her system. She only hoped she wouldn't suffer terrible withdrawals.

Now that she thought about it, she would need to contact the volunteer house as well. She might give Raoul a call. He had given them a card with his telephone number in case of emergency. If she could just find a payphone, she thought, as she pulled out the card and a few coins from her pocket.

Scanning the buildings which now surrounded her, she scrutinised them all, down to the last minute detail. Directly in front of her stood a large building with a spacious entrance which obviously resembled a supermarket. The locked double doors and the darkness inside pointed to the fact that it was closed. Of course. She had been so consumed with getting as far away as possible and finding a police station, it hadn't even occurred to her that the shops might be closed. She had long since lost all track of time. Checking her watch, she realised it was now 1am in the morning. All the surrounding buildings in the vicinity were also closed save for a small dingy fast-food joint that reeked of chips and could not have appeared less appetising if it tried. Now, she stumbled on to one long street, to all intents and purposes it appeared to be the main street in the town. Jean could only imagine it must be a lively street by day as it was lined with small quirky cafes and clothes shops selling the traditional garments that Nepalese women wore.

She thought through her options. Raoul in the volunteer house had always impressed upon them the importance of safety and it wasn't safe wandering the streets at this hour of the morning. He had given them his number to contact in an emergency and perhaps that should be her next move. This was that emergency. At the very least, he might be able to point her in the direction of the local police station. He claimed to know the area very well after all.

Spotting a payphone up ahead she ran towards it, yanked open the door and hurried inside. A small private booth boasting a rusty interior, it really wasn't the most welcoming. The phone was so dirty it looked riddled with infection and the fragile chain barely held the receiver to the main box. Jean was sorry she didn't have some hand sanitiser with her but this wasn't the time to be worrying about such trivial matters. Thankfully, she had managed to hold on to a small bit of loose change in her pocket. Carefully lifting the receiver, she slotted the coins in, dialed the number and waited for it to ring.

"Hello" came a sleepy voice on the other end of the line.

Of course. It was after 1am in the morning, not exactly sociable hours. Raoul must have been fast asleep.

"Raoul, it's Jean. I'm in trouble and I need your help."

Rubbing his eyes and glancing at the clock, it took Raoul a moment to register who was calling at this late hour.

"Jean, what is it? What's the matter?" he asked.

Jean had never been more delighted to hear a familiar voice, a friendly voice on the other end of the line. Raoul would help her. He would know what to do.

"It's me and Maggie. We were abducted." she said, speaking at the rate of knots.

"What? Goodness Jean, that's terrible. Are you okay? Are you hurt? Is Maggie there with you?" she heard Raoul asking her.

"No, she's not, they've got Maggie."

"Who's got Maggie?" Raoul asked, sitting up and wide awake now.

"I DON'T KNOW!" she bellowed down the phone.

The woman in the bed beside Raoul stirred but turned on her side and fell back to sleep. She was a deep sleeper, bless her.

"Where are you?" asked Raoul.

"I don't know. I'm in some town in the Himalayan resort, I think. We definitely didn't travel too far……then again, I was knocked unconscious so I don't know……I don't know where I am." Her thoughts were coming out in spurts now and she was making little to no sense.

"Okay, okay, slow down. Tell me what happened?"

"We were abducted by a group of men and taken to a brothel. I managed to escape but Maggie is still there."

"Oh my God." Raoul replied now. He had to sit down for a moment, that had knocked the wind out of him. He had not anticipated this, nothing in his wildest dreams could have prepared him for this.

"Were they foreign men or local men?" he asked now.

"How would I know? Foreign I think but I was too busy trying to get away from them."

"And they definitely operated a brothel?"

"Yes, I was there. I saw the whole set-up for myself."

"You're sure?"

"Yes, why is that so hard for you to believe? It does happen in this part of the world you know. I read about it.

I never thought it would happen to me though."

"Alright, tell me exactly where you were abducted? You both travelled the full journey on the bus, yes?"

"Yes, we did. We got off at the correct stop for our hotel, the Himalayan Inn Hotel. We checked with a local woman where to get the tuk-tuk, it was only further up the road on the same side, and then it was on the tuk-tuk that everything changed."

"So you never checked in to your hotel at the Himalayan Inn?"

"No."

"Did you see or hear anything unusual? Anything out of the ordinary?"

"No, nothing. Then again, I wasn't expecting this. I don't know what I'm going to do." Jean said desperately. "I'm sorry, I didn't know who else to contact." she finished quickly.

"Have you any idea where you are and I can come get you?" he asked.

"No, I just ran from the brothel and tried to find civilisation."

Jean scanned the area around her. There appeared to be some houses, a grocery store, a banyan tree. It was rural but she had certainly arrived in to an area of human habitation. "Even though I think I might be close to a village...... maybe... I'm not sure."

"It's alright Jean, we'll figure something out." Raoul chanted soothingly in to the phone and Jean chastised herself. She didn't know what she expected him to do. It wasn't like he lived just around the corner or could perform miracles. She berated herself for her ridiculous idea.

She heard him sigh momentarily on the other end of the line.

"Jean, it's really not safe for you to be wandering around the streets at this hour. You need to get out of there."

Raoul leapt out of bed now, he was pulling on his pants and searching frantically for a clean shirt. Being miles away, he felt completely helpless.

"Well, what else can I do? Tell me what to do Raoul." she said, irritated now. She didn't need to hear him proclaiming her danger, she needed help. Even if she hadn't worked out how yet.

A shadow fell across the payphone causing her to shiver, distracting her. A man dressed in a dark hoodie and, slacks started pacing back and forth behind her, fumes of smoke billowing out in front of him. He had a funny gait as he tried to ride all his coordination on his Nike runners. The guy was obviously drunk, but appeared to be intent on something, like he was waiting for someone, waiting for her.

"Raoul, you need to come now." she pleaded desperately into the phone. In all her life, she had never felt more alone.

"Jean, of course I'll come for you but if you're somewhere in the Himalayan resort as you seem to think you are, I'm hours away, you know that. It will take me several hours to get there. You remember yourself and Maggie had to take a four-hour bus journey from the volunteer house." he reminded her.

"But where am I supposed to go in the meantime?" she asked.

"That's what I'm trying to plan in my head right now." he replied quickly.

"I guess I was hoping because you organised the trip you might have some contacts down here." she said, crying down the line now unable to stop herself.

"I might have some." he said thinking fast. "Jean, listen to me. Have you any idea what village or town you're in?"

Then like a vision erupting before her, a recollection of overheard conversation came to her. Pokhara. That was it. Through whispered conversations somewhere she had definitely heard her captors mention this town.

"Pokhara. I think they mentioned Pokhara. That's where I am."

Raoul thought fast. "Are you able to get to your hotel – the Himalayan Inn? If you could safely get there, wait for me and I'll come get you as quick as I can?"

"I guess I can try." Jean replied meekly, not relishing the thought.

"If you think you're in Pokhara, you shouldn't be too far from your hotel. Try to make your way to the hotel safely and I'll meet you there."

"But won't the men from the brothel look for me there?"

"It's possible, but it's the best chance we've got." he replied.

Raoul was on his feet now, running down stairs and switching on the kettle. He wasn't going anywhere without a coffee.

Where were his car keys? He didn't know what he had done with them. He ran swiftly back upstairs to search for them hoping he didn't wake the children.

He scoured his entire bedroom, fishing in pockets of pants he had worn over the last few days. Nothing. He checked his wardrobe. Nothing. He ran downstairs to check the hall table Nothing there either.

"I'm going to have to find a police station around here somewhere first. I need to alert them and help them to find Maggie." Jean said and suddenly she was uneasy. She couldn't just abandon her best friend. There wasn't a bone in her body that could do that. She had to alert the police and get help.

She glanced out the window and watched as a car pulled up outside the payphone, music practically blowing her eardrums to shreds. Shielding her face in case any of them saw her, she saw the young man who had been pacing up and down outside step in. He had obviously been waiting for them.

"You don't want to go there." Raoul continued.

"And why not?" she demanded. "I need help if I'm going to find Maggie." That was it, her mind was made up. The fog in her brain was lifting and suddenly her path was clear. She wasn't going to go to the hotel and wait for Raoul. She would find a police station first. The earlier the police were made aware of what had happened, the better surely. It was the obvious thing to do.

"Because the police in this country are corrupt, they won't help you. Believe me."

Finally, Raoul located his car keys downstairs on the kitchen countertop.

"I can't do it by myself."

Jean was disappointed with Raoul. It was easy for him to sit there and tell her not to go to the police. He wasn't in the situation she was in - vulnerable, alone and terrified.

"Of course you can't!"

The kettle piped to boiling point and Raoul poured himself a hot cup of coffee. As the scalding water licked the cup, this freshly designed kitchen represented the life he had carved out for himself. He had worked hard to build a comfortable home here in Kathmandu for his wife and family and he was proud of it. He scribbled a note for his wife to let her know he would be gone for a few days.

Grabbing his jacket from the banister he gulped down his coffee almost as instantly as it had been made.

"Well, are you going to help me then?" she shot back at him, annoyance rising.

"I told you. Make your way to the hotel and I'll meet you there in a few hours."

"But I can't. I have to find Maggie. If I don't alert the police right now, she could die."

"Jean, I'm getting into my car right now and I'm coming to get you." he said, as he shut the front door behind him and went out into the night air. "Find your way to the hotel, you should be safe there."

"But you're all the way down in Kathmandu, you won't be here for hours."

"Jean, will you stop being so stubborn and listen to me, it's the best option we've got." Raoul insisted. "And don't go to the police, I've told you, they're corrupt."

"What else do you expect me to do?" she was sick of him now and was impatient to get him off the phone. "Goodbye Raoul, I'll see you in Pokhara in a few hours." she said as she slammed down the receiver. She was stressed now and was fast running out of options.

Well, that was a complete waste of time. So much for Raoul being the emergency contact. Even though he worked with an abundance of clients for booking accommodation and transport he didn't seem to have anyone to call on in an emergency? What a liar. She had expected better. She didn't know what she expected him to do but she had thought he might be able to find some kind of resolution. She couldn't make her way to the hotel and wait hours for him without alerting the police. Maggie could be dead by the time he arrived. She might already be dead for all she knew. Jean shuddered. She didn't want to think about it. It looked like she was completely on her own.

She yanked open the door of the phone booth in a fury trying to decide what to do. Glancing at her watch she felt despondent at the late hour. It was all very well for him. He wasn't alone and vulnerable in unfamiliar territory in the dark of night. There was no way in hell she was going to stay here and wait for him. She didn't care what Raoul said, she was going to find the police.

As she bolted along, in search of some sign of police presence, she passed pottery shops, Buddhist places of worship and various quaint antique shops. With all these distractions, it was easy to forget that she was a young woman alone in a foreign country and it was dark. Her earlier resolve had deserted her as she continued to pound the streets aimlessly searching for a police station. She was beginning to get anxious. It really wasn't safe to wander these streets by herself and she could be miles from the nearest police station. Although her intellect told her she was obviously in the main street of a town so there ought to be one close by. The air felt hot and humid as she carried on walking, all the while maintaining a sense of purpose and a brisk pace. She began to perspire. At this time of year, the temperatures rarely dropped far, even at night. She didn't know where to turn next. She kept sneaking a glance over her shoulder, almost as though she expected to see Kamal and Sajit chasing after her at any moment. Try as she might, that level of paranoia was difficult to suffuse. She had spent the last few days in captivity, constantly on edge. She couldn't just switch it off. If she couldn't find a police station tonight, the next best option was to find a hiding place. After what seemed like an eternity, she eventually managed to stumble across a police station in the centre of the town. She was safe now.

CHAPTER 8

A little bit run down but it wasn't the most foreboding of places. Jean thought if she were a criminal, it wouldn't impede her crime in the slightest. That concerned her. Looking at it now, she felt almost midget-like as she took in the brown brick exterior and the small windows that looked in need of a decent lick of paint. Through a small little archway lurked the front door. She dashed inside in search of a uniformed policeman. Entering the building, she found herself in the middle of a giant hall bathed in a beaming light and whitewashed walls filled the space around her. Putting her hands to her forehead she peered into the night sky through a round concave glass roof. Wooden floorboards creaked underneath them, all the while threatening disintegration.

Shielding her eyes from the piercing light, she scanned the hall. It was busy even at this hour. All around her policemen were marching their prey in and out of the different rooms, their victims were kicking and screaming in protest. She witnessed one sturdy policeman pass through with a young boy who Jean couldn't imagine was more than seventeen years of age. With his hands in cuffs behind his back, he was screaming torrents of abuse and trying to kick out at the figure of authority he so obviously resented. He was so anti authority, he spat full in the face of his captor. This boy was still a child, yet already he was a seasoned criminal. The police officer remained calm and onwards they marched through a set of double doors out the back.

Off to her right she noticed a large office space decorated with a blue swivel chair and a broad study desk. On the desk stood a load of files all bundled together one on top of the other. Beside that was a mug stained after copious cups of coffee and a dell computer. Paper remnants and short post-it notes littered the desk rendering the place untidy. In the background, the distant hum of the radio could be heard. Not that Jean could understand it, the presenters were all speaking Nepali. A policeman was standing over his desk searching through all the pieces of paper when she entered. Interrupted from his work, he looked up and proceeded to greet her. A man in his mid-to-late thirties, he spoke with an air of authority but his demeanour portrayed a kind, human side to him.

"Please, come in." he said, ushering her in and sitting her down on the small two-seater couch in his office. "I'm Detective Rashid. Can I get you a cup of tea or coffee or some water Ma'am?" he asked. She could see him taking in her rough unkempt appearance and the note of desperation that must have been oozing from her. He was evidently coming to the conclusion that she was the victim of some terrible crime.

Jean was touched by his sincerity. It was all she could do to mumble a quiet 'no thank you'. She had spent the last few days bred in captivity being treated as anything other than human. It was a radical change now to be treated with dignity and respect.

Detective Rashid looked at her now his eyes burning into hers, waiting for an explanation. He could see she was wildly distressed but he needed to tread carefully. He saw these kinds of victims pass through his office all the time. If they were pushed too far, they would clam up and reveal nothing. "Do you want to tell me your name?" he said eventually.

"Jean. Jean Sayers." she mumbled in a voice that sounded completely alien to her.

"Nice to meet you Jean. Do you want to tell me what happened?" he probed gently, all the while watching her body language for any signs that he might be pushing her too far. "I'm assuming you didn't just wander in here by mistake?" he said as he closed the door and sat back down at his desk. His heart sank as he watched her body descend into lockdown. She crossed her legs, folded her arms and cast her eyes down at the floor, avoiding eye contact. Detective Rashid recognised this as the classic signs of clamming up.

Detective Rashid had seen it all before. Whenever victims of physical or sexual abuse presented themselves in his office, invariably they had endured unbelievable trauma and they didn't want to talk about it. They wanted help but found themselves unable to open up unless they were given a little gentle persuasion.

"No." Jean replied shortly before slumping back into her chair.

In spite of herself, all her defences sprung up out of nowhere like a moth to a flame. She might as well have built a brick wall around herself without the slightest intention of letting anybody in. She found herself reluctant to trust anybody, even the police officer. What was wrong with her? She found herself completely incapacitated, unable to divulge anything that had happened. Her mind spun into overdrive as hundreds of thoughts whirled around her head. Over and over again, she played out the scenes from the Brothel, unable to erase what she had witnessed from her mind. All of those poor unfortunate girls who had been there for months, even years perhaps, without any prospect of ever being found. And there was Maggie. She was still there under the evil spell of Kamal and Sajit.

"Jean, I can see that you have obviously been through a terrible ordeal. But I can't help you unless you tell me what happened." he pleaded with her. "You're safe now, nobody can hurt you."

Jean instantly stood up in fury, kicking the couch as hard as she could. How dare he suggest that he understood her. He couldn't even begin to understand what herself and Maggie had endured. Some of these people were egotistical maniacs in her book gorging on their power and loving the ride. He sat in his office day after day, earned a big fat salary and went home to his wife and children. What did he care about some more foreign girls getting tied up in the Brothel industry? Meanwhile, Maggie was still there, trapped in that life forever.

She was shouting at the Detective now. "I might be 'safe' as you say, but what about Maggie? She's still in that filthy place and it's all my fault." she said, collapsing down onto the couch again in a torrent of tears. "It's all my fault. I should have looked for her before I left. How could I leave her there? What kind of friend am I?"

"Jean, you did the right thing. You had to save yourself first; there's no use in two of you going missing is there?"

"Don't you preach to me from your high horse. You haven't got a clue what you're talking about." she ranted, unable to stop herself. Once the river had burst its banks, it was impossible to stem the tide and she was in full swing now "Have you any idea how those people treated me? They tied my hands and feet and locked me in a cell in a basement. I was given a hole in the floor to go to the toilet and what I was fed wouldn't feed a bird. But the worst part was they treated me like vermin, like I was some piece of meat they could just have. So forgive me if I fail to appreciate you preaching to me."

She paused for a moment before getting up and making to exit the office. "I don't know why I even came here. My best friend is out there and I should be searching for her. Clearly this place will be of no use to me."

"Jean, please calm down." Detective Rashid begged, getting to his feet and rushing to the doorway before she could make her exit. "Tell me what happened and I promise you, we will do everything we can to find your friend. I know it's difficult, but please let us help you."

Finally Jean was reassured and took her place back at the couch. There was a moments' pause before she spoke.

"I've just escaped from a Brothel. I'm fine, obviously, but my friend Maggie isn't. She's still there." she said, as tears stung her eyes. Finally, the enormity of what happened was hitting home and she could hide from the pain no longer. "Please help me find her." she finished.

"Of course. But first, we're going to need to take a statement from you. Is that okay?"

Jean simply nodded, unable to speak at this point. She was exhausted, completely depleted of all her resources.

"And." the detective continued, once he was satisfied that she had understood him thus far. "We're going to need to know everything about your friend. We're going to need you to tell us when you last saw her, what she looks like, what she was wearing, height, build, everything. Okay?"

Jean nodded again.

"Do you have any photos of her or could you describe her to a sketch artist for us?"

Jean snapped out of her daze and looked up at the policeman. Was this guy for real? Of course she would be able to describe Maggie to a sketch artist. She was her best friend. What kind of friend would she be if she couldn't even describe her? She gave the Detective the benefit of the doubt as she realised he was only following police protocol. And she decided to cooperate fully.

"I don't have any photos with me but I could definitely describe her to a sketch artist for you." she answered.

"Great! Now, the next thing I'm going to ask you to do is a little more difficult. Your captors, do you think you'd be able to describe those to a sketch artist?"

"I couldn't forget them if I tried." Jean replied, a shudder escaping her entire body.

****

Back at the police station, Jean provided the police with statements and relayed as much information as she possibly could. She left nothing out, recounting every minute detail of her ordeal. She might have been in a state of complete distress and exhaustion but once she began, the whole sorry saga came pouring out of her like a burst dam. As three policemen, colleagues of Detective Rashid's gathered around her, they lent a sympathetic ear. A few probing questions were fired her way but nothing that would push her over the edge.

As promised, she described each one of her captors to a sketch artist with as much detail as possible. When he showed her the finished product, she was satisfied that the drawings accurately reflected the faces of her captors - Abdul, Sajit, Babu, Kamal and Anoushka.

They faltered at a number of items, however. Since she had no idea where she had been taken, she could not provide them with an address. She offered to travel with a police officer in a car to try to locate the brothel but once they ventured outside the town, the landscape seemed to resemble nothing but a large barren wasteland. She hadn't realised just how far off the road it was. Somewhere in her memory she recalled the opaque white colour of the marquee. Not exactly a colour that would stand out in this barrage of wasteland.

Since she hadn't been raped, they were limited in DNA evidence. They provided her with fresh clothes, ordered her to take a shower and hand over her old clothes. She only hoped they would find something that would help to incriminate her captors and lead police officers to them. And Maggie. She felt like a convicted criminal as they took swabs from her mouth, took her fingerprints and picked under her fingernails. She was forced to wave goodbye to any shred of dignity as she was asked to pee in a small bottle for traces of drugs in her system. Finally, they took photographic evidence of her injuries which were mostly bruises to her face and arms. She had a dark line of bruising around her neck, wrists and ankles as well from the chains they had used when she was locked in the cell. They took photographs of her arm where she had been injected with heroin. By the time she was finished she had seen several members of the team ranging from the medical examiner to the sketch artist to the psychiatrist. She was exhausted and just wanted to curl up in a ball. But she couldn't, she needed to feed off her adrenaline and keep going. Even as Detective Rashid advised her to get some rest, she knew she couldn't.

They stood in Detective Rashid's office now as he informed her of the latest developments. She was distracted by a painting that looked ominously like Maggie, as he spoke.

"We have been in touch with the Irish Embassy." he informed her. "And they have agreed to fund a week's stay in a hotel here while you help us with the investigation. They have also agreed to fund flights for your parents to fly out for 5 nights. They will arrive late tomorrow night."

Jean spun around now to face Detective Rashid, admiration for the painting forgotten.

"My parents? I only live with my Mum. I don't know my dad, he left when I was small." she said, very confused by what Detective Rashid was telling her.

"I have been informed that she will be travelling with a man named Noel. He is your biological father, I believe." he said.

"Oh!" she replied, rather puzzled. "But I haven't seen him since I was a toddler. In fact, you could say I never really met the man."

"But you obviously remember him?"

"No I don't. I probably have some vague recollections but I don't really remember him. What the hell does he care? He abandoned us." she spat, forgetting for a moment that she was sitting in Detective Rashid's office and letting the anger she had kept locked away for so many years course through her.

"Well he obviously does if he's prepared to travel half way across the world to see you."

"And he thinks that will make up for everything does he? He's nothing but a worthless piece of shit." she said shaking now with the full force of her anger. "He doesn't just get to come into my life and claim me as his daughter."

"Give the man a chance. At least sit and listen to his side of the story." he said gently.

"After what he did to us? You must be joking. He practically left us in the gutter. He abandoned us when we needed him most. I have worked hard to get where I am today and he does not get to be a part of it." she ranted.

Detective Rashid merely sat down in his chair and sighed. He had of course experienced this before. A police station was after all a place where many family woes came to a head. He had been unprepared for this one and found himself at a complete loss as to what to say. The young girl had clearly made up her mind and there was nothing he could do or say to make her change that.

"If you don't patch things up with him now, you might regret it when it's too late." he offered.

****

The recollections she had of her father were pitifully vague. Occasionally she experienced fleeting glimpses where she could almost see him in her minds' eye but nothing more. His absence had however left a void in her life so big it could never be filled, unearthing itself in many shapes and forms. The financial hardship that epitomised her childhood. The silence of a house that would never resonate with the booming sound of a man's voice. The little girl that would never know the safe loving arms of a dear father or the sacred bond between father and daughter. It was the simple things she supposed - the absent birthday cards or the presents that never came. It was all the little milestones he had missed as she grew up - the first time she rode a bike, her first day at school, her first communion. These were painful reminders of what she couldn't have. Yet she still harvested the knowledge that somewhere out there her father was living his life. Did he ever think about her? Did he even care? Was it really too much to ask for a father figure in her life?

School pageants and birthday parties were the worst she reflected. The effect of her fathers' departure from her life had floored her in one tumultuous wave as her classmates began to notice. After the first school pageant when she was seven, she had gone from enjoying a plentiful supply of friends to being the school outcast overnight. As all her classmates flocked to their parents, babbling with excitement in the aftermath of their performance, it was glaringly obvious that Jean's father was nowhere to be seen. All the other mothers and fathers had made a special effort to come out that night to see their children perform, why hadn't hers? Her mother, devoted mother that she was, had turned up to support her. She recalled envying her classmates the stable family life she craved, often awash with jealousy that they had both a mother and father. Stability was what she craved the most she supposed as she reflected back on it now. All she could do was look on with longing as she watched her classmates flock to their parents, babbling with excitement after the pageant, where she knew they were the absolute centre of their parents' world. Why couldn't she be the centre of her father's world? Did he find her repulsive?

Suddenly all the girls were whispering about her behind her back and all eyes were on her as she took her seat in the classroom. In the school yard, her arch-nemesis Eve McGowan took great delight in spreading the word that "Jean had no Daddy" and she instructed the other children not to play with her.

"Don't play with Jean girls, you'll only be associating with the wrong kind and she will bring you bad luck." had been Eve's most famous chant.

While Jean was well able to challenge Eve on her ridiculous assertions, the damage was well and truly done. All her classmates turned their back on her and sided with Eve, forming what could only be described as a deadly cult. They all avoided her as though she possessed some contagious disease that might cause them to drop dead at any moment. She remembered taking the school bus home one day when the bus was full. Some of her classmates sat in seats with an empty seat next to them. As soon as she approached, they deliberately placed their school bags atop the empty seats, denying her the opportunity to sit down. Recognising rejection when it stared her plain in the face, she stood near the front of the bus for the entire journey home. As the girls filed off the bus one by one, they all sniggered at her, declaring her the school reject. As if that wasn't bad enough, one of them also poured an entire bottle of Lucozade into her school bag covering her books, copies and pens in the thick, sticky liquid. She had run home, hot tears of frustration streaming down her face. She could not understand what was so wrong, everyone seemed to be out to get her.

Everyone except Maggie. She had been the only person to play with her at break times, the only person willing to be her friend. Yes, she would be forever grateful to Maggie for that awful period in her life. If it hadn't been for her, she would have had no one. Their friendship for life was sealed.

To her innocent eyes it had seemed bitterly unfair that she had no daddy to call her own. His sheer rejection had been the most difficult to accept and she had spent her formative years thinking she must have repulsed him so much he had been forced to leave. She blamed herself. In fact, she remembered making a bargain with God one night. If He would only make her dad come back into her life, she would spend the rest of her days forever indebted to Him. Her mother did her best to lavish her with love and affection and shield her from the worst of the sense of abandonment. But children are naturally inquisitive making them highly perceptive. And Jean was no exception. Outgoing and precocious to a fault it had been quite the revelation to discover at an early age that not all children came from such a dysfunctional family dynamic.

She had spent her whole life trying to make up for his absence, never quite managing to fill that void. Hard and all as she tried, nothing came even close. No, there was no way she could forgive and forget. She had worked too damn hard to allow this imbecile of a man to think he could just waltz back into her life whenever it suited him. He abandoned his own flesh and blood and that was all she needed to know.

How could she ever forgive her father for the trauma he had inflicted not only on her, but her mother, who she knew was grieving internally. She had too much anger stashed inside her, she would never forgive him and she didn't see the point in meeting him. She had better things to do with her time than listen to his sorry excuses for abandoning her. Why should he be granted access to her world now because it suited him? In her mind, it would be the greatest possible betrayal she could inflict on her mother and she wasn't ready to do that.

Jean turned to face Detective Rashid head on now. She knew what she was about to say would displease him but the decision lay with her at the end of the day. Holding firm in her resolve she spoke clearly and eloquently, her tone implying that she was not open to negotiation. It was final. "Tell the authorities I will see my mother Pamela Sayers, but I refuse to see him."

****

A little while later, Detective Rashid was trying to convince Jean to get some rest amid a flurry of protestations. It had been more than twenty-four hours since she had turned up at the station, traumatised and alone. Looking at her now, the sheer magnitude of her fatigue betrayed her in every way. It was evident in the heavy motions by which she carried herself, the bags under her eyes, the pale drawn skin, and her wild and bushy hair. The girl needed a decent night's sleep.

They sat now in his office once more. He had just witnessed her almost collapse as she paced up and down the waiting room. He had taken the initiative to bring her into his office after that.

"Look, you have been through a terrible ordeal. I think it's about time you went to your hotel and got some rest."

He had already supplied all the details, booked her in, and had made several attempts to persuade her to leave. He was reaching the end of his tether. The girl was a liability.

She shot him a fierce look, her dark eyes boring into his. Her indignant expression leaving him in no doubt he had just made a preposterous suggestion. Her pupils shrunk to a fraction of their original size and he half expected her to start screaming hysterically. For a brief moment, as he fleetingly calculated her body language, the air rang heavy with the scent of delirium.

"No way. I can't rest, not until Maggie is found." she said defiantly. She turned away from him and folded her arms, attempting to dismiss any further discussion on the matter.

"I'm insisting on it Jean, you're no good to us in this state." he said in his firmest voice. "I promise you we will do everything we can to find her. If I have any news, I will contact you immediately."

"Sir, can I ask you a question?" she asked, spinning back around towards him so fast a gust of wind might have just blown up in his face.

"Of course, you can."

"Have you children?"

"Yes." he said simply, wondering where this conversation was going. "Two daughters."

"If one of your daughters went missing, would you wait around and let your colleagues here try to find her?"

Detective Rashid sat back in his chair and took a moment to answer.

"No, I don't think so. I'd try to find her myself." he said truthfully.

"Exactly! So I am proactively helping in this investigation whether you like it or not." Jean said as she rose to her feet. "And I will find her by myself if I have to."

And then, she promptly turned on her heel and stormed out of the office.

CHAPTER 9

On the final leg of the journey. Noel sat back in his seat as the usual safety announcement and demonstrations wafted over him. He tossed and turned like an impatient child scrambling to get out. He took a series of deep breaths to calm his nerves and shut his eyes in preparation for takeoff. He hated flying. He really couldn't fathom how some people travelled all over the world for a living. Fishing in his pocket he found what he was looking for - his bottle of rescue remedy. Opening the bottle with his stubby fingers he discreetly deposited some of the liquid into his mouth and he waited for the anxiety to leave him. He must have drunk a bottle full of it by now. Fastening his seat belt securely around him he found a comfortable position and waited for the plane to taxi down the runway.

"Noel, are you alright?" he heard Pamela ask him.

"I'm fine." he lied. He didn't know why he had lied. He supposed it was just a moment of impulsion. They might not have seen each other in twenty odd years but Pamela could still read him like a book and he could feel her x-raying him now. She was probably silently guffawing at his cowardice. She knew him far better than the lame attempt at false bravado.

They had just boarded the plane from New Delhi to Kathmandu and this was their third flight in the space of twenty-four hours. They had endured a rush out the door arriving at Dublin airport for their flight to London and then on to New Delhi which would be the main leg of their journey. This flight, which would transport them into

Nepal's capital city, would only take two hours. They would get a taxi to the Embassy once they landed.

All around him, his fellow passengers chatted excitedly about the trip that awaited them. Most of them tourists, some had come for the sole purpose of hiking in Mount Everest. Others had come to explore the many temples and Buddhist places of worship Nepal had to offer. It was quite a surreal experience to find himself out in this part of the world. Thousands of miles away from home, it was a world he saw on the news or read about in the papers but a world that he really knew very little about.

As the moment he hoped he would finally meet Jean grew increasingly closer, the more apprehensive he became. Like a thick layer of cling film, it began to bubble up inside him until it stuck to every groove. He tried to suppress a gnawing fear that she would reject him, despite all logic telling him otherwise. As far as Jean was concerned, he had abandoned her in her hour of need and she had endured the humiliation of a fatherless childhood. He had missed every single birthday ever since, been glaringly absent from every single milestone in her life and she was riddled with doubt and insecurity as a result. The damage he had inflicted was enormous and could never be undone. He could picture it now. The fury, the venom, the hostility that would be hurled at him. And he deserved it. But was there any way he could ever make her believe that he had never stopped caring? He had to at least try. He would regret it if he didn't.

****

His mother had run out on his family with another man when he was ten. A chronic alcoholic he had never quite decided if it was a blessing in disguise or not. He could remember coming home from school on several occasions to find his mother passed out in the bathroom from alcohol poisoning. The house would be a mess with empty wine bottles strewn all over the place, crumbs on the kitchen countertops and litter everywhere. The breakfast dishes wouldn't have been touched, no dinner prepared for him or his sister. Other days he might come home to find a mass of broken China plates evidently thrown to the floor in a temper. In the middle of winter, the fire wouldn't be lit, the heating wouldn't be turned on and there would be no sound of the washing machine turning. The clink of a wine glass would be the only sound to indicate how she had spent her day.

Noel and his sister had to make their own lunches for school and wash and iron their own school uniforms. Their mother would insist they did all the household chores like hovering, dusting and polishing, cleaning the bathrooms and preparing the dinner so it was ready to switch on when their father came home from work. She never once helped either of them with their homework, their spelling and grammar, bought them school books or other such paraphernalia. Their father did that. On the days when he arrived home to find her conscious, that was a good day. He used to live in a permanent state of fear of a dark day. Those occasions when he would find her unconscious. Sometimes he woke at night to overhear a heated argument ensuing between his mother and father. He used to hate it, all the yelling and screaming and his mothers' drunken slurs. At times, it would get extremely violent and his mother would lose her temper and throw whatever was at her disposal to the ground.

As an innocent, naïve child he convinced himself that if he performed better at school, if he did more chores around the house and transformed himself into a well behaved, child, he would make his mother happy and she would stop drinking. For several years he put extra time and effort into his schoolwork, he practically ran the household making sure it was spotless and he worked his way up to become one of the star players on his local hurling team. Anything that would appease his mother. And for a while it appeared to be working. She wasn't drinking, the fierce rows had ceased and she even prepared delicious snacks for them when they arrived home from school. He finally began to feel like they were a normal family unit again.

After a Sports day at school, Noel had practically run home full of excitement to tell his mother how terrifically well he had performed. He had won a silver medal in the 200m sprint and he was chuffed with himself. It was a gloriously sunny day and he sprinted fast and furiously through the park that led to the pathway to his house. He hardly noticed the daffodils and the tulips sprouting up all around him as he ran. All he saw was a sea of green, so intent was he on telling his mother the good news. He bolstered in the door shouting as he went:

"Mom." he shouted. "Mom, guess what? I got a silver medal at school today."

His heart sank as he saw his mothers' unsteady gait emerge at the top of the staircase, her thick brown hair unbrushed, her eyes wandering unable to focus. Not a scrap of make-up dotted her face and she was wearing yesterday's clothes. As she looked at him now, clinging on to a bottle of wine as though her life depended on it, she had a wild look in her eyes.

"Hello Noel." she slurred, barely able to speak. She was intoxicated. "Come and give Mommy a kiss." she said clambering down the stairs to greet him. How she made it down in one piece he would never know.

"Hi Mom." he replied despondently, completely taken aback to see her drinking again. He had thought he was doing enough to make her happy but clearly he wasn't.

"How was school?" she asked.

"Good mom, I came second in the two hundred metre sprint. I got a silver medal."

"Second place?" she asked. "Sure, that's useless. How come you didn't come first? Or are you just a loser like the rest of them?" she said now as she stepped down the final stair and strode straight past him into the kitchen.

"I did my best Mummy." he protested.

"Well, you're best clearly isn't good enough darling." she said as she helped herself to another generous gulp of wine. "Mummy always wants you to come first."

"Mummy, you've been drinking again. I hate it when you drink." he snapped, not at all pleased with that last comment.

"Oh my dear it's not uncommon for adults to enjoy a drop of wine, you'll learn that when you're older." she said, gently brushing aside the issue of her drinking.

That spelled the beginning of the end of his mother and father's marriage. She had run away with a fellow drunkard after that. It had broken his father and he was never the same man again. Despite all of their problems it was clear he had worshipped her until alcoholism had taken hold.

One thing was for certain, Noel had never trusted women after that. Without him realizing it, the effects of his mothers' rejection had manifested itself in his relationships with women. He had been programmed into believing that all women were domineering and overpowering because he didn't know any different.

And so, when it came to Pamela, he had never believed that she truly loved him, that she could commit herself to him for life. In his eyes, the postnatal depression had merely served as the 'get out' clause he needed before she hurt him, albeit at the expense of Jean.

****

"Ladies and Gentlemen, we have begun our preparation for landing. Please make sure your seatbelts are securely fastened and your trays stored in the upright position," the flight attendant announced.

And so, it was with a dangerous concoction of relief and trepidation that Noel stepped off the plane when it touched down in Nepal. Arriving in the country was a little disorientating with the time difference. Nepal was six hours ahead so it was now just approaching noon. Pamela and Noel already felt like they had been up for days on end.

They took a taxi from the airport. Passing shanty towns and slum villages along the way before being catapulted into the heart of the city, it was obvious they had a different way of life here. Noel had been flabbergasted at how little the taxi cost when he made to pay the driver. Doling out his rupees it had seemed a miserable amount of money, so he had given a tip.

Their first stop was the Irish Embassy in Nepal. It was a swanky modern building clearly situated in an upmarket area of town. This quarter of the capital was home to a slew of foreign embassies and the red brick building stood tall and proud, Irish flag protruding from high above. Glass windows and some low-slung flower baskets added some much needed embellishment to its frontal exterior. A small makeshift garden stood directly in front. Pamela wasn't a gardening expert by any means but she could see a colourful display of flowers lying saturated on the ground. Monsoon season was clearly here in full swing. The entrance was up a short path through a large set of automatic doors.

Once inside, the embassy had a much more corporate feel. Plush carpets, glass doors and the latest model of computer all spoke volumes of a firm that was reeling in the cash. Noel and Pamela made their way towards the smiley faced Receptionist who sat behind a large desk.

"Hello, how can I help you?" she asked in a friendly Irish accent and they felt like they were back home in Ireland again. Blonde hair swept neatly off her face, and caked in make-up she was as Irish as they came.

"Hello. We're Jean Sayers' parents, an Irish girl that was reported missing down in the Himalayan resort the other day." began Pamela. "I understand the Department of Foreign Affairs has been in touch with the consular assistance team here and we're here to meet them."

"No problem at all folks." the friendly receptionist replied. "What's your own name?"

"Pamela Sayers and Noel Brady." Pamela volunteered.

'Okay, if you just take a seat for me, someone will be with you shortly.' she said, as she typed furiously into the computer screen and picked up the phone beside her.

As they left the Receptionist babbling away into the receiver, they made their way over to the luxurious three-seater couch to wait. Pamela wasn't sure of the colour - turquoise maybe. It complemented the walls she supposed, which were a lovely shade of off-white and gave the place a warm, cosy feel. Magazines littered the miniscule coffee table in front of them spouting the latest celebrity gossip. Pamela was about to take out her phone to send a text until she remembered she was on the other side of the world with no coverage. They would have to visit a phone shop to get a special SIM card. What if the police were trying to ring her with news of Jean?

Moments later they were greeted by two men, both members of the Irish consular assistance team. Decked out in suits and formal attire, they looked more aptly dressed for a business meeting as opposed to capturing two missing women. One was plump and short, wore dark spectacles around his eyes and introduced himself as John Nash. The other man was tall with more of an athletic build and identified himself as Paul Cargo. Both of them could be anywhere between thirty and forty-five but Pamela took a wild guess that John was the more senior of the two. As they greeted them with full Irish accents, it was great to have the feel of a home away from home. She was grateful for all the help they could get.

They were led down a long corridor into a sterile meeting room where the door swung swiftly closed behind them. As they sat down at the cold conference table, Pamela felt sure she could feel a chill going straight to her bones. Glancing around the bare walls to check if there was a window open or a draft coming from somewhere, she eventually surmised there wasn't. There were floor to ceiling windows allowing bright shades of light to infiltrate into the office, offering picturesque views of the area. A telephone in the centre of the table, presumably for use during board meetings or conference calls, and a large jug of water, cemented the office vibe. Over in the far corner stood a number of paper coffee cups, some stirry sticks and sachets of tea, coffee and sugar. Good to see Ireland's campaign on the green front was reaching all corners of the globe. In this room that was devoid of personality, she turned her attention to John and Paul.

"Sorry to be meeting you under such circumstances." John, the short plump one began.

"Thank you for meeting us." Pamela said.

"I'm sure it's a terribly distressing time for you both. Now, we are going to provide any assistance we can." he finished, his face moulding into one of empathy and concern.

"Are there any updates on Jean or Maggie's whereabouts?" It had been a long journey to get here. There may have been some developments over the last twenty-four hours. It was a possibility.

"Yes, there is." It was Paul who spoke now, the tall, athletic one. "We are happy to tell you that police in the local Himalayan resort contacted us to say Jean showed up there earlier today."

Pamela couldn't believe her ears. Just like that, they had found her. She stared at Paul dumbfounded. Beside her, she could feel Noel's head practically tear off its hinges and his eyes bulge from their sockets.

"She's ok?" she squeaked, more for reassurance than anything else.

"Yes." replied Paul, with a smile on his face.

"Is it definitely her?" Pamela was beside herself. She couldn't control the onslaught of questions that were escaping out of her mouth now.

"She has some cuts and bruises and some contusions to her forehead but she's alive and well. They will keep her in for questioning and they will require her assistance on the case, but she's safe." Paul finished.

"Oh thank God." Pamela breathed a sigh of relief. The sheer elation swelled every inch of her body. It was all over now and their little girl was safe.

"It's not often we get to be the bearer of good news, but today is one of those days." Paul said in kind dulcet tones. "You should count yourself one of the lucky ones."

As she went to embrace Noel, they held onto each other for dear life. Almost intuitively she sensed that he had been every bit as concerned as she had. He felt every ache, every bite of food like sawdust, every phone call the one to declare their demise. Regardless of what had gone before, Jean was his daughter too.

"And Maggie? Is she with her?" Pamela asked now.

Paul and John shot a look at each other as if contemplating what to say next. There was definitely a shift in mood and the tone of the meeting had taken a turn for the worst.

"What is it?" Pamela asked now, her concern for sweet little Maggie growing by the second.

"Unfortunately, Maggie hasn't been found. Preliminary reports from the police say that Jean was being chased and she didn't have the opportunity to find Maggie so she ran from her captors herself."

"So where is she?" asked Pamela.

"Police believe she is still at the compound." Paul finished, almost hating himself for saying it. It was a horrible position to be in, they had found one of the girls and not the other. They must look like a complete joke. Paul was also cognisant of the terrible burden this placed on Jean.

"Oh God." Pamela said now. If she hadn't been sitting down, she thought she might have collapsed, her elation of just a few moments earlier eradicated entirely. Beside her, she could feel Noel's head swirling too, lost in thought. Suddenly, this wasn't an occasion of joy, it was bittersweet. They wouldn't be able to celebrate officially until they found Maggie.

"Well, what do we do now?" Pamela asked.

"Police are continuing their investigation and following up on any leads." John said now. "They have Jean with them, so hopefully she will be able to provide some detailed assistance."

"That's a lot of pressure on her." Noel spoke now.

"It is." agreed, John. "But the police are well used to handling situations like these. They will be very tactful." he reassured them.

"Sounds like women go missing up there all the time." said Noel. "What are they doing to make it safer, to stop this happening in the first place?"

He was a man of few words but when he spoke, he didn't mince his words.

"Noel, now is not the time." Pamela protested.

"You're quite right of course." replied John. "Unfortunately, it is a hot target for abducting women, tourists especially. But tourists want to see the Himalayas, they want to go hiking and they want to experience it. It's a very popular attraction here in Nepal."

"I bet it is." Noel said now, almost accusingly. "A very hot spot for predators too."

"Can I speak to her - please?" said Pamela, before Noel had a chance to argue further down this line.

"Of course."

John picked up the phone, dialed a number and spoke to someone Pamela could only presume was the local police in the Himalayan resort. Hearing him speak perfect, fluent, Nepali in a completely different accent was like some strange outer body experience. After a few moments, he handed the phone over to her.

"Jean is on the line." he said.

Taking the phone in her hand, Pamela nervously placed the receiver to her ear. It was Jean who spoke first.

"Mom?" Jean whispered, choking on her words.

A cloud of dust might as well have enveloped the room as they both choked on the emotion that threatened to engulf them. She had never been more grateful to hear her daughter's voice than in that very moment.

"Jean." cried Pamela. "It's so good to hear your voice. Are you alright?"

"I'm fine Mom, but they still have Maggie."

"Are you safe?" Pamela enquired. It was a silly question, she knew, but she still needed verbal reassurance.

"Yes, I'm safe. I'm in a police station. Mom, they've still got Maggie." Jean insisted again, but it seemed to be falling on deaf ears.

"I know love, I know." Pamela said, trying to comfort her.

"What am I going to do?" she asked.

"Your father and I are coming to get you. Stay at the police station, you'll be safe there."

"What about Maggie?"

"We'll find her too, don't worry."

"Where are you?"

"We're at the Irish embassy in Kathmandu."

"Okay, you're hours away. Maggie doesn't have that long. What are we going to do?"

"Stay where you are."

"Maggie will be dead by the time you get here Mom." Jean protested now.

"Okay, okay. Tell me what happened?" she probed gently.

"I was knocked unconscious and when I woke up, she was gone." she replied.

Pamela's heart began to beat at the rate of 100 beats per minute at the obvious ordeal that Jean had been subjected to. But she heard Jeans' voice continue talking on the other end of the line and knew she had to be strong.

"I managed to get away but I don't know where Maggie is." Jean was saying now.

"Oh Jean, that's terrible. What a horrible ordeal."

"What are we going to do?" she repeated again.

"Let the police do their job love, they'll find her." replied Pamela.

"No, they won't Mam, not from what I can see."

"Jean, I'm telling you now, stay where you are. Let the police do their job."

Pamela was stressed now. Her daughter could be so difficult to deal with sometimes, she was unbelievably headstrong.

"It's not over yet." said Jean defiantly.

"I know it's not. We'll find Maggie too, I promise."

"Thanks Mom." she stammered before composing herself and calming down. "I'm going to have to give some statements and the whole lot here so I'm going to have to go. I will ring once I have any news."

"Alright, stay safe darling and we'll see you soon." Pamela repeated.

Pamela Sayers put down the phone. She was absolutely thrilled. She wanted to jump up and down with sheer joy and elation and run out into the streets shouting that Jean was safe. She had never known such euphoria in all her life. She was so consumed with a new found energy and she needed to expend it. To her this was a new lease of life and a burgeoning hope that she had all but lost in the short period of time since Jean had been reported missing. She had to pinch herself to be certain she wasn't dreaming.

Hearing her daughter's voice on the other end of the phone had been better than winning the lotto. In her mind she had imagined a whole host of scenarios, each one of them worse than the last. She had imagined everything from Jean being sold to a Sheikh right up to receiving the dreaded phone call that her daughter had been found in a refuse bag somewhere. The police in Ireland had informed her statistics on these types of cases were not in her favour and to brace herself for the worst. How fortunate was she that her Jean had transpired to be one of the lucky ones?

The lack of sleep had been the worst she reflected. The endless tossing and turning, the breaking out in cold sweats and the absolute incapacity to rest. She had woken up from a light hazy sleep during her flight and for a split second she could not recount anything of the horror of the days before; but then it had all come flooding back and a new pain had hit her. She had barely been able to eat with worry. Her stomach had tied itself up in knots, too volatile to consider eating anything.

As she had prepared to disembark the plane earlier, the complexion that stared back frightened her. She barely recognised herself. Her face was drawn and haggard succumbing to the intensity of time. Her eyes stood obediently in their sockets but they were dull and lifeless. They say the eyes are the window to the soul and in Pamela's case they certainly were. They betrayed her usual carefree persona and spoke volumes of the pain and sorrow she had been subjected to. She hadn't bothered to wear any make-up, hardly taking the time to comb her hair. It had seemed pointless and trivial while her daughter was missing half way across the world.

They had stood on the brink of losing Jean for good and Pamela genuinely could not imagine a future without her. Her only daughter made up her entire universe and she had never loved anyone as ferociously. Jean had taught her what it meant to love unconditionally. She wouldn't have the strength to cope if she were to lose her.

Now, as she looked up at Paul and John, she was anxious to get a move on.

"What happens now?" she asked.

"We will organise a driver to take you to the police station in the Resort." John said. "It's about four hours away. We can have one ready for you in twenty minutes if you want to get a coffee and something to eat perhaps. We have a canteen in the building here which is fully available to you."

Pamela groaned inwardly to herself. Another vehicle, another form of transport and more travelling. Putting her best foot forward, she reiterated her thanks again and said her goodbyes along with Noel before making her way out of the room. Coffee sounded delicious.

****

Abdul stood in the middle of the marquee showing a potential client around. Over the past few months, he and his team had worked hard at infiltrating new blood into the business. Abducting young women at the Himalayan resort had proven to be a stroke of genius and they had struck gold. So many young women went hiking there, either on their own or in pairs, from all over the world. Add to that the relative ease with which they could be lured into a false sense of security. It was pathetic really when he thought about it. Last week Sajit and co. had captured two sexy Brazilian women, tall, tanned, toned and with sun tinged golden locks, Abdul had struggled to maintain his professionalism. He had wanted to kiss them, caress them there and then and he fought hard to quench his desires. When they turned out to be two innocent seventeen-year-olds it was like rubbing salt in his wounds and it made him want them even more.

Now, as his mobile phone rang and he saw the familiar number flash up on the screen, his stomach churned. He knew what this phone call would be about and he was not looking forward to it.

"Abdul, you idiot. Did you let one of those Irish girls escape?" the voice on the other end of the phone shouted.

"No." insisted Abdul. Lying was always his first tactic.

"I don't believe you, you little shit. The police have been on to us looking for Maggie Adams and Jean Sayers. What the fuck has happened up there?" asked the voice, panicking now.

"Calm down, it's only one of them that's missing."

"Yeah, and how long do you think it's going to be before the police realise that I led them to you."

"They're never going to have any proof of that. They were traveling to the Himalayas and they're not going to suspect anything."

"And what if they do? I could lose my job. I could lose everything."

"Oh, will you stop, you will not. They will have no proof. Besides, she doesn't suspect you're involved in this. It's myself, Sajit and the rest that she will identify. I don't know what you think you have to worry about."

"But she will talk Abdul and that will lead to probing. As you rightfully say she can identify you and she has the power to destroy us. I mean, don't you realise that?"

"Of course I realise it, you, fool. What do you take me for?"

"She's a loose cannon. What are we going to do with her?"

"Nothing."

"Find her and kill her."

"Don't be so stupid."

"Well, have you got a better idea? I'm telling you she will talk. She is not going to go quietly. She's going to come back to find her friend."

"We'll be ready for her if she does."

"You promised me you would never let this happen again."

"Yeah well, I lied." he said, and he hung up the phone in a temper.

Abdul looked up and discovered that his client was gone. He was glad as he needed to be alone right now, he needed space to think. In fact, what he needed was a good scotch to calm himself down. He turned, made his way out of the marquee, marched across the scorched earth and up to his office where he poured himself a stiff scotch. He had put a brave face on the phone call feigning bravado and an ego to boot but in reality, he was sick with worry. She would talk to the police, the police could find their hideout, raid the brothel and seize the business that he had worked so tirelessly to create. This girl that had escaped was indeed a loose cannon and with just a few words she could potentially annihilate them. It had happened once before many years ago when two girls had managed to escape from the brothel and gone to the police. They had been operating down south in Tibet at the time and had been forced to move location. He was beginning to think he would have to do the same now.

As he mulled over the situation in his mind recounting every minute detail, he cursed himself, he cursed his team, this warehouse and everything in it. In red hot fury he flung his glass of scotch in full force at the wall. Why did this have to happen to him? Just as his business was flourishing and he was getting back on his feet. He had disagreed with the man on the phone earlier but now as he sat pondering the alternatives, he realised there were none. The young Irish girl that had escaped was dangerous, she knew too much. If he didn't act fast, she would only be his downfall. He could not let that happen. There was nothing else for it; she would have to be found and when she was, she would have to be killed. Or make her disappear, never to be seen again. He had connections, he could easily arrange either outcome. Satisfied now with his decision he picked up the phone and dialed a number.

CHAPTER 10

Jean found giving evidence daunting and challenging. It was like this whole new world had opened up to her, the kind that you were only exposed to if you were unfortunate enough to be a victim of a crime. Although nothing overly intrusive, she felt as if she had been placed on a conveyor belt of forensic tests. First the medical examiner had taken a swab from the back of her throat and her nose, before taking fingerprints and samples from underneath her fingernails. If that wasn't bad enough, she was obliged to hand over her clothes for inspection as well. Jean turned her nose up at the replacement clothes she was being forced to change into – a tatty pair of bright orange scrubs that looked like they were well past their sell-by date. It was definitely not her finest hour. She may as well have been a convicted criminal. Once that was finished, she was escorted into a small room where she was greeted by another Detective who introduced himself as Detective Rabdo Manning. Tall and striking with dark facial hair and gleaming brown eyes that appeared to twirl in their sockets, Jean estimated his age at approximately mid-thirties. Detective Manning took her hand in a firm handshake and gestured for her to sit down in the vacant chair at one side of the table while he sat down at the other.

The room was grim. Dark and gloomy, it had been the scene of interrogation for many of the worst criminals in the country. Grey walls loomed large and tall around her with a small window at the back to breathe life into the room. The chairs were old and shabby and as she watched Detective

Manning shuffle through his case file, she couldn't help but notice the rust that was fast developing on the table. The dents caused by years of thumping the table with the force of a fist as many criminals protested their innocence and the multitude of dark brown circles served as a reminder of the countless victims that were brought tea or coffee in the aftermath of their ordeal. As dismal as this room appeared, one thing was for sure, it had character.

"Now Jean, I know this is difficult for you, but we are going to need you to tell us everything and start right back at the beginning from when you arrived in the Himalayan resort, what you saw, what you heard, when you became suspicious something wasn't right."

Jean hesitated. She was reluctant to go through it all again. It was too painful. The things she had witnessed over the last few days had traumatized her beyond belief. To witness a whole secret hideout containing hundreds of intelligent young women condemned to prostitution and drugs had been more than she could endure. And then there was the guilt. Should she have left Maggie or should she have gone to look for her? Would she ever find her now? Finally, with a subdued sigh, she began to tell her story.

"My best friend Maggie and I had just arrived in the Himalayan resort. We asked a local woman where to get the tuk-tuk to our hotel. She told us where our stop was, we thanked her and went to our stop to wait."

"Was that far from where you got off the bus?"

"No, just a few hundred metres up the road on the same side." replied Jean dismissively. "But the odd thing was that same woman went in to the shop, then she came back out running after the tuk-tuk we were on. Like she was following us."

"Okay Jean, I'm going to stop you there. You're saying you approached this woman. She gave you directions, then followed you?"

"Well, initially she went back in to the shop after helping us. But then yes, she came running back out trying to catch our tuk-tuk."

"Did she seem trustworthy?"

"Yes. She did at the time. I guess we both probably felt safer approaching a woman – for obvious reasons."

"Was there anything unusual about her? Did anything stand out?"

Jean tried to cast her mind back but it was so difficult.

"Well, I didn't think of it like that, but no, nothing unusual. She was just like any other local woman. I obviously didn't know she was part of this gang, did I? She didn't have 'abductor' written on her forehead." said Jean, getting hot under the collar at the Detectives insinuation that they had been naïve, careless and foolish.

"Alright, alright, keep your cool."

"And what happened then?"

"A tuk-tuk arrived and Maggie and I climbed aboard. Then we saw that same woman come running out of the shop, looking to climb aboard the tuk-tuk. We screamed at the driver to stop and they did. Only I didn't realise the only occupants of the vehicle were Sajit, Kamal and Babu. Men from the brothel working for a man named Abdul."

"Telephone call." the Detective said more to himself than anyone else. His eyes began to dart around the room and she could see him processing a lot of different thoughts in his head trying to make sense of them all. His face etched into a frown, he silently rambled on with his musings.

"What?" Jean said, clearly interrupting his reverie.

The Detective fixed her with his gaze now, having been brought back down to earth.

"That woman, do you know her name? She clearly made a phone call to alert the men that ye had arrived in the resort when she went back into the shop."

"Are you having a laugh? That's preposterous. That theory is so far-fetched you could shove it up your own arse." Jean insisted, shocked at the incredulity of it all. What were the chances?

"I'm serious. It's important to know if this abduction was random or preplanned. That will really help us with this investigation."

"I'm sorry, but there is no way there was any forward planning to this. Obviously they are stationed there on a regular basis and they just randomly select young women to abduct. There is no way they were specifically waiting for Maggie and I."

"I wouldn't be so sure about that. Some of these brothels depend on the tourist trade for abducting women. Because Nepal is not the kind of country you can lure young females to with the promise of a better life and Nepalese women are so well protected by their husbands, the most cost-effective way of abducting women is to target high-profile tourist attractions. But some of these Brothel bosses have connections with various other outside sources as well."

"Is that so?" Jean replied, still not convinced. Suddenly Jean sat up straight in her chair.

"Wait! She WAS following us. Oh my God, she set us up. That's what she was doing in that shop. She was ringing the rest of them to drive the tuk-tuk over."

Jean had completely blocked that part of the puzzle from her memory. Even though she had spoken to this woman in the brothel, she had completely forgotten due to the trauma of the last few hours- or perhaps the drugs she had been given.

"It certainly appears that way but let's not jump to conclusions just yet."

"But why else would she have gone in to that shop? That makes perfect sense. We were set up." Jean's mind was spinning now, desperate to piece all the puzzles together.

"We'll need to check them out, that's all I'm saying. Clearly this woman was involved. But we will need proof. Anyway, you still haven't answered my question. What was this woman's name?"

"Anoushka." Jean replied obediently. She almost spat the name out, she detested it so much.

"Can you describe her?"

"Yes, I've already described her to a sketch artist." Jean informed the Detective. "Small, low-sized woman with dark black hair and big brown eyes. She was probably in her mid-thirties or so."

"Okay." said the Detective as he jotted down some notes on his notepad. "And what happened then?"

"It all gets a bit blurry at this point." exclaimed Jean, racking her brains for any minute details she could remember. "One minute the tuk-tuk was just moving through the town, next thing I know Maggie and I are hit over the head."

"Right, can you describe the tuk-tuk? What size or what colour was it? Was there a registration number on it?"

"I thought there were no driving laws in this country? Why would it have a registration number?"

"There aren't, but there might have been a number on it somewhere that might help us to locate it."

"Well, I don't think I noticed any registration number on it. It all happened so fast I didn't think to look. Besides those tuk-tuks are always covered in dirt from the roadside."

"Describe the tuk-tuk for me." the Detective asked patiently trying to get her to focus.

"It was like any other tuk tuk; small, dark on the inside, able to seat about six people in the back and one other passenger up front. There was a small opening at the back where people could get on and off. They were very light vehicles and able to move extremely fast. And when it moved, it became enveloped in a cloud of dust."

"Alright, and these men on board definitely hit you and Maggie over the head?"

"Yes."

"What's the next thing you remember?"

"I remember coming round in this huge gorgeous mansion. Our hands and feet had been bound and we were helpless."

"Who was there?" interrupted the Detective, cutting to the chase.

"Sajit, Kamal, Babu, Anoushka and the brothel boss. He was revolting."

"What did they do with you?"

"Abdul just basked in the light of his power and inspected us for suitability for his brothel. Then he ordered us to be knocked unconscious again."

"And where did you wake up this time?"

"In a cell. And Maggie was gone." Jean cried tears swimming very close to the surface again. She must be emotionally spent at this stage.

"Take a glass of water." instructed the Detective, clearly very aware of the impact this was having on her. "And she was with you up until that point?"

Jean picked up the glass of water on the table and took a sip as instructed before replying. She could feel a lump forming in her throat.

"Yes." Jean replied. "They took her and I don't know what they did with her. She could be lying dead in a ditch for all I know."

"Let's hope not. We're going to do everything we can to find her." the Detective said in a calm soothing voice. "Can you describe this place to me?"

Jean shrugged her shoulders. "What's there to describe? I was locked in a cell in some kind of abandoned outhouse in the middle of a barren wasteland. When I was allowed out, I was shown around a setup marquee full of young women being taken advantage of or to be drugged and prepped for my first client. Oh, and there was a torture room as well, that was particularly impressive." she said sarcastically.

"Did anyone give you any specific information? Like tell you what they were going to do with Maggie or any of the other girls?"

"No." Jean replied. But as soon as the words were out of her mouth, a light switched on in her brain and she remembered something. "No... wait. I remember Sajit saying something about Maggie." she began, struggling to gather her thoughts. "Something about them being very impressed with her, so impressed they were going to sell her to the Sheikh. I think he was lying though."

"The Sheikh." Detective Manning stopped writing and looked up sharply from his notes. He tried to compose himself instantly, not wanting to convey to Jean how alarmed he was, but it was too late. Jean had already spotted the horror in his eyes.

"That's bad, isn't it?"

"Well, it certainly gives us a much narrower time frame." he said, not wanting to indicate how disastrous this could potentially be. Yet he knew Jean couldn't be fooled, she was far too intelligent for the wool to be pulled over her eyes.

"What kind of time frame?" Jean asked, afraid to hear the answer.

"Generally, we have a ninety-six-hour window from when women are abducted to when they decide to sell them to the Sheikh."

"So many of those hours are gone already. Please tell me you'll find her?" Jean pleaded desperately with him.

"We'll do everything we can." Then changing the subject, he said. "And your first client…." a little unsure as to whether he should finish the question or not. "What did he do?"

Jean shifted uncomfortably in her seat. She had wiped every detail of that horrible incident from her mind and now thanks to the man sitting before her, it had come flooding back. She felt every bit of disgust again as though it had just happened.

"No offence, but I don't want to talk about it." Jean said, folding her arms.

"Look, I know this is difficult for you Jean, but it's important that we know everything so we can build a case." the Detective said patiently.

"I know that, but like I say, I don't want to talk about it."

"Jean, do you want to help us find Maggie or not?" the Detective said bluntly, his tone suddenly sharp, all compassion and empathy momentarily gone.

"Of course I do. That's why I came here isn't it?" Jean replied, standing up instantly in her chair and beginning to pace the room. This interview was not helping her, it was merely building up a kind of frenetic energy inside her vying to be released. She continued to pace the room until she was satisfied she had expended all the energy within.

Detective Manning looked on knowing from experience that this young woman was fighting her internal thought processes. He had seen it so many times before. All of these young women were victims of a terrible crime and they would never be the same again.

"Then you've got to tell us everything." he said gently after a few moments.

Jean collapsed down into the chair utterly deflated. She had wanted to forget the whole ordeal but she supposed the police needed to know. Taking a deep breath, she cast her eyes down at the floor.

"They drugged me with heroin. They brought me out to one of the cubicles in the marquee." she began pronouncing every word carefully and speaking in a low voice. "After a while a man of about fifty appeared through the curtain. He didn't even say hello, he just kissed me and caressed me like I was some trashy piece of meat. He kissed me full on the mouth and then he… he… he." damn it, she couldn't say it.

And she was up again, pacing the room. Why was it that it suddenly appeared to be closing in on her, she was sure she could see the walls physically moving, moving towards her. If she didn't get out, she would be crushed under the weight of it all. And the air, it was putrid, hot and heavy. Was there no air to be found in this room? And this Detective dude, why was he asking her so many questions that she didn't want to answer. Was he stupid or something? It was much too painful. She couldn't cope; it hurt too much. She was a proud woman and it disgusted her that she had been violated in such a way, narrowly escaping rape. And she had abandoned her friend in her hour of need, what kind of person was she? Blind panic gripped her now and the room began to spin before her eyes, her pulse rate quickened by the second and she felt an enormous surge of adrenaline take hold of her body. She started banging on the door, yelling at the top of her lungs and she couldn't stop.

"Let me out of here." she screamed, ramming both fists on the door. "Let me out of here now."

In a flash, Detective Manning stood up from his chair and he was at her side, pleading with her to calm down.

"Jean, it's alright, you're safe here. No one can hurt you now." he said, all the while trying to take hold of her hands to stop her from banging on the door where she would inevitably disturb other investigating officers. "Please…… just calm down and take a seat." he insisted.

As Jean finally felt the frenetic energy and the momentary surge of adrenaline leave her body, she was able to feel relaxed again. She did her best to hide her embarrassment at her behaviour but she did apologise profusely.

"I'm sorry Officer." she said, casting her eyes down at the floor, refusing to look at him.

"You have nothing to be sorry about. You have been through a terrible ordeal Jean, it's only natural that your emotions are all over the place while you process the enormity of what happened."

"Thank you for being so kind to me." she said. Internally she was almost laughing at herself. The old Jean would never have made such a statement. It would have killed her. Kindness? Who needed that? Kindness was only for misfits she would have said. And yet, here she was half way around the world thanking a complete stranger for being kind to her? What an ironic twist of fate. Yes, she had been hardened by life and she had found compensation in a shallow and superficial persona. Everybody thought she had plenty of friends but the truth was her only real friend was Maggie.

"Are you okay?" Detective Manning asked.

"Yes I'm fine." Jean replied.

"Okay so start again, what did that man do to you?"

"He……… he caressed my breasts." she said, feeling sick to the pit of her stomach and swallowing a lump in her throat. The Detective didn't blink. She couldn't decide if this was his way of trying to remain neutral to stories he must hear all the time or a complete lack of empathy. She decided not to concern herself with it. Now was not the right time.

"Anything else?" he asked.

"No." spat Jean. "But he would have………you know……. if he had half the chance."

"How did you escape?" the Detective asked, steering the conversation forward.

"Well, he was just unzipping his jeans and about to undress me when we heard a commotion coming from outside." She began to feel faint from the efforts of reliving this nightmare. She couldn't believe that she was telling someone about it. "I still don't know what it was but I didn't hang around to find out. Seeing that he was momentarily distracted, I made a run for it."

"Then what?"

"I just kept running and running. Part of me felt like I should go back for Maggie but I knew I would be no good to her if I went back by myself. I needed help. So I just kept running until I stumbled into the next town."

"Have you any idea how long you were running for?"

"No, I was drugged, I had lost all sense of time. It could have been twenty minutes or it could have been three hours. I don't know."

"Did you see any others escape?"

"Yes, there were about four or five other girls making their escape too. But Maggie wasn't one of them." she finished sadly.

"Do you have any idea where they were going?"

Jean thought for a moment. She remembered that night so clearly. In each and every one of their faces she had seen the clear intent of escape. They had all shared that same desire. But as for where they went, she didn't know.

"No, I don't." she replied simply.

"Okay, you're doing great. I just have one final question." the Detective began. "If this was a preplanned abduction, is there any particular reason why they might have chosen you and Maggie?"

"Well, for the obvious reasons I guess – we're young, we would have stood out as tourists. I don't know." she replied, thinking fast, not entirely sure what he wanted to know. "Please, just find her." she pleaded.

"We'll try. But in the meantime you should get some rest. We will call you if we need you or if we have any further news, I promise. You'll be the first to know."

"Okay, thank you." Jean replied, finally relenting to the sleep deprivation that had taken hold. She had provided all the evidence and told them everything she knew, there wasn't anything more she could do for the moment. It was time to get some rest.

****

Jean fell into an uneasy sleep in the waiting room at the police station as thoughts of her father clogged her mind. Jean had always known she came from a dysfunctional family. She was acutely aware of the fact. But she wanted to know more about her father. Her mother had been the exact same whenever she asked about him. One morning after a swimming lesson, Jean finally felt brave enough to ask. She was twelve years old. She had taken the liberty of preparing lunch for both of them in anticipation of what was to come. As they sat down to eat their soup and sandwiches, Jean carefully broached the subject.

"Mam, I wanted to ask you something." she began as she lifted a spoonful of soup to her mouth. "Tell me about dad? Please?"

She waited with baited breath, totally unsure of what kind of a reaction she would receive.

As she observed her mother, it was more than obvious that she didn't want to reveal anything. Although her mother did her best to disguise the unease she felt, her body language spoke differently. Pamela instantly put the soup spoon down, crossed her legs and folded her arms. Her jaw tightened and her whole body began to seize up. Time seemed to stand still as Jean waited for her mother's reply.

"What do you want to know that for?" her mother asked eventually.

"Because all the other kids in school have a mom and dad, but I don't. And I want to know why that is?" she squealed.

"Well Jean, sometimes Daddy's are such bad people you're better off without them." she said in a tone laced with bitterness and resentment. Her mother seemed momentarily lost in translation seemingly indulging herself in memories of him. Then she seemed to remember the food that was in front of her, picked up her spoon and began to feed herself again.

"But I want to know about him." Jean demanded abandoning her food.

"Your father was a good-for-nothing moron." her mother interjected, cutting across Jean. "Now I don't want to hear anymore about it."

"But Mam, he's, my father. I want to get to know him."

"Jean, you're a child. How could you possibly know what you want?"

"That's a stupid thing to say."

"I'm telling you now, if you try to meet your father, you will be bitterly disappointed and you will only get hurt. It's better this way." her mother said.

"Well, I wouldn't know, would I?" Jean argued, unable to stop herself. "Because of you I don't have a father. It was probably you that drove him away in the first place." she finished in an accusatory tone. The truth was Jean blamed herself but she wasn't going to tell her mother that. Besides, it was easier to place the blame somewhere else.

"Jean please, I'm begging you. Just stop." she insisted.

"Why couldn't you be normal? Why couldn't you be like Maggie's parents and all the other kids at school who have two parents. I'm sick of being stuck with just you, it's not fair." she cried.

Jean had made several more attempts to find out about her father but every time she did her mother went into lockdown refusing to divulge anything. What was easy as a child was difficult as an adult. As she progressed into adulthood, she began to fear rejection and hurt, so she had never thoroughly looked for him - not that she had much information to go on anyway. She kept procrastinating and the more she procrastinated, the more difficult it was to contact him. What if he didn't live up to her expectations? What if he let her down again? And so, the years had slipped away without her realizing it – until now.

Now, with the imminent arrival of her father, part of her wanted to relent. It would be so easy to forgive and forget and build a relationship with him. It was what she craved most in the world. And at a time when she was at her most vulnerable, she craved it even more.

****

"What do you mean you've lost her?" Pamela demanded of Detective Rashid. "I spoke to her on the phone just a few hours ago and she was here, perfectly safe."

"Yes, I am aware of that Ma'am, but unfortunately we had a disagreement and she left." he said.

Herself and Noel had just arrived at the police station after disembarking from the motor vehicle that had transported them here. Even though it had been a long journey and they were exhausted, the journey had been filled with talk of Jean. Together, they began to reminisce over old times and Pamela had dutifully filled him in on all the details since. Pamela revealed what Jean had been like as a little girl and just how terrible the teenage years had been as they travelled. She painted a beautiful picture of their daughter with very similar characteristics to Noel.

"She's very feisty." she had teased. "That's definitely you."

They were on cloud nine, full of excitement at their imminent reunion with Jean. Ensnared by the trappings of exhaustion, delirium and jetlag that follow a long haul flight they had come to take her home.

Now as they sat in the Detective's big spacious office, they were being met with reports that she had walked out of the police station in a temper. As she sat with Detective Rashid in front of her and Noel to her right, she couldn't believe what she was hearing.

"And you just let her go? What the hell were you thinking?" she yelled at Detective Rashid, standing up and knocking her chair sideways.

"Jean is a fully grown woman Ma'am." the Detective replied calmly, not flinching for a second. "We could not make her comply with police regulations against her will."

"Why did you not go after her?" Pamela asked.

"That's against police protocol." Detective Rashid fired back.

"Where the hell is she then?" said Noel in absolute fury. "Are you so incompetent you can't keep her here?" Noel said, his hands curving into little balls as he spoke.

Noel had been devastated to learn that Jean had fled the police station. Of course he was nervous but he had been excited to meet her. At first he had thought she was just being her usual hot tempered self but now he understood. As he met the police, their attitude appalled him and their investigation left a lot to be desired. Even when Jean and Maggie had been reported missing, the police had been very slow to act. Now, opportunities for vital evidence had been missed and they were searching for a brothel somewhere. They didn't know where. Everything they did was slow with no sense of urgency about them. From what he could see, they did not put themselves under pressure, they did not hurry forensics or warrants through and gauded about the office as if they had all day. Did the police not deal with these kinds of missing cases all the time? Surely they knew they weren't going to find anything here? Why were they not out looking for Maggie? No, he completely understood why Jean had run. If it had been his friend on the line, he would have done the same.

"I cannot hold her here against her will but I did give her a lift to her hotel." Detective Rashid protested, weary now. "Unfortunately though, when I went to check on her again a short time later, she had left."

"Well, where is she gone?" demanded Noel.

"We don't know at this current time."

"I thought you were supposed to be protecting her." Pamela said. Detective Rashid's arrogant attitude was infuriating. Or at least that was how she saw it through the realms of her current tunnel vision.

"We were."

"So what happened?"

Detective Rashid sighed to himself. He didn't mean to be unprofessional but he was beginning to lose his patience now. How many times was he going to have to explain this whole sorry saga to Jean's parents? Jean had made her choice, she ran, there had been absolutely nothing he could do to stop it. He didn't like it anymore than they did.

"I've already told you. She expressed significant dissatisfaction with the progress of the police investigation. When I refused to allow her to the site where herself and Maggie were abducted, she left. I'm sorry Ma'am." the Detective apologised.

"Oh, sorry doesn't cut it." Pamela fumed. "Have you any idea how headstrong my daughter is?" she asked.

"As a matter of fact, I do." he replied through gritted teeth.

"Thanks to you, we have no idea where she is and she's in danger now again."

"I'm sorry Ma'am." Detective Rashid said, a little more sympathetically now. "But I really couldn't stop her."

"I know." cried Pamela. "I know exactly what she's like."

Pamela put her head in her hands. What the hell were they going to do now? Only mere hours ago they were safe in their little cocoon, believing their nightmare was over. Now, in a matter of seconds they had been swept like the tide right back in. Back to where it all began.

"What can we do?" Pamela said, finally relenting and taking a seat in Detective Rashid's office. She recognised defeat when it stared her in the face.

"Well, you can start by doing a video plea. It might help persuade Jean to return to the police station."

In the light of the office, the Detective was a scrawny guy, who looked in dire need of a hot meal. His hair was cut short over his ears and he was clean shaven.

"Yeah of course, we'll do anything." she replied. "Anything that might help."

"We also want to appeal to the abductors to let Maggie go. But first, let's tackle getting Jean back here safely."

"We want to help any way that we can." she heard Noel echo beside her.

"Alright, that's great. Let me get that organised for you." Detective Rashid said.

"What do we do? What do we say? We've never done anything like this before." Pamela said.

"Don't worry, we'll go through that and explain everything to you. Please excuse me a few minutes while I set that up."

Detective Rashid disappeared out of the office to speak to his colleagues, leaving Pamela and Noel alone. They sat in silence a moment and Pamela could feel Noel brooding over something beside her.

"What's wrong?" she asked, pre-empting him.

"Do you think this is going to work?" Noel asked standing up, walking over to a little cabinet in the corner and investigating the myriad of trophies on display. Picking one up, he turned it over in his hand and appeared to focus all his attention on it.

"It's got to be worth a try." she replied.

"Hey, looks like this guy was some cop. He got policeman of the year in 2017."

"I think we can trust him then. Can you leave his trophies alone please?"

Noel ignored her and carried on reviewing all of Detective Rashid's glittering silverware.

"I don't know, this seems like a longshot to me." Noel continued parting with another of the Detectives trophies. "Even if she sees this, is Jean really going to come back here?"

"I don't know." Pamela replied. "I don't know."

A large picture stood on the wall of Detective Rashid's office and Pamela found herself drawn to it. Dressed in his traditional police attire, the picture seemed to mirror her own mood right now as it was impossible to detect a definitive smile but it was similarly difficult to detect a serious facial expression. It was a very odd picture to have up on the wall. Just hours earlier her daughter had stood in this office alive and now they seemed to have lost her all over again.

"Is this going to play right into the abductor's hands? I mean they might go and kill Maggie in revenge. Are we doing the right thing?" he asked.

"I don't know any more than you do, but the police deal with these kinds of criminals all the time so we've got to trust them. Why did she have to leave anyway? She could have been perfectly safe here at the police station but no, she had to go and take matters into her own hands."

Noel had moved on from investigating the Detectives trophies and had graduated to the books that sat on the shelf. Some dusty, some torn, some mouldy, others brand new and highly legible, it boasted books spanning generations of police force activity. Selecting a book of interest, he carefully took it down trying to ease his agitation.

"But why leave?" quizzed Noel, his attention partially on the book.

"She wanted to find Maggie." Pamela replied, matter-of-factly. "Noel, we've been through this already."

"I know, but she's no good to Maggie out there in the middle of nowhere, is she?"

Pamela had had enough.

"Oh for goodness' sake, can you just stop being so negative for once in your life. She wanted to find Maggie and that's the end of it."

"Alright, alright, just saying." he replied. Noel dutifully conspired to read the book he had selected, carefully opening it on page seven and silence descended on them for a few moments.

Noel was right of course. It could be a fruitless waste of time and resources. But the level of desperation Pamela felt right now was at fever pitch and she was willing to do anything.

She was exhausted beyond belief but she knew she wanted to help somehow. She had no clue what to expect. She hadn't sat in front of a camera a day in her life. Would this be like a press conference? Would it be a simple video? Would they have to speak in front of a load of reporters? She hoped not. Although thankfully it hadn't quite made front page news yet. Pamela reached down for her bag and took out her hairbrush and her make-up. Carefully placing them on the table, she took out her small compact mirror and brushed up her foundation.

"How are you so calm?" Noel asked her moments later, as she applied some mascara. She considered herself lucky to have luscious long eyelashes. They were her best feature.

"I'm not." she replied. "I'm just doing what I have to do."

"What do you think of this guy? Can we trust him?" he said, picking up a pen from the desk and fiddling with it. He needed distraction and the police books had bored him already. Searching for a new energy to take his mind off things, his eyes landed on a scissors and a sheet of paper cut down to size on Detective Rashid's desk. Inadvertently he searched the desk for any clues. Anything that might suggest this guy was anything other than innocent.

"Noel, will you calm down." Pamela said.

"We need to be careful."

"What are you suggesting?" she asked, wondering what he was getting at. Did he know something she didn't?

"I'm not suggesting anything." he replied. "I'm just saying we need to tread with caution."

Pamela opened her mouth ready to respond but put her make-up down instead.

As if right on cue, Detective Rashid entered the office with his entourage in tow and Noel quickly sat back down. The man that would film them making their plea was introduced as their communications officer, Sol. On first impression, everything from his oversized spectacles to his lopsided ears screamed this guy was a nerdy individual. His tasteful facial hair and modern dress sense offered little in the way of redeeming his features. The camera in his hands alluded to artistic endeavours and technical abilities of the highest order. A smile spread out on his wet lips as Detective Rashid introduced him and he offered a limp handshake.

The family liaison officer was next on their radar. His eyes creased into a smile almost disappearing into his forehead as Detective Rashid introduced him as Usman.

He profaned his hand for one of the firmest handshakes Pamela had ever received.

'We are going to do everything we can to locate Jean and Maggie.' he assured them with a wide smile.

As the team set to work around them, Pamela felt like she was in her very own horror film. The camera was set upon a tripod where it quivered a moment before succumbing to the stillness. What could only be described as wings flanked the camera. Two huge lights were set either side, dimming and brightening in equal measure, as they were carefully manipulated by the cameraman.

Meanwhile Usman briefed them on the next phase of the procedure.

"Okay, what we want to see here is two heartbroken parents. We need to see two parents united in their grief. We are relying on Jean so we want to appeal to her to contact the police station."

"What do we say?" Pamela asked.

"You don't need to say much, it's best to keep it short and to the point." Usman replied patiently.

"I've never been in front of a camera before so I'm a little nervous. I've no idea what I'm doing."

"The best thing you can do is forget about the camera and remind yourself that you are doing this for Jean. We'll all be right there with you."

"Do we get notes on what to say or anything?"

"No, it's best if it just comes straight from the heart. It won't seem rehearsed." Usman replied.

"Okay." replied Pamela cautiously.

The cameraman was still diving over his camera, testing the lighting and adjusting the focus. Detective Rashid was busy discussing the case with his colleague.

The desk was cleared and a second chair placed behind it. Feeling like fish out of water, Pamela and Noel were instructed to take a seat behind the desk. The light was blinding, dashing, a severe flash upon the eye. A sweltering heat protruded from the camera filling the space, a hissing sound emanating from its insides. It was difficult not to be distracted.

As a sea of expectant faces awaited their every word, Pamela and Noel didn't know what to do, where to look or how to act. Vacant expressions upon their faces, neither one of them could disguise their discomfort. Both of them looked aimlessly around the room, scanning the walls before glancing at each other. Funny how Pamela had never noticed the rustic rouge of the room before now. Every minute seemed an eternity, all the energy in the room transfixed on them. Pamela recoiled at the thought of getting up on stage to recite a poem let alone stand in front of a camera. It was unlike anything they had ever done in their lives. In desperation Pamela looked to Usman for some guidance. A simple nod and a smile were all the encouragement she needed. After what seemed like an age Pamela grabbed hold of Noels hand and finally began to speak.

"Jean, if you're out there somewhere, please come back to the police station. We're not angry with you. We miss you and we want you back here safe and well. We love you."

As Pamela was hit by a wave of emotion, she turned towards Noel and squeezed his hand tight indicating that he should say something.

"Jean, it's Dad. Please come back. Your mother is in bits and we need you here. Please come back safe and well."

"Our lives are not the same without you. We're begging you, please come back." Pamela finished.

And just like that, it was all over. The lights went out, the buzz of the camera disappeared and the lump in Pamela's throat lessened. The cameraman immediately began dismantling all his tools, Detective Rashid was discussing elements of the case with his colleagues and planning the release of the statement. With all the activity and all the people, Detective Rashid's office had never seemed so small.

Usman was straight over to them with words of encouragement.

"Well done guys, that's not easy."

"No, it's definitely not. Thank you for helping us with this." Pamela said.

"Yes, thank you Usman, we couldn't have done it without you."

"My pleasure."

A little while later, Pamela and Noel sat in Detective Rashid's office, tired and satisfied with their work.

"You've both had a long journey. You should go to your hotel and get some rest." Detective Rashid was saying to them now.

"I can't sleep, not when my daughter is missing." cried Pamela. "You do know where she's gone, don't you?" she asked. "She's gone back for Maggie."

As advised by Detective Rashid, they had checked in to their hotel, before plotting their next move. As discreetly as she possibly could, Pamela grabbed a map off one of the Detective's desks on the way out. It detailed a map of the local area but also the big terrain of land they believed Jean had run through to get here. Skew markings roughly drawn indicated where they suspected the brothel might be but it was quite obvious they had no idea. It could be anywhere on that terrain.

They found Jean's hotel room thanks to the information supplied by the embassy and knocked on the door several times. But Jean wasn't home.

It was half past one in the morning now local time. Desperately trying to form a plan in her head, Pamela suggested they get a few hours' sleep.

"Let's get some sleep Noel, we need it. We're of no use to Jean in our exhausted state." she said. "We'll get up first thing in the morning and make a plan."

And with that, both Pamela and Noel settled down to a restless night's sleep in their individual rooms, cleverly arranged by the embassy. Tomorrow was another day.

CHAPTER 11

As soon as she left the police station, Jean bitterly regretted her decision. She had nowhere to go, nobody to turn to and about fifteen Nepalese rupees to her name.

She had emerged out of the police station into the same small quaint little village. Arriving there late at night, she had noted little of the surrounding vicinity. All around her now stood dull, gloomy, rundown shops, galleries and boutiques all perched one on top of the other. They were crammed in so tightly it was difficult to distinguish them. Off-whites, creams, browns and greys danced in front of her eyes. Shopkeepers perched at the edge of their stores desperate to entice passers-by. If circumstances had permitted, she might have been tempted to have a browse for they sold all sorts of treasures – colourful bright sarongs, delicate Buddhist ornaments, intricately woven tapestries and exquisite silks and satins. Cosy looking internet cafes, mobile phone shops and small little cafes where one could enjoy a masala tea also adorned the streets. Tuk-tuks, motorbikes and cars roared past on the shoddy roads leaving a cloud of dust in their wake. All around her passers-bys babbled away excitedly in their native tongue. Glancing up at the sky above her she could see it was dull and overcast and she could feel the sun's UV rays searing through the clouds. The first rays of morning were trying to burst through.

To her right she could see little muddy paths that led into slum areas, shanty towns and squatter settlements, once again reminding her of the overwhelming poverty.

Evidently, this was where the densely populated low income districts of the area resided. Even from where she stood, she could see the muddy paths, the children playing hopscotch in their bare feet and cycling on bicycles that looked close to cracking under their scrawny frames. Yet they were oblivious to the outside world and all its privileges. The infrastructures that represented home were nothing more than shabby, poorly constructed huts subject to mass overcrowding and no access to sanitation. She had never been an overly emotional person. If she was honest, usually she was more concerned with herself than with others. If it was not for her current predicament, she might have been able to turn a blind eye. But as she glanced over at the children holding hands and dancing around in a circle, she couldn't help feeling a certain sadness that these children didn't know any better. What would have become of her if she had been born into this?

Jean was most aggrieved with Detective Rashid and his team. Even just thinking of the incident that had forced her exit made her blood boil. Their blatant disregard for finding evidence, the callous way they went about trying to find her as though she was just another number and their lack of progress had infuriated her.

She had been about to leave the police station having gone to the bathroom to freshen herself up when she spotted a team meeting. As bold and brass as they came, Jean did not need an invitation and ensconced herself tactfully between Detective Rashid and the other lead, Detective Manning. In an open-plan office a team of five were hovered in a semicircle around a large screen that presented a snapshot of all the information they had to date.

Directly behind them stood four desks, each one of them littered with policy documents, protocols and information pertaining to Maggie's disappearance. Off to the right stood a door indicating the lead Detective's office; Detective Rashid's office was off to the left. In one corner of the room stood a water fountain and tea/coffee making facilities while the other corner boasted a bookshelf. The books were layered so thick with dust, they looked like they had been there for centuries. At her feet a carpet that had been a deep pink to begin with but worn down to a softer version lined the floor. No doubt it had borne the brunt of the Detectives' stress over the years and a high footfall. A tall life-size lamp in another corner bathed the room in a soft light flooding it with an almost homely feel.

Jean's heart sank when she saw the sparsity of information in front of her now. The hard cold truth was they knew very little. Jean had been unable to provide an address that would lead them to the brothel. She only knew her captors by their first name and while she knew what they looked like, there was absolutely no way of tracing them. The police had tried everything, checking all illegal immigrants over the last few years and matching them with her description but there was nothing that looked even remotely like them. It was so painstakingly frustrating that she could visualise these men clearly in her minds' eye yet she had little or no information capable of incriminating them. She couldn't even recall seeing a number on the tuk-tuk for crying out loud. Investigating officers had looked at various records pertaining to drivers operating tuk-tuks in the Himalayan region but that had proved nothing. They didn't even have any rules of the road so why would they bother keeping a list of registered drivers with a full driving licence, Jean reasoned. It was free for all here as far as she could see. Anybody could present themselves at a tuk-tuk company, claim to be a driver and take one away, no questions asked. The very same could be said of taxi drivers. Were any of these outlets regulated? Doubtful she thought.

These men were clever, kept themselves well under wraps and had obviously been operating illegally for quite some time. On the plus side, no DNA evidence had come back yet and Jean was only hoping and praying that it would give them a lead. Without a lead, Jean could feel the case quickly turning to ice. If they continued like this Maggie would be long dead before they ever got to her. Time was moving on and it didn't take a genius to realise their efforts here were proving futile. They needed to be proactive now and start searching. The logical thing to do was revisit the place where they had been abducted. And so, Jean rounded on Detective Rashid, keen not to waste any more time.

"We should begin by going back to the site of the abduction." she insisted, not paying any heed to the disbelieving expressions on the Detective's faces. She knew full well that she had just interrupted them all mid-flow but she didn't have time for niceties. "Isn't that where you should begin? I'm telling you, I could identify those guys in a heartbeat if I saw them."

They were really beginning to annoy her with their procrastination. Why weren't they out searching for her instead of wasting valuable time and resources standing around discussing a case that was on a dead-end to nowhere? There were no police officers out scoping the land for a possible brothel and there was no one up at the Himalayan resort where they had been snatched. Anoushka might be purring waiting to pounce on her next prey. Her foremost desire was of course to find Maggie but this case was also rendered a debacle if they did not prevent the culprits from succeeding in another abduction. Jean would recognise Anoushka instantly and she had begged and pleaded with Detective Rashid to let a police officer escort her to the site where she might turn up. It was summer time after all, there were bound to be more female tourists they were planning to groom for abduction. If they were lucky, they would catch her red-handed, arrest her and bring her in for questioning. Even better, follow Anoushka's movements, and the van they used to transport the abducted girls which would eventually lead them to the brothel. But Detective Rashid dismissed her idea outright claiming it was a waste of police resources as there was no guarantee she would be there.

"But Mr. Rashid, it could lead us to Maggie." Jean protested. "We have to make some bold choices if we are to find her."

"Jean, I've told you, I won't sanction it and that's final. Besides, even if we do manage to catch Anoushka in the act and bring her in for questioning, do you really think she will tell us anything?"

"So, we just let her carry on and abduct more girls, do we?" Jean protested, absolutely horrified and dumbfounded by Detective Rashid's complacency.

"Jean, enough!" Detective Rashid exclaimed in a tone that indicated his word was final. His stiff posture, eyes narrowed in frustration and his stern gaze bore little resemblance to the man she had met when she had come in here last night, barely twenty-four hours ago. That man had made her tea. She understood it wasn't her place to be intruding on a team meeting, of course she did. But someone had to play devils' advocate for Maggie's sake. Didn't they?

"So how do you propose we find her then? Have you got any better ideas?" she shot back at him, with a waspish lilt to her voice. It was a deliberate expression of her dissatisfaction with the case.

"We're handling it Jean, please just trust us." Detective Rashid sighed wearily.

"Trust you?" she said, almost laughing at the incredulity of it all and fed up with being brushed aside. "My best friend is out there lost, alone, probably so hooked on heroin by now she doesn't even realise she's having sex with some random man. She could be beaten to death, murdered or even sold to a Sheikh and you're telling me to be calm?" she finished, screaming at the top of her lungs.

She was shaking violently now, the anger within her building block by block until she couldn't control it anymore. She had seen them flinch and shift uncomfortably as the full force of her ferocity reached its peak. She had not meant to lose her temper but the complacency of these men astounded her. Did they even care? She wondered how these men slept at night. Obviously, she was directly involved in this case, but if she was responsible for solving crimes or saving people from disastrous situations, she didn't think she would be as far removed from it as these Officers appeared to be. She couldn't help but wonder if it was because Maggie was a woman? Would they have shown the same complacency had it been a man?

Another one of the Detectives, a grey-haired man in his early fifties tried to calm her down.

"Miss Sayers, I can assure you, we are doing everything we can." he said through a thick Nepali accent. It was the wrong response because this only served to infuriate her further.

"Really? What are you doing exactly?" she said, her eyes moving swiftly in his direction. "I don't see anybody out there searching for her. Apart from that time I escorted the police officer to try to relocate the brothel, no one has made the slightest attempt to find her. I don't know why I came here in the first place. I was stupid enough to think you would be able to help me."

Detective Rashid sighed sympathetically and fixed her with a look that radiated warmth and empathy. In spite of his earlier brusqueness, she suddenly made the startling discovery that he too was crestfallen. He wanted to find Maggie just as much as she did. She almost felt a tinge of guilt for the way she had acted now.

Just then another police officer intervened, becoming increasingly irate with her. Clearly, he was not impressed with her indignation. At five foot five his tiny frame did little to repel her and in fact had the opposite effect. It almost made her laugh. His attempt to compensate for his short stature with a fierce glint in his eye and an authoritative attitude had minimal effect. Taking one giant stride, he stepped towards her.

"Look here, you don't know these people. They are a very dangerous breed of criminal and think nothing of killing in an instant and they lure women into drugs and prostitution."

"But -," she tried to interrupt, but he kept on talking.

"They load these women up with so much cocaine, heroin and amphetamines they don't even know their own name. We have to tread very carefully. One wrong move and your friend could be dead. Is that what you want?"

"No, of course not." she shot back in revulsion.

"Then shut up and let us handle this." he spat.

Jean was so appalled by this man's attitude and the way he casually suggested she knew nothing about the case, it took her a moment to find her voice. Even worse was the fact that Detective Rashid didn't appear to notice. He made a few mild-mannered attempts to silence him but nothing more. Well, if they thought she was going to sit back and be silenced they were wrong. That was not her style. There were some days when she loved that she had been born with the gift of the gab and today was one of them.

Speaking directly to the rude police officer now, she vented.

"How dare you suggest that I know very little about this group. I was abducted by them, I spent hours and hours in a cell doped out of it on heroin and God knows what else, I was taken to their seedy marquee where alongside lots of other young women I was almost raped, so don't you dare suggest I know nothing about them. I know a hell of a lot more than you. And quite frankly I'm astounded that you even suggest I know nothing." she finished, almost panting at the fury of it.

A deep silence descended on the room in response to her outburst. The silence rang so loud you could have heard a pin drop. All of the police officers gathered avoided making eye contact with each other and glanced aimlessly around the room unsure of where to look. Jean was aghast at their cowardly behavior. Clearly, they were not accustomed to having an opinionated woman around and they didn't know what to do. Men, they were full of shit. She made no apologies for it. A subservient, obedient woman with no opinions of her own she would never be. She was damned if she was going to change now.

And with that Jean made to leave before adding:

"You know what, I don't have time for this. I'm going to find her myself." she quipped before storming out of the open-plan office without as much as a backward glance. That ought to show them she thought to herself. She didn't need their help. It was clear she would get no satisfaction here.

Now as she stood outside the police station, she weighed up her options. She had never been the practical logical one. Ultimately, she needed to get back to the brothel. But without knowing where it was, how was she supposed to get there? She had no transport and she doubted whether tuk-tuks or buses took that route. From what she remembered, the brothel was in the middle of nowhere spanning miles and miles of sparse land. Then she had to consider the obvious implications of going back. She might not escape this time. But then she had to go back for Maggie's sake. She couldn't leave her there to rot. What kind of a friend would that make her? There was nothing for it but find her way back to the hotel and wait for Raoul. Together, they would try to find their way back to the brothel and rescue Maggie. Finally. It would all be over.

Her only problem now was how would she get herself to the hotel? Standing outside the police station, she decided there was nothing for it but to thumb a lift. She had no change for a taxi and no other means of transport.

****

Detective Rashid sighed sorrowfully to himself and looked on feeling completely bereft. He combed his hands through his hair as he contemplated a more assertive effort to try and stop Jean leaving the police station. On some level he couldn't help but feel that he was failing her if he didn't at least try to persuade her against it, but her mind was made up. He knew his client well enough to know that once she had decided on something a whole army of kinsmen couldn't dissuade her. She was as resilient as they came. He had been humbled by her strength of character and her fearless courage. No, he couldn't blame Jean for her natural desire to find her friend even if that did mean blatantly disregarding the efforts of the police. He knew he would do the same.

He thought of his two young daughters at home and their uncanny zest for life. They were just six and nine. If anyone were to rob them of that profound innocence, he thought he just might break every rule in the book, find the person responsible and rip their heart out. Yes, he firmly believed any human being was capable of such deeds given the correct circumstances. But he feared for her. A young woman roaming around these streets on her own was far from safe. As he admitted defeat and resolved that he was powerless to stop her, he couldn't suppress a burning feeling that this was not going to end well.

No, he had to at least try to help her. He couldn't have her roaming the streets. She couldn't have gone very far and he would at least give her a lift to her hotel. She would be safe there until they found Maggie. He just hoped she would take him up on his offer.

****

Leaving all dignity and self-respect behind, Jean stuck her thumb out in search of a lift. She felt sure this wasn't an unusual sight but she was nervous all the same. She had no choice. She was completely alone now. With her thumb out, she resigned herself to the fact that she would be here for some time.

All of a sudden, she saw a small cream car approaching. Urgently holding out her thumb for dear life, she squealed with delight when it indicated in and began slowing down. As the car came to a grinding halt, she saw it was Detective Rashid.

"Will you at least let me give you a lift back to your hotel so I know you're safe?" he said, pulling down the window.

"Alright." she resolved.

Reluctantly, she opened the car door and jumped inside. Together they travelled the short distance to the Himalayan Inn Hotel and Jean was surprised to learn they couldn't have travelled far at all with their abductors. But it had seemed like hours.

On the drive there, Jean vaguely heard Detective Rashid informing her that any expenses incurred for food or accommodation would be covered by police authorities and the embassy until they found Maggie. At least that was one less thing to worry about she supposed. She wouldn't have long to wait now anyway until Raoul arrived. She had already called him for help.

Detective Rashid dropped her off with a plea to stay where she was, advising her that she would be safe here and a promise to check in on her later.

CHAPTER 12

True to his word, Raoul arrived at the hotel less than an hour later. She had never been so relieved. He had come for her after all. He would help her to find Maggie. He knew he cared for her as much as she did. As his toned physique strode in to the lobby, she ran to him, squeezing him so tightly she almost broke his ribs.

"Raoul, oh thank God." she said. "Man, am I glad to see you."

"We've been so worried about you." Raoul said. "Are you alright?"

He fixed her with his dark concerned eyes and she could feel the tension flow out of her body. He had found her. At last, she was safe. With Raoul by her side, everything would be okay.

Finding a quiet corner of the lobby where they could talk out of earshot, Jean filled him in with as much information as possible.

"They've taken Maggie and the police are doing precious little to find her.' she told Raoul now, relaying the events of the last forty-eight hours.

She had lost all concept of time ensconced in the events that had unfolded. Between passing out and running across miles and miles of terrain, there was no way of telling how much time had elapsed. Her only defining concept lay in the distinction between night and day.

"What have the police said?"

"That they're doing everything they can. But all I see is teams of police officers around a whiteboard drinking coffee." she replied.

"Have they scoured the area?" he asked.

"They are saying they have, but I don't believe them. Meanwhile, Maggie is supposed to rot away in a filthy brothel." she replied.

"Have they any idea who's behind all this? Names, addresses, anything that could identify them?"

"No, they know they're dealing with drug trafficking and women but that's about it. They have no leads, no evidence, nothing. I'd nearly do a better job solving the case myself."

"What do you want to do?"

"I want to find Maggie myself." she said resolutely. "You were right about the police." she added quickly. "They were useless."

"But how? How are we going to find her?" asked Raoul. "I thought you said you don't know where the brothel is?"

"I don't." cried Jean desperately, thinking fast but all hope fading quickly. "I have no idea where it is. Maybe if we start by returning to the bus stop where we were abducted? That might help us?"

"Alright, we can do that." he said.

"Do you know where the bus stop is from here?" she asked.

"As a matter of fact, I do. Alright, we might talk to some of the locals there, see if they saw anything unusual or heard anything. Then we can take it from there."

"Let's go get her."

They left the lobby then and made their way out to Raoul's car. Easing gently out, Raoul checked his wing mirror as he indicated out and eased into the early morning traffic. It must have been very early because they met very few cars as they drove along the bumpy roads. Jean thought her bum must have been almost to the floor as she felt every bump. She gazed out the window as they passed a series of run-down buildings. It really was a quaint little village with rustic stone walls and brightly coloured flowers scourged along its edges. Any buildings they passed looked fit to collapse, tufts of green moss interspersed between the higher and lower decks. The rickety windows looked so fragile, it was a wonder they hadn't already collapsed onto the street. The air smelled of decay and desperation. They passed a man roughly in his fifties arriving at his shop door ready to open up for the day's trade. A man under duress of his early morning run passed them wearing a mask and Jean found herself doing a double take. It was still a strange sight for her to behold. Her eye was drawn to a woman walking her baby in a pram. A vision in colour, Jean couldn't help but wonder what she was doing out at this hour.

"Where are we going?" she asked.

"I thought you wanted to find Maggie."

"Well, yes, I do."

"Then let's do that."

"But I don't know where this place is. How do you propose we find it exactly?" she asked desperately.

"You mean the brothel?" he asked.

"Yes, I mean I literally have no clue where it is. I just hope we get to her on time. But thank God I have you. There's no way I could do this on my own."

She became acutely aware that Raoul might be depending on her to find the brothel and she wouldn't be able to guide him. This was causing her to panic. She was growing frightened now, retreating into herself momentarily like a little girl. She really hoped it wouldn't be too late. Shaking herself out of her melodramatic thoughts, she steadied her busy mind. One step at a time, she told herself as she heard Raoul talking now.

"Just like we said. We find the bus stop you both got off at, talk to some of the locals and take it from there." he said to her, a look of slight confusion on his face. Had she completely forgotten their conversation earlier?

"Okay." she said, biting her lip as though she were unsure.

"Have you any idea what direction you ran?" he asked.

"Raoul, I was terrified and running for my life. I haven't got a clue which way I turned. All I know is I emerged on to a barren wasteland and I just kept running."

If she could not remember what direction she ran or where the brothel was then they really did have to start from the very beginning. There was no point driving around aimlessly trying in vain to locate a brothel. That would only be wasting valuable time. Time they didn't have. Stick to the plan he told himself and on he drove to the bus stop for the Himalayan Resort.

"Did the captors follow you?" Raoul asked.

"Yes, they did. But I couldn't think too much about that. I had to stay focused on getting out of there and getting help."

"Of course you did." he replied.

"Raoul, we really need to get to her as quick as we can." Jean finished urgently. She had visions of driving around for hours, both unsure of where they were going. Still, it was bound to be better than running around aimlessly by herself.

"Tell me again what happened? I want to go through it one more time."

"They brought us to a brothel, Raoul, and they drugged us." Jean cried. "I had a narrow window of opportunity to leave and I made a run for it. I had to."

"I understand." said Raoul.

"I had to alert the police and get help. I know you didn't want me to, but I had to. If I didn't, we were never going to be found."

"It's a good thing you did."

"I'm a horrible person." cried Jean. "How could I just abandon my best friend like that?"

"You did what you had to do to survive, Jean. Don't be too hard on yourself."

"But what does that say about me? My friend could be dead now and it will be all my fault."

"Jean, you've been through a terrible trauma. Take it easy." Raoul said in a gentle, soothing voice. "We won't stop until we find her, I promise. Everything will be fine."

As the empathy poured out of him, Jean could feel herself relaxing a little more. From the first day they had met at the Volunteer house, both Jean and Maggie had warmed to Raoul. He played the dual role of being one of the staff in charge and also being their friend perfectly. He had a special way with the footfall of volunteers that passed through the house and everyone loved him. Of course, he had charisma and charm to boot, but it wasn't just that. There was a kindness and a sincerity to him that almost implored you to trust him. The way Jean did now. What luck had befallen her.

They left the small little village leaving the hotel behind them. Now, as the first light of day was breaking, she became intimidated by the rolling green hills that seemed to be growing more rural by the minute. Luckily, Raoul knew the area well. Where were they she wondered?

Passing her a drink of water and a sandwich, Jean grabbed it gratefully and took a long gulp. It seemed like hours since she had been fed at the police station and she almost forgot she was hungry.

Suddenly that familiar nauseous, woozy sensation washed over her and everything began to blur in front of her. Her body began to stiffen until she was unable to move any of her limbs. All of a sudden it clicked. The bottle of water. She had been drugged. But no, it couldn't be. Not Raoul. Then everything blacked out.

****

Jean came to in a shabby make-shift tent. Dark, bare and small it had no redeeming qualities. A sliver of light penetrated through at one end and she crawled on all fours, following the direction of the light. Still woozy from the drugs, she tried to steady herself as she glanced out through the opening.

The familiar expanse of land stretched before her, almost beaming gold in the early morning sunlight. It was enough to send her over the edge into jitter territory. With a jolt her worst fears were confirmed and she realised she was back at the brothel. The marquee set up on the right and the abandoned warehouse where she had been held in captivity on the left. The premises that only hours earlier, she had vacated.

The warehouse, or the torture chamber as Jean called it, was exactly as they had said - abandoned. Broken cream paint dotted the exterior serving as evidence that it hadn't seen the lick of a brush in years. It wasn't a massive warehouse. It could easily have been mistaken for a regular bungalow. She could see it all now in proper daylight.

Rusty steel windows ensured no captors could escape the horror. It looked so dilapidated and stank of such neglect, it was hard to believe anything sinister could have been going on.

The marquee beside it, once presumably white, now stood like a mouldy grey fortress, home to a hive of activity. Jean could only speculate that it must be able to hold about thirty women, maybe more. Four giant black pegs stood at each corner to ensure it remained upright and a partition opened to the front.

Here, stood a man in uniform. Jean would have said he looked rather lost and forlorn if she didn't know any better, standing outside a barely-there marquee in a sea of wasteland. Holding a rifle between his two hands, however, it was difficult to see how anyone might stand a chance against him. Yet there he stood, guarding those entering and leaving, ensuring none of the clients caused any trouble.

She must have been positioned near the front of the brothel as she had a perfect view of the guard from where she was.

As she plotted her next move, she realised she would first need something to defend herself with. What if that man tried to shoot her? If she tried to escape the brothel or escape with Maggie, he would certainly use his gun. But there was nothing of use in this shabby tent in which she had been unceremoniously dumped. She had nothing to defend herself with and she could feel the panic rising in her again.

And her memory was hazy too. She was struggling to piece together the events that had led to her return. Back at this marquee set-up. In this brothel. And she found herself wondering what part of the brothel Maggie was in. What had they done with her? More importantly, was she still alive? Focus, she scolded herself. Think back and try to remember. But she was exhausted, sleep deprived, drugged and famished which made remembering even more challenging. The last thing she remembered was….

Just then, Raoul appeared at the entrance to her makeshift tent.

"Welcome home." he said with a sneer. "I hear somebody's awake."

Of course. Raoul. She had completely forgotten. Raoul had deceived her by pretending to help, then drugging her. That was how she had ended up back here. He was one of them. She froze in terror.

Before she had time to react, Raoul slapped her hard across the face with such force, it knocked her off her feet. The man that had been keeping guard appeared to assist him and before Jean knew what was happening, they were manhandling her out of the tent into one of the spare cubicles in the marquee. Jean struggled against them with the little energy she had left in her body but she didn't stand a chance against two strong men.

"No, let me go." she screamed. "Let go of me."

As they forced her down onto a tattered bed in an empty cubicle, a third man came along to assist them. As he held her down, Raoul grabbed a syringe nearby and injected her straight into the arm.

Not Raoul. He couldn't possibly be one of them. Not kind, gentle Raoul. He was the most popular staff member in the volunteer house and was always concerned for their safety. She thought he was the only person she could trust. Now this? How could he do this to her?

"Don't worry Jean, you'll be just fine." he soothed, stroking her hair.

Yes, Raoul was Abdul's most revered sidekick and he boasted very close ties with the brothel leader as together they had worked on various assignments over the years. Naturally, some of them proved more successful than others. Their arrangement was simple. Abdul depended on him for his inside knowledge at the volunteer house. Thousands of unsuspecting volunteers passed through every year and they were so transparent when they came to Nepal, he could read them like a book. And he took advantage of it.

He remembered starting out in this business, in his younger days, trying to persuade women into a getaway car. How naive and inexperienced he had been. His skills had flourished since until he successfully played the dual role of friend in need and perfect villain.

He had taken the job several years ago purely for access to young women. The kind of women Abdul needed to diversify his camp. They had employed other methods of course but none had operated as smoothly. With his squeaky clean record, he had won over the volunteer bosses with his charm and vivacious personality. They hadn't suspected a thing. With a persona that would transgress the most stoic of resolutions, he was ideally placed organizing trips away for the volunteers, offering a beautiful vantage point for everything they were up to. All he needed to do was build a strong rapport with the women they were planning to abduct. They trusted him implicitly and it would never cross their mind that he might be luring them into a trap. He thrived on it. He was a self-confessed adrenaline junkie and he was proud of it. There was the other advantage too of course, the volunteer house offered him a hideout from the law.

Growing up in Nepal, he never felt good enough for his father. He was a conniving little bully. He had always despised exam results day because he knew he was in for a beating regardless of the grade achieved. If he didn't achieve first place in sporting events, that was a dead ringer for an extra lash of the whip. He never invited friends over to his house because he could never tell what kind of reception they might get. The resulting impact was a heart that turned cold to any feelings of compassion or empathy. He couldn't pinpoint exactly when it had happened but somewhere along his formative years, he had stopped caring, stopped feeling these feelings. In fact, he didn't think he felt anything anymore and so he became a loner. He had acquired a decent set of social skills though. Enough to sway these ladies head first into their worst nightmare. Yes, there was a reason he was number one in Abdul's book, he was highly accomplished in his field. And he intended it to stay that way.

"No, please don't. I trusted you." Jean spat at Raoul. "I thought you were helping us."

Raoul merely laughed a horrible callous laugh as he beckoned for the others to join him. Like sheep following their Master, they all joined in, as if they found the whole thing hilarious. Jean couldn't hide her revulsion.

"You silly girl. Did you really think this was all just a mere coincidence?"

"Yes!" cried Jean. "I told you, I trusted you." she finished, as the familiar sensation of the drugs thundered through her veins making their presence known. Her arm throbbed once more and for the second time she wondered how she had ended up here again.

"Of course not, you idiot. I orchestrated the whole thing." he bellowed. "What wasn't part of the plan was your escape, that was never supposed to happen."

"No." cried Jean. This couldn't possibly be happening. Could it?

"After you rang, I guessed you'd go running to the police like a scaredy cat."

"I did not." protested Jean.

"Well, whatever. All I had to do then was show up at the hotel and pretend to be your friend. Easy as that."

"Why?" asked Jean.

"Why?" bellowed Raoul as if stumped at her stupidity. "I had to pretend I wanted to find Maggie to earn your trust. Although the beauty of it was you already had it in your head you were going to go back for her anyway so really, I had very little work to do. It actually worked out perfectly." he chuckled, very pleased with himself.

"You arrogant bastard." she roared at him, unable to contain herself. "I thought you were going to help us."

Digging deep to find the worst of her spit, she spat at Raoul full on in the face. A moment of fury and a slap across the face before he carried on.

"Oh, stupid little tourists, what do they know of the world." he drawled. "Imagine how pleased Abdul will be when he learns I have you both here again. He'll be a very happy man. And this time, you are not leaving."

"You can't keep me here. Or Maggie." she began to protest but the drugs were hitting her hard now and she was growing weak.

"Oh, but I'd miss you too much to let you go, a sweet little girl like you." Raoul said teasingly.

Jean felt sick to her stomach.

"You never mentioned what a fine piece of meat this one was Raoul. I'd nearly have her myself." she heard the man that had been standing guard say as he laughed heartily at her expense.

"You'd be welcome to her." Raoul replied. "Once we… tame her… a little bit."

"Screw you." she yelled at them all in frustration.

Jean's head began to swirl and she blacked out as the drugs took hold.

****

A big yob of a man sat perched in the centre of a big conference room in a hotel, his heavy frame spilling over all four corners of the chair. Dressed in his long white tunic and colourful garment atop his bald head, his big claw clutched the buzzer in his hand. He would need that, he thought to himself. Beside him sat a large jug of water should he get thirsty. They really were so kind here, he mused. He sat facing a large stage and waited patiently for the parade to begin.

As was customary, there were a number of girls waiting backstage, all eager to impress. Sure who wouldn't want a life of riches and luxury with him? They'd never have to worry about a thing. What girl wouldn't want that?

Yes, he always enjoyed this part of the game. It was fun, always worth the visit and the process was simple. The team worked tirelessly to find new blood and present him with a number of women. He would review each one carefully and select the most desirable. He would take advantage of his selected prize for his own sexual gratification first before trafficking them into India and selling them off to a brothel. Being a Muslim Sheikh from India had its perks, he mused.

Women in his own country were forced into arranged marriages and were rarely seen in public without their husbands so his contact with them had been reduced to this. He of course, had suffered a similar fate, sentenced to a loveless marriage. It was purely a business arrangement. Sex was perfunctory, rare and he was lucky if he came. Besides, it wasn't uncommon for men to seek gratification elsewhere. And so, he found himself ready to pick from the best. Who would have the honour of sharing his bed tonight, he thought, as he rubbed his hands in glee.

The lights dimmed and brought all focus to the stage. An announcement came over the tannoy via a female voice, welcoming him to Nepal and advising him to sit back and relax. As he watched in front of him, the first girl was presented for his consideration.

"First up, we have Elise de Janier, 18, fifty thousand pounds, Nationality: French; Eye Colour: Blue; Purity: Certified."

The girl was tall, slim with long blonde hair and very attractive in her silver bikini and heels. She was slightly wobbly on her feet due to a combination of drugs and heels. The man felt himself grow hard as he watched her standing there with so much flesh on display. He was not accustomed to this where he came from and this display never ceased to be a revelation for him. His eyes feasting on her voluptuous breasts drinking her in, he could easily take her to bed and reach perfect heights of orgasmic satisfaction. He lowered his eyes noticing her perky buttock as she waddled around the stage. And she had such a good figure too, she definitely must have been a size eight. Rubbing his chin perplexed, something was holding him back. He decided to hold off pressing the button for this one. This was going to be a difficult decision for him.

The next girl didn't excite him. She was short, rather dull with mousy brown hair and his team knew to take her off stage when they saw his reaction.

The girl that subsequently crossed his path had him in a trance.

"Purity: Certified." was all he heard the woman say over the tannoy in his excitement.

She was absolutely stunning. She paraded across the stage in her leopard print bikini and pink kitten heels. A real turn on. He felt himself growing hard again and he was burning with desire now. He definitely wanted her in his bed. There was nothing for it, he would have to jack himself off right now. He slid his hand down to his genital area and began to rub. Gently rubbing himself, he reached out with his free hand to grab onto the side of the chair, as he was transported to a state of complete bliss. His breathing coming hard and fast, he began to perspire as explosions of pleasure pervaded him all over. Rubbing harder and faster now, his attention fixated on the girl, he finally ejaculated, reaching a very satisfying climax. Yes, he had to have her.

Reaching for the buzzer, which had fallen to the floor in the midst of his euphoria, he slammed his finger down for girl number three. He didn't need to see any more, he wanted her. "Yeeessssss." he screamed.

"Girl number 3, one hundred thousand pounds, sold to the Sheikh." came the woman's voice over the tannoy.

CHAPTER 13

Noel and Pamela were at a loss. They had travelled halfway across the world and they didn't know where to turn. They were in this completely unfamiliar country with no idea of the landscape, no idea of the people or the customs they kept. They didn't even speak the language. They had been brought here on the brink of a terrible tragedy that threatened to ruin their lives.

The police investigation appeared to be in pieces. They had found Jean, and then they lost her. What kind of a police force was that? They appeared to be more interested in standing around discussing the case and drinking coffee than actively searching for the brothel or collecting evidence. The successful outcome of any police investigation depended on the action taken in the first twenty-four hours of someone being reported missing. Even the ordinary fool on the street knew that. They had been terribly slow to take action, wasting valuable time. Was it any wonder Jean had run off in frustration? She would have done exactly the same. Like mother, like daughter, Pamela thought.

Pamela ran through the options in her head. They could contact the Irish Embassy she supposed, but realistically she didn't think that would achieve much. They seemed happy to leave the investigation to the police.

They were clearly in the vicinity of where Jean had escaped. The police had said that Jean had run all the way from the brothel to the nearest police station. Pamela knew her daughter and knew how her mind operated. Jean could be shallow and superficial in lots of ways but she was a loyal friend. She would not have left that sham of a place lightly knowing she was leaving her friend behind. It would have been her plan to raise the alarm, get help and go back for Maggie. Call it mother's intuition, but she just knew.

As they digested a bit of breakfast that morning, Pamela explained to Noel what she wanted to do.

"Are you serious?" declared Noel, incredulous. "You want to hire a car and scour the local area like a bunch of misfits?"

Both of them had barely slept a wink and presented themselves for breakfast looking haggard and drawn. They were first to arrive and had the dining room to themselves. Small and dark, it didn't boast much comfort. A small spindly table, shabby chairs and brown painted walls did little to avert the gloom. A lamp in the corner compensated for the lacklustre light. Misted windows rendered the air hot and stuffy. Now, Pamela was anxious to set out the agenda for the day.

"Well, do you have a better idea?" she barked at Noel, annoyed. Sometimes she wondered if he even wanted to find Jean. That wouldn't be hard, she supposed, given that he had been missing for most of her life. "In case you hadn't noticed we're on our own. The police are not scouring the area. There's a brothel operating right under their nose and because they're more interested in drinking coffee, these traffickers are being given free reign."

"Yes, but Pamela, you're not thinking this through." Noel advised. "We're two tourists in a remote little village in Nepal. We're going to stand out a mile if we're just driving around going nowhere. People will be suspicious."

"I know." agreed Pamela.

"Plus, we haven't got a clue where we're going."

"But we've got to do something." cried Pamela, putting down the boiled egg she was eating, no longer hungry. Not that she was eating or sleeping much anyway. "Besides, I've got the map from the police station, that's got to count for something." Pamela finished and Noel was certain he saw a little glint in her eye.

She produced the map from the back pocket of her jeans and placed it on the table. It was a map of the entire Himalayan resort.

"Now, that's more like it." replied Noel cheerfully, clearly very impressed. "When did you get that?" Noel said as he settled down to study it more carefully.

He saw the police station had been marked with an 'x'. There were some rough scrawlings written all over it and in an empty space there were two 'x's identified. The x's signified Maggie's rough location, he surmised, as he skimmed over the scrawling's at the side. Somewhere written on the map he was able to make out the word 'Pokhara'. It was well outside the village, a couple of miles perhaps. This was obviously where police officers believed Maggie was, and where Jean was heading. If they could just follow the map, they might find Jean. He had never been more grateful for his supreme map reading skills in leaving cert geography. Did he ever think he would see the day it might come in useful?

But why had the police not gone directly to the Brothel if this was where they believed Maggie was and Jean currently on route back to? Did they not have a warrant? Were they corrupt? Or did they simply not have enough evidence? Either way neither he nor Pamela were waiting around.

"I took it from the police station as we were leaving last night." she said as she watched him figure out the map. "I found it on one of the police officer's desks, I thought it might help us."

"Excellent." replied Noel and he excitedly relayed his findings from the map.

"So do you think you might know where she is?"

"I think I have an inkling. It looks like it's a few miles outside the town." he said. "It might be nothing, it might be something."

"That's good enough for me. My little girl is out there somewhere and if the police aren't going to search for her, then I will." she said, a little dejected now and the mood changed.

"She's my little girl too." moaned Noel, looking up from the map now. "If anything happened to her without me ever having been a part of her life, I don't know what I'd do."

"Nothing's going to happen to her Noel."

"How do you know that?" he said suddenly, a sharp edge to his voice. "Don't make promises you can't keep."

"Okay Okay, forgive me for trying to remain positive." Pamela shot back at him, a hint of anger in her voice. "We have to believe she's still alive Noel, we can't give up hope. It's the only thing keeping me going."

"I know." Noel said despondently. Placing his face in his hands, he was clearly battling some inner turmoil. "I should have been there. I'm such an idiot. I took it out on you because I was angry and she suffered."

Under normal circumstances, Pamela wouldn't have tolerated his self pity for being an absent figure in Jean's life.

As far as she was concerned, he had brought it on himself, but she recognised she had played her part in it as well. If post-natal depression hadn't claimed such a vice-like grip on her, things could have been very different. They might even have been happy. She could see he really regretted making such a mess of everything now and the prospect of losing his daughter was bringing it into sharp relief. Taking his hand, she stared him directly in the eye.

"We're not going to lose her." she assured him. "Our tears are not going to help her now, we need to be strong." said Pamela, blinking back the tears herself.

Pamela could feel the relationship they had when they first met bubbling up under the surface again. White hot anger and years of pent-up fury had been replaced with friendship and affection as they came together in search of their daughter. Both of them were now committed to the same end goal of finding Jean. She was very grateful to have him by her side through this whole fiasco. It would have been a very long trip to make on her own and the company was nice. Indulging in a wave of nostalgia she allowed her mind to wander.

She was just seventeen when she met Noel, she remembered. To be sweet seventeen again. What a magical time. She was young and carefree with no responsibilities or accountability to anyone. No children or elderly parents to concern her. Whenever Pamela reflected on that period in her life, she always remembered it with fondness. They were some of her best years.

She was in her final year of school with aspirations of becoming a journalist. Her days were filled with school, study, homework and chatting with her parents in the evening. They had been so good to her that time. She was studying non stop, primarily focusing on English. If she wanted to study journalism, she needed a decent grade. Her parents ensured a constant supply of heating, made her hearty dinners and endless cups of tea. It had been so easy to study in that warm snug environment. Up until then she had been the model A-grade student. Until she met Noel.

One evening she decided to take a break from the mundane routine when her best friend Una insisted on going to the cinema.

"I'm bringing Cathal." Una had declared on the phone as they discussed their plans. Cathal was Una's boyfriend of the hour and she never lost an opportunity to tell anyone who might listen. "He's bringing two of his friends for you and Orla." she finished, breathing a sigh of contentment.

Una had only been dating Cathal for three weeks but already she was head over heels in love. Pamela almost didn't recognise her best friend. Who was this starry-eyed stupor of a woman? She didn't know whether to be insulted or pleased at the prospect of Cathal tagging along with his friends. Were they trying to set her up? She didn't need to be set up and was perfectly happy on her own thank you very much. It was bound to be better than sitting next to the two of them playing tonsil tennis though, she resolved.

That was until she saw Noel.

True to his word, Cathal met them at the cinema flanked by two of his friends, Noel and Eamon. Devilishly handsome with dark brown hair and chocolate brown eyes to melt, Pamela and Orla were falling all over him. They had to practically fight over who would get the coveted seat beside him. Poor Eamon didn't even get a look-in.

Noel smiled pleasantly at them both, the corners of his eyes creasing as he introduced himself, his voice dripping with depth and melancholy. Could he be any more attractive? Pamela had vague recollections of almost fainting. On the other side of Noel, Orla was nursing two wobbly knees as well.

"Back row seats." Una announced.

After stiff competition, Pamela eventually won the seat beside Noel.

"So, have you any interest in this film?" he said conversationally, as they sat down.

"A period drama?" she replied. "You must be joking me. I'd rather watch paint dry."

"Me too. Any chance we can escape through the fire exit?" he said, glancing around the cinema, looking for the nearest exit.

"I don't think so. Una would have me for the slaughter if I left now."

"Yea, Cathal would too. I don't know why though. It's not like they're going to notice. They'll just be playing tonsil tennis all night." he said, smirking, a hint at humour in his voice.

They had chatted away amicably as they waited for the film to begin and they had to be told to shut up so engrossed were they in conversation. Out of the corner of her eye, she could see Orla shooting daggers as poor Eamon suffered the fallout. She wasn't even trying to engage him in conversation, too preoccupied with everything that was happening at the other end. The things you get away with at seventeen. It was all Pamela could do not to take hold of Noel's hand and rub her nose in it. She'd never be that mean, would she?

Afterwards, conversation flowed over the lacklustre screenplay.

"That was so badly written." she had protested to Noel as they left the cinema.

"Awful, I was really really bored."

"So was I. I could have written a better screenplay myself. And to think that buffoon got paid for it."

"I know. I wanted to get up and walk out about twenty minutes in."

"Yeah, me too."

"Ah damn, we should have walked out together then."

"Definitely."

"I mean, what was that?" he asked of the film, his mind a haze of bewilderment.

"Pure trash that's what." Pamela replied honestly. "I mean, there was no character development, no humour, no story, no sense of having any empathy for any of the characters. The whole thing was just dull."

Noel paused a minute surprised at her outburst. He turned to look at her as though sizing her up.

"Do you write?" he asked.

"Yes I do." she exclaimed. "Not professionally mind, but I do love to write."

"What do you write?"

"Everything. Poems, short stories, stories that are a bit longer than short stories…...whatever takes my fancy." she finished. "What about you?"

"Yes, I do actually." he replied and Pamela felt Noel rise higher in her estimation - if that was possible. He was already well up there. "Mostly short scripts and things but it can be a bit of everything."

Una and Cathal had enjoyed their evening of tonsil tennis, Pamela and Noel had thoroughly enjoyed meeting each other so all in all it had been a successful evening out. The only one who wasn't impressed was Orla who wore a permanent frown on her forehead, save when Noel politely asked what she thought of the film. She had flashed him her broadest smile, showing her full range of teeth and said:

"I enjoyed it very much, thank you."

Noel took Pamela out the next week, much to Orla's dissatisfaction, and they became the best of friends. Ever since they first met, they had always felt at home in each other's company. She had never felt more comfortable around anyone and she quickly began to fall in love. Epitomising the stereotypical teen, she began to neglect her studies as she gradually spent more and more time with Noel. She couldn't get enough of him. Her parents grew very concerned but she ignored their pleas to return to the books. It was only an exam at the end of the day. Her grades slipped and she wasn't accepted onto the Journalism program despite spending months and months preparing a portfolio of her work. One month later her world was rocked when she discovered she was pregnant. Together, they decided they were going to keep the baby and she was happy with her decision. Telling her parents, however, was the hardest thing she ever had to do and she had been wracked with nerves. As predicted, they threw her out and she was forced to move in with Noel. In a matter of hours, her cosy home life had been swiped from under her feet. That was probably the beginning of her downward spiral, she thought. Unable to see a future with any kind of prospects, she began to sink into a black hole. Young and juggling a new baby along with depleting finances she didn't know how to cope.

That same man was sitting in front of her now. She wondered if he still wrote? Epilogues, prologues, poems, screenplay - anything. She hoped he did. She had suffered severe writer's block years ago and hadn't written anything since. He was still the sweet caring man that had been repulsed by that film all those years ago. The only difference was life had been hard on him, he had suffered a series of setbacks and they had taken their toll. She knew he resented the lack of involvement in Jean's life. He hated being robbed of the opportunity to form a father/daughter relationship with her. It pained Pamela now to confront the hurt she had caused, because she had, and it was all her fault.

He had tried everything to locate them in those early days but she hadn't budged. He had persevered and persevered but she had remained steadfast in her resolve, never giving an inch. Inevitably he got tired of living his life on a shoestring and had decided to move on. Who could blame the man for that? He had not abandoned his daughter. It was she who had denied him access. Her post-natal depression had been so severe she hadn't been thinking straight. In a blind panic, she had fled the house with Jean when she was just a toddler, severing all contact. It was the only action she knew to take at the time. But could she ever tell him the truth?

Now, as she returned back to the present, Noel was speaking.

"I just can't stand the thought of it." he moaned. "She's out there somewhere on her own trying to locate her friend and we have no idea where to begin."

"We've got the map Noel, we have some sense of direction now hopefully." pleaded Pamela.

"Yeah, but we could still be on a wild goose chase to nowhere."

"But we've got to try and can't just sit here and mope."

"What kind of sick bastards are they anyway. What do they want with her?"

"We know exactly what they want with her, the police told us that." replied Pamela.

"Yeah…" said Noel. "If they so much as lay a hand on her…" he continued, not caring to finish his sentence. His hand brushed off the cool exterior of his revolver and his mind surged with thoughts of what he was going to do.

Yes, he had been delighted with his purchase. It had been surprisingly easy to get the neat black revolver that was now sitting fully loaded in his lap. Easy once you know the right places to visit. Walking into the shop had been a strange experience. The man behind the counter was the stereotypical big burly man with tattoos covering every square inch of his body and piercings in every available orifice. Noel couldn't help but wonder what he actually looked like. He almost had a lump in his throat as he asked for the gun and the shop assistant had dutifully presented him with the shiny revolver.

He loved the feel of it, loved how his fingers fitted in to the trigger perfectly, like it had been kitted out for him. He didn't know if it was purely psychological or not but the power trip it brought him was like nothing he had ever experienced before. Yes, the weight of it in his hand unleashed a sense of power inside him but also made him feel like a criminal. He found it quite surreal that he should be in a position where he needed it, but he was.

Flying over to the other side of the world he had wanted a safety net. Neither he nor Pamela knew the scale of what they were dealing with and he had wanted to be prepared. Whoever had taken his daughter would not show them any mercy and neither would he. One thing was for sure, he would not hesitate to use it.

Pamela was anxious now, fidgeting, her mind in turmoil trying to determine the next course of action. Every second of procrastination could cost Jean her life. Suddenly, her mind was made up.

"You know what, I don't care anymore. I'm going to find a car to hire and I'll bloody find her myself. You can come with me if you want but don't try to stop me."

Pamela leapt up from the table, drained the last dregs of coffee and marched straight out to the reception area with a purpose. Noel had always admired this fiery persona. It had been both the making of them and their downfall. Draining the last of his coffee, he put it down on the table.

"Pamela, wait." he exclaimed, getting to his feet and following her into the lobby.

Within the hour, they had visited the local car rental and secured the keys. Selecting the cheapest model they could find, they didn't know whether to admire or detest their latest contraption. It stood like a small beige brick in the garage. Caked in dust, one would think it had spent the day at the local rally and they would do well to see out the windscreen. The wheels were almost flat and looked like they might come off at any minute. All they needed was a puncture and they were finished. The stench of petrol told them they had been given half a tank by the car rental company. Good, thought Pamela. With a bit of luck, they wouldn't have to top up for hours.

There was just enough room to fit into the driver's seat and the passenger seat.

"It's a good thing we're not big." Noel had exclaimed as soon as the salesperson was out of earshot.

"You should count yourself one of the lucky ones." Pamela had replied, not paying too much heed as she climbed into the car. "You're driving." she barked out the window at him.

"You know, this really dents my ego, driving a banger like this." Noel complained, still standing at the car and giving it the glance over.

"Oh, for goodness' sake, will you just shut up and get in?" she cried, annoyed now at his childish attitude.

"Will you lighten up woman, I was only joking." he barked as he clambered into the car and made use of every inch of available space. Eventually, heads slightly ducked, they were in.

Now to begin their search.

Forcing herself to think logically, two things were certain. Fleeing the brothel, Jean had to be running. Pamela couldn't imagine there would have been any form of vehicle at her disposal. It was possible, but unlikely. If she was running, the distance she could cover would be severely curtailed. Even if she ran for an hour or two, she couldn't have gained massive ground. A couple of miles maybe. But which way to move first?

She had the map of course, and they would follow that route first but if that turned up nothing, then what? She wanted to have a plan B in place.

"Okay, let's start by following the directions on the map and hope that turns up something." she said to Noel now as he started up the ignition.

"Alright." agreed Noel. "And what if it doesn't?"

"We're going to have to keep driving in all directions until we find this damned brothel, simple as that."

"But where do we start?" asked Noel.

"You're guess is as good as mine. We're probably going to have to start with the local town to get our bearings and improvise from there." she said. "But let's not worry about that yet. Let's follow the map and hope that steers us in the right direction."

Turning to Noel, she beckoned for him to pull out as they started their journey along narrow dusty roads. Grappling with driving on the right hand side of the road, they did their best to navigate their way. Entering the local town which had no traffic lights or clear direction for giving way to traffic, Noel proceeded to drive through some bustling streets and bumpy, unkempt roads. Navigating bikes, tuk-tuks and all other forms of road users, they drove out of the town. Following the map, they took several wrong turns and Pamela had to stop at a shop and ask for directions. She had barely understood the directions delivered in a thick Nepali accent and broken English, but they had managed to follow them. Eventually they had steered on the right road out of town. Now, as they drove along, they, saw lines of banyan trees and valleys of green. Pamela thought they had entered an ocean of tranquility. The country really was beautiful, it was such a shame they couldn't appreciate it.

Finally, still following the map, they came across a vast expanse of land. Bleak and deserted, it didn't look like much. Just barren wasteland, stretching on for miles. Pamela thought there must be acres and acres of land here. It was a huge terrain of disused land from what she could see. In fact, it was almost as if nobody ever came out here.

Pamela had noticed there weren't many people following them when they took the turn-off.

"That's it, that's it." Pamela said now as she pointed at the sparse area of land up ahead. "Let's pull up and check the map."

"I'm pulling up! I'm pulling up!" Noel said.

"That's got to be it, that's got to be where she ran from." Pamela said, her head moving from the map to the land in front and back again. "What do you think Noel?"

Noel studied the map again, trying to get his bearings and deconstruct the map simultaneously. After a long pause, he said "According to the map, it definitely seems to be, yeah."

"Let's go." Pamela insisted and with that they both scrambled out of the car and set off walking at a brisk pace.

"We're close, so close." Pamela whispered almost to herself as she began walking. "Where are you Jean?"

What they didn't realise was that the car had been fitted with a GPS tracking system.

****

Abdul's mobile phone rang. Looking distastefully at it, he contemplated declining the call. He didn't have time for this right now. He had just finished for the day and would be making his way over to the compound shortly.

Abdul was in the hotel conference suite in the local village, just a stone-throw away from the compound. With wall-to-wall luxurious surroundings, no one would ever have guessed that such catastrophic events were unfolding in such close proximity.

He was very fortunate. The hotel owner was a client of the brothel and in exchange for silence on his misdemeanours, he permitted the use of the hotel on occasion. It was probably one of the best business deals he had ever negotiated. Not that it happened very often because they were constantly moving and they primarily operated from abandoned warehouses and marquee-style set-ups. But the Sheikhs liked their comforts.

He had just had a Sheikh in town viewing a number of girls and he had selected the pasty one on the floor in front of him. Yes, the hotel conference suite had served him well, he thought. It was the ideal opportunity to parade the girls around when the Sheikh decided to make a spontaneous visit. It was a form of entertainment after all, Abdul decided, used as an excuse to show them off.

Of course, the girls would all be drugged so he always had a number of staff on hand and they had just taken four of his girls back to the compound. The girl that remained with him, well, the Sheikh had taken a real shining to her. And whatever the Sheikh wanted, the Sheikh got.

Oh, it could be important so he picked up his mobile phone deciding against his earlier irritation.

"Yes?"

"Abdul, we have her, the Irish girl that escaped." an excited voice said on the other end of the line.

"Excellent! Lock her up, make sure she can't escape again and I'll come and get her. I'll be leaving here shortly."

"Of course, Sir."

"And Kamal, don't fuck it up this time."

"Yes Sir!" said Kamal and the line went dead.

He clicked off his phone and turned his attention back to the job at hand. Bending down, he made sure he was at eye level with the girl in front of him.

"Now Maggie, what shall we do with you? The Sheikh wants to buy you, isn't that wonderful?" he teased.

Maggie was on her knees, her hair scuffled and a trace of blood in her mouth thanks to some punches Abdul had thrown her way. She was swaying from side to side and had to use her hands to steady herself. She had tried desperately to make her escape after the Sheikh's showcase but instead earned a series of punches from Abdul.

"No…" stammered Maggie.

"I'm sure he'll take exceptional care of you." he said, taunting her now. "You were special Maggie, he liked you."

"Stop it!" Maggie cried.

"Have you any idea the amount of money the Sheikh is paying for you?" he said, running his hands along her cheek and down along her chest into the deep curvature of her breasts.

"Get off me." said Maggie, though it sounded like a disembodied voice as the room was swaying in front of her.

"Because of you, I will have another hundred thousand rupees to my name. Do you have any idea what that kind of money can buy?" he asked.

Maggie didn't reply.

"No, of course you don't." Abdul continued with contempt. "That's the problem with you tourists, you get everything you want handed to you on a plate. You have no mass on anything. I am only making the money I deserve."

"By drugging women and turning them into prostitutes… that's disgusting." Maggie said gasping for air and barely able to speak. "You make me sick."

"Get up." he demanded suddenly.

"Get up." he demanded again, dragging Maggie to her feet. She put her back against a wall to try and steady herself.

"Such beautiful prey." continued Abdul, leaning in closer, his mouth just inches from hers. "Perhaps he might buy your friend too, now that we've got her."

"No..." was all Maggie could get out, such was the effect the drugs were having on her. Her brain was dead, her body like lead, almost like it was detached from her.

"Ehhh....eeehhhh......eeeehhhh" he chanted in a mocking tone. "Have you nothing more to say Maggie?"

Maggie did not reply.

"That's a pity." he said, talking in a slow drawl. "Your friends' parents sure had a lot to say."

"I won't reason with a lunatic." Maggie spat, making a determined effort not to rise to his bait.

"Oooh touché!" Abul replied, enjoying himself. "I daresay we will miss you around here." he continued, as he turned away from her and started pacing up and down the room again.

Suddenly grabbing her hair and pulling her head back with force, he leaned in close, menacing eyes protruding from their sockets. Maggie's mind swirled in terror as she winced in pain. Why had Jean come back? Between intermittent bouts of clarity, Maggie had gathered that Jean was after escaping from the compound. She had been relieved. Now, as Abdul informed her of her subsequent recapture, she wondered what would happen to her best friend. She shouldn't have come back. These animals would make her pay and she feared what the repercussions would be. They were in way over their head and she didn't want anything to happen to her. If she had managed to escape, she, should have stayed away.

This was a side to Jean that only Maggie knew, loyal to a fault, and she knew it only too well. Maggie remembered the time Jean had shunned a big basketball match and scouting opportunity to be with her on her father's anniversary. It was his fifth anniversary and Jean's basketball team had made it to the All-Ireland finals, due to be played on the same day. There were going to be leading scouts there, ready to offer the best players a one-way ticket to America. Jean was one of their star players and had been hotly tipped to win a much-coveted scholarship.

But Jean had refused to go, much to the chagrin of her coach and team mates. Maggie had utilized every trick in the book to entice her to go but Jean wouldn't budge. Maggie even gave a false date for her father's mass, but Jean, smart and savvy as she was, had figured it out. There was no fooling her.

Jean had arrived at her house, producing a home made apple tart and beautiful wreaths for her father's grave. She had also presented her with a card, imprinted with Maggie's favourite photo of him. The caption read: "Maggie, I am watching over you, always."

Maggie had been touched. Nobody had ever been so kind and it meant a lot. Her mother was great, of course, there was no denying that. But Maggie felt she had never really gotten over her father's death. She had never really moved on and so it was great to have a friend who cared.

"What are you doing here?" Maggie asked, noting that she was all dressed up instead of dressed down in her sports gear for the match. "Are you insane?"

"I'm not going to the match." she had insisted. "They can play without me."

"No, they can't and there is no way in hell that's happening." Maggie had insisted. "They need you. Will you go?" she had said, trying to show her out the door.

"I told you, no. You need me here."

"I really don't, I'll be fine. Will you please go to your match? I'll call you later."

"No, I'm not going." Jean said, putting her foot down.

"Please Jean, I can't have that on my conscience." Maggie said. "It's really not necessary for you to be here. I appreciate it, but please, go."

"When are you going to start thinking of yourself and realise that other people actually care about you? You're my best friend Maggie, I know today is a really hard day for you. Who cares about that match?"

"What about the scouting opportunity?"

"If they want me badly enough, they can come and get me. They know where I am." she said confidently as she swanned into the house and Maggie closed the door after her. "Besides, I'm too late now, the bus is gone."

Jean was, of course, referring to the bus that would ferry the team to the basketball arena.

"I feel terrible. Won't your teammates hate you?"

"Probably, but they'll deal with it. Besides, that really cute cousin of yours is coming, isn't he? What's his name again? Brian, is it?"

The scouting opportunity never arose for Jean but she never complained. She had remained content playing amateur basketball and never felt she had missed out on anything. For Jean, it had been more about a love of the sport than a desire to make a living from it. Maggie still felt bad about it though. She would never have stopped her friend fulfilling her dreams.

That was the kind of friend Jean was. She was so feisty and outspoken though, she hoped she didn't get herself killed.

"Leave… my … friend … alone." she managed to stammer finally, barely able to get the words out with the pain.

"But… but …. but … what's the matter Maggie? Has the cat got your tongue?" Abdul snarled, releasing her head and slapping her hard across the face.

"Take me. Leave my friend out of this." she managed to get out more forcefully this time.

"You know, I don't really understand why you're so loyal to her. I know you thought you were the best of friends but she abandoned you, now you're being sold to the Sheikh. She's not such a good friend after all is she?" he mused, clearly trying to provoke her.

"Jean is the only friend I've got." cried Maggie in despair.

"Really? Shall we go and ask her then?" he said.

He was about to grab Maggie by the arm when Raoul and Sajit burst into the room in a blaze of panic. Shiny foreheads sat atop their stern faces and they couldn't have been more transparent if they tried. It was obvious they needed to speak to Abdul immediately.

"Abdul, we need to speak to you now. It's urgent." demanded Raoul.

Raoul embodied every inch of his heritage dressed in khaki pants with bulging biceps protruding through his black sleeveless vest. Sajit, meanwhile, looked like something out of the Terminator films, guns poking out of his low-slung trousers and his t-shirt barely covering his chiseled torso. Their combined fitness levels would have easily matched Olympic standards.

"Oh, what now?" asked Abdul in frustration as Maggie slithered to the floor.

"We've got word that one of the Irish girl's parents is in the vicinity and they're close to discovering our hideout."

"Which one?" enquired Abdul.

"Jean's parents, Sir."

"The one that escaped" replied Sajit. "Where are they?"

"We're not exactly sure. We have a confirmed GPS tracking of them just off the land over an hour ago but we don't know their exact whereabouts right now."

"Where is the GPS tracking coming from?" asked Abdul.

"It's from a car they hired at a local rental company; they parked up well over an hour ago."

"And nothing since?"

"No sir. We believe they are on foot in pursuit of Jean."

Abdul began to laugh and once he began, he couldn't stifle his laughter.

"And you think her parents are going to find us here and overthrow us? I don't think so boys." he replied with arrogance.

"With respect Sir," interjected Sajit, "if they discover our hideout, the whole brothel is busted and we will lose our clientele."

Abdul walked right up to Sajit now, their faces barely inches apart.

"Let them come. These two will be no match for us. We will see to that." Abdul said, laughter subsiding.

"How do you propose we do that?" Raoul asked.

"Set a trap." commanded Abdul. "You boys are intelligent. I trust you will know what to do."

"Certainly Sir, leave it to us." said Raoul. And with that, Sajit and Raoul made to leave the room.

Turning back to Maggie, he dragged her to her feet once more.

"Time to get you ready for the Sheikh." he said, as he tugged her arms behind her, and together, they made their way back to the compound.

CHAPTER 14

Noel and Pamela had been walking for well over an hour, their legs growing heavy and tired. Sweat was dripping from every pore, their hair matted to their faces from the intense humidity and their bottles of water were long drunk.

They had parked the car a little further back and started making their way to the brothel by foot. They planned to retrace Jean's steps with the limited information they had gleaned from the police. Jean had run from the brothel late at night, it was dark so directions were sketchy to say the least but they were willing to take their chances.

This probably wasn't the most practical move but they had been forced to take matters into their own hands. Stopping for a moment to catch her breath, Pamela took a good look around.

All she could see for miles around was barren waste land. There was no vegetation, no crops, no fluttering birds on the shallow breath of wind. All was silent. The skies above them painted a grey picturesque landscape on the horizon, creating the illusion that it could rain at any given moment.

How did Jean run all this way? It only enhanced her realisation of how terrified she must have been and how determined she must have been to seek help.

Pamela exhaled in despair as she tried to decide what to do next. They could be here for hours or days even wandering around aimlessly with no direction. Did they continue on and hope they eventually found this brothel? They had brought supplies of food and water with them but that would run out. The mounting pressure she felt that every minute Jean was in that brothel was another minute spent in danger continued to dominate her thoughts. Time was not a luxury they could afford.

"Jean really ran all this way?" Noel asked in disbelief, reading her mind.

"It looks like it."

Turning to Noel, she went to make a plan.

"Noel, what are we going to do?" she asked. "We can't keep traipsing around here for hours. We don't have that kind of time."

"Well, what do you propose we do?" replied Noel, looking at her like a lost little boy.

Pamela started to get annoyed. Why was it always up to her to make the plans, make all the decisions? It really irritated her. She was as clueless as he was and didn't know the area any better than he did. She would really appreciate his help right now.

"I don't know." she replied in a panic. "I don't know what to do."

She looked in every direction, desperately scouring for clues that any living breathing thing inhabited this space because right at that moment it didn't look like it. Beside her, she could see Noel doing the same thing. Pamela did her best to remain optimistic but in this bleak location, it was difficult not to let the despair of the land feast away at your insides. It had been a longshot she knew but she had wanted to come here and search for her daughter.

The rain started bearing down on them, full pellets of rain, courtesy of the monsoon season then. They were just about to give up when Pamela spotted something a little way off into the distance. An abandoned warehouse. A marquee set up beside it. Pamela did a double take to be sure her eyes weren't deceiving her. She badly needed a trip to the opticians.

"Noel, I think this is it." Pamela shrieked, pointing towards the warehouse and marquee in the distance. Suddenly she was alive on her feet and pumping with adrenaline. "Call the police - now."

Overcome with a sudden burst of energy, Pamela took off full steam ahead towards the warehouse.

"Pamela, wait!" cried Noel, running after her.

Pamela ran as fast as she could, the long walk they had just endured a distant memory. Vaguely aware of Noel in the distance behind her, she kept her sights focused straight ahead, the buildings looming ever larger. As Pamela veered closer to the warehouse, she caught sight of a figure lying out front.

She could just make out the body of a girl lying flat on her back, her hair an unkept mess behind her head. The girl lay ghostly still and from this distance Pamela couldn't tell if she was dead or alive. Why was she out front? Would she not be kept in the marquee or the warehouse? It didn't make any sense.

Pamela was still running, getting ever closer, gaining ground all the time. Her muscles ached, her breath rattled out of control and her legs burned from endurance, but she kept going.

She was getting closer.

Glancing over her shoulder she saw Noel was well behind her, trying to speak to the police as he ran. Pamela swung her head back around and gasped as everything came into focus. She recognised those clothes, the bright colourful nylon pants, the pretty white blouse, the sparkly sandals. They were all too familiar. Pamela upped her pace sprinting steadily on.

"Pamela, what is it?" Noel bellowed from behind her.

Allowing herself a closer look, her worst fears were confirmed as she realised the body of the girl in front was Jean. She lay ghostly still and Pamela couldn't determine if she was dead or alive. Pamela was almost there now, running like the wind towards her. It was only a few split seconds but it seemed like hours. Finally seeing Jean's leg twitch, Pamela breathed a sigh of relief and took the final leap across the flat terrain towards her daughter.

"Jean, it's Mum. I'm here, you're safe now. I'm going to take you home." Pamela said, crouching down beside her and grabbing her daughter in a tight bear hug. She glossed over her for any hint of cuts or bruises. There were many of course but she was alive. Everything else was secondary.

Jean sat up, still wearing the clothes she had gone hiking in. Glancing down at her tattered, torn and blood-stained clothes, she tried to focus. Putting her hand to her head, she felt a slight dizziness but was otherwise fairly cognisant. The effects of the drugs must have worn off.

"Mom, what are you doing here?" asked Jean, gazing at Pamela in shock. The last person Jean had expected to see out here was her mother.

"I came to find you sweetheart, that's what I'm doing here. I'm going to get you home safe and sound." replied Pamela stoically.

"Mam, they've still got Maggie." Jean said urgently, a sense of panic to her voice. "I'm not leaving without her."

"I know love." said Pamela, cradling her daughter once more, trying to allay her fears.

"I have to find her, I just have to." she pleaded, tears starting down her eyes.

"Sssshhh, we will." said Pamela.

Catching up with them, Noel gently came to a halt gazing at the daughter he had never known. She was so beautiful. How he had longed for this day. He had imagined several different scenarios in his head but none of them had come close to this. He wished he was meeting her under better circumstances, of course, but this was it. He wasn't getting a choice in the matter.

"Dad." she said, looking at him, taking in every feature. Jean watched him approaching, unable to believe this was the man who had walked out on them all those years ago. Jean had always resolved that she would never speak to him, she would never have anything to do with him. But seeing him standing in front of her now, red-faced, sweaty and out of breath, her resolve softened. It was uncanny, she had always imagined they would be like awkward strangers but this man did not feel like a stranger to her. She felt an instant connection with him, like all those years hadn't elapsed and they could pick up right where they left off. Pamela had tactfully moved out of the way and allowed them to have their moment.

"You came all this way?" she said finally.

Noel, meanwhile, felt like he was being x-rayed and didn't really know how to conduct himself.

"I did. I didn't want to miss the party." he ventured, always trying to diffuse a fraught situation with a lame joke. There was a moments silence before he asked. "Are you hurt?"

"No Dad, I'm okay." she smiled.

"Good, you're safe now." he said, kneeling down on the ground beside her and giving her a big hug. After a while, Pamela joined in on the hug and for one fleeting moment they were just like one big happy family. Even if it was deceptive.

Noel found it quite surreal to be meeting his daughter for the first time, in her most vulnerable state, outside a brothel in the middle of the oceans of wasteland, but he was. And it was bittersweet.

He was looking at her and he found himself lost for words. She was a grown woman now. Even after all this time, he felt bereft of all the absent years, years he had not been a part of. Did he say sorry? He had never wanted to be the estranged father. It was a role he had never envisioned himself playing. He had been robbed of his obligations as a father and he hated it. Of all the regrets he had in his life, this was by far his blackest.

The girl before him was a stranger. In other ways though, he felt like he knew her. Time had elapsed but, there, in that vast ocean of space, it was insignificant, like pages turning in a book. He was very proud of her and of everything she had become.

"You know, that really is a touching story but I don't have time for games." said a foreign voice.

Stopping in his tracks, Noel looked up at the man standing in front of him. He was holding a gun to his head.

"Sajit." cried Jean. And before she knew it, Kamal had a gun to her head and Babu had a gun to Pamela's head. It was like they had come out of nowhere.

What kind of idiots were they? All three of them had been so engrossed in their reunion, they had completely neglected to stay alert. They were right outside the brothel and still in danger. They shouldn't have let their guard down.

None of them had noticed all three men lurking quietly nearby.

"Have I got the story right?" teased Sajit. "A father that never saw his daughter but now wants to make amends." he finished as he wielded his gun dangerously close to Noel. One wrong move and Noel was dead.

"You don't know the first thing about me." said Noel, anger coursing through him again. He really needed to get a handle on it.

"Actually, I do." Sajit was saying now. "You see that's where you're wrong; I know quite a lot about you."

"Sajit." repeated Jean. "Please, just let us go."

Sajit appeared to be taking on the role of ringleader for this exercise and so she decided to appeal to him.

"I'm afraid I can't do that. I have orders to bring you all back inside. Bind their hands." he barked at the others.

He was very pleased with his carefully laid trap, executed to perfection, even if he did say so himself. He knew the area so well it didn't matter if he was on a flat terrain of land or up a huge hill, he knew all the great hiding spots. He also knew how to launch an attack on unsuspecting civilians. It was preposterously easy he thought, dripping with arrogance. Abdul would be sure to award him a raise for his efforts and his pockets would be lined with gold. He would look forward to it.

"Get up! All of you." cried Sajit as he continued to hold the gun to Noel's head. Together, they manhandled the three of them to their feet.

"Sajit, please." cried Jean as her arm was practically torn out of its socket. Kamal was extremely rough and her arm hurt like hell, making her scream.

"Shut up." he threatened, pointing the gun at Jean. "Or I'll shoot. Now walk." he ordered.

Lowering their guns against their backs, Sajit, Kamal and Babu marched behind the three of them. Gently steering them in the direction of the brothel, they were led into the warehouse on the left. Jean could not believe she was back here again. Was her nightmare ever going to end?

They were led down a dark corridor into a room. Black with darkness, Jean had to blink several times to allow her eyes to grow accustomed to it. Then someone switched on a lamp and there he was. Abdul. He sat, perched on his throne, all powerful, like a cat ready to pounce. You could have cut it with a knife such was the density of the air. It was thick with fear.

Jean didn't like it. The office was a gloomy run-down collection of old furniture and ancient antiques. She had definitely seen better offices. Beginning with the mahogany desk Abdul was currently sitting behind, off to her left she could see a withered bookshelf spouting tattered books and reams of torn pages. The little lamp that was currently bathing the room in light was caked in dust. A small number of tables and chairs lay scattered around the room, turned upside down. They looked almost adorable in their kids' sizes. A large blackboard held pride of place across the top wall and she noticed a few paintings strewn on the floor as well. They had almost been imprinted black now, they had been there so long. Had this once been a primary school, Jean wondered?

"Well, well, well, what have we here?" asked Abdul now.

"As you wish Sir, the Irish girl and her parents." announced Sajit as he thrust them forward on to their knees in front of Abdul.

"Thank you, Sajit." called Abdul.

Looking from Sajit to Noel and Pamela to Jean, Abdul's cold dark eyes bored into theirs. He was clearly delirious to have them under his thumb. He had them exactly where he wanted.

Sajit, Kamal and Babu stood directly behind each of them like puppeteers as they let Abdul do the talking.

With big, extravagant moves, he made to get up from his desk, towering over them. Ensconcing them in a circle as they remained on bended knees, he made to address Noel and Pamela.

"Now, what brings you all the way out here? I dare say you shouldn't have wasted your time." he began, speaking in a slow voice, pronouncing every word.

"We came looking for our daughter." replied Noel. "You abducted her, remember?"

"Ah yes, that's right." said Abdul, stopping for a minute and stroking Jean's face in mock tenderness. "I'm afraid I just couldn't resist."

"Don't touch her you sick bastard!" cried Noel.

"She's just so pretty." Abdul hissed.

"Stop it, or I'll kill you." said Noel. As he lunged forward, unsteady with his hands tied, Sajit caught hold of him, ensuring he could not intervene.

"Sit down." said Abdul in a patronising tone. "Don't be getting yourself all worked up."

"You leave my daughter alone, you twisted pervert." Noel bellowed furiously.

Abdul moved away from Jean and started circling the three of them again. He really was determined to make a show of this.

"You flew halfway across the world, navigated the Nepalese landscape, walked for miles and for what?"

"It will all be worth it to get our daughter back." said Noel, through gritted teeth.

"I'm sorry, perhaps I haven't quite made myself clear. You won't be getting her back. Not when I'm through with you." he finished.

"What is it you want?" demanded Noel. "Do you want money?"

"Noel, don't!" Pamela interjected, terror written all over her face.

"Dad, no." called Jean.

"What do I want?" replied Abdul, putting his hands to his chin in mock thought.

"Oh, cut to the chase, what are you, some kind of Pimp?" asked Noel, frustration quickly rising like bile again.

Abdul laughed, looking at the others as they laughed and jeered along with him.

"Am I a pimp? What do you think boys?" he said in jeering tones and flashing his eyes at his subordinates, clearly finding the whole fiasco hilarious.

"I would think so, Sir." Sajit replied, going along with the joke.

"Quit messing around and tell me what I've got to do to get my daughter back? What's it going to take to get her released?" interrupted Noel, getting more frustrated by the minute.

As quickly as it had begun, the laughing stopped and Abdul's expression changed. He was teasing now, expertly delivering his malice and he made no attempt to hide it.

"But she's not really your daughter, is she?" taunted Abdul. "I mean, biologically yes, but not really."

"What the hell are you talking about?"

"Well… she doesn't call you 'Dad' the way most daughters do. Oh, that's right - because you've never been there for her."

This hit a nerve with Noel. His failings as a father and feelings of inadequacy coursed right through to the most vulnerable part of him. This was hitting him where it hurt the most. How did he know? Damn it, Abdul was not going to get away with this.

He knew he shouldn't rise to the bait but he couldn't help it. A swirling hot anger took over and he had to get up and wrestle Abdul to the ground. He shouldn't have bothered really, as the minute he had leapt to his feet, Kamal and Babu went to restrain him. With his hands bound, he was no match for any of them.

"You evil son of a bitch." cried Noel. "I'm a hell of a lot more than you'll ever be."

"Touché! Touché!" said Abdul, loving the spectacle. "Clearly I have hit a nerve."

"Please, just let me take my daughter and her friend and let us get out of here. What do you want with her? With us?" demanded Noel.

"You see young Jean here has been scouted by a Sheikh in the absence of the other Irish girl that was here. Oh my, what a tragedy." continued Abdul lightly, enjoying the whole charade.

Jean's blood ran cold. This couldn't mean what she thought it meant, could it? From what she could tell, herself and Maggie were the only Irish girls in the brothel. But these guys were working day and night in the Himalayas, so there was surely a good chance it wasn't Maggie. Why had he brought it up though? He was definitely insinuating something and whatever it was, it wasn't good. Jean concluded that he was just trying to provoke her.

"What other Irish girl?" Jean asked. Damn it! She hadn't been able to resist.

"You didn't hear? Oh dear, another time then." teased Abdul, feigning a yawn, as if bored. "But I have arranged for your transfer."

"If you have hurt Maggie, I swear to God, I'll kill you." shouted Jean.

Jean scoured the ground beneath her, searching for anything that might double up as a weapon. If this indeed had once been a school classroom, there had to be something here. A small scissors, a sweeping brush, a duster for that blackboard - anything that might help them escape. She half expected to find a mini torture set somewhere in the room but she couldn't find any. Nothing visible to the naked eye at least. What they really needed was something sharp to sever their ties. Scanning her eyes around the room, she searched like she had never searched before. Eventually her eyes landed on small scissors lying perfectly on the floor. Perfect, that would do. As discreetly as she could she drew the scissors close to her with her big toe. Making sure to keep one eye on Sajit, Kamal and Babu - they were too busy gloating anyway - she quickly moved it over towards Noel. Catching his eye, he affirmed his knowledge of her movements.

Abdul was laughing his head off, dismissing Jean's comment like a feather of dust off his shoulder. He was used to these threats. They didn't bother him.

"Your petty little threats don't scare me darling." Abdul mused. "Now, what to do with the pair of you?" he said, fixing his gaze on Noel and Pamela once more.

"Let us take the girls and get out of here." pleaded Pamela, suddenly finding her voice.

"No… that won't work I'm afraid." replied Abdul. "You see, I can't just let two people who have discovered my brothel, free to talk to the police. I'm sure you'll understand that I will be in a lot of trouble." he finished, his voice laced with arrogance.

"Well too bad for you we have already spoken-" began Pamela.

"- we won't say anything." interjected Noel, cutting across her. "If you let all of us go, we won't say anything. We give you, our word."

"What kind of a fool do you take me for?" said Abdul calmly. "Do you not think I've heard those promises hundreds of times before?"

"Please? We don't want any trouble. We just want to go home."

"I can't let you do that." replied Abdul.

"Why not? Please, I'm begging you."

"It's too late now for your desperate pleas. I might just have to kill you both." said Abdul, with a demonic look in his eye. He took a gun out of his back pocket and was brandishing it like a man possessed. "I'll just have to finish you off."

"Nooooo." cried Pamela.

Pamela was frantic. This could not be how she would die, she refused to meet her death in this kip. But as Abdul pointed the gun at her it was hard not to believe this was the end. How were they going to get out with their lives? Beside her she could hear Jean's protestations and Noel calling for them to shoot him first. Abdul was having none of it.

"You first, My Lady." he said. She looked up at him towering over her, a spiteful grin spreading across his face. Would this be the last thing she would remember before she fell to her death? His finger curled neatly around the trigger and he flexed his wrist, poised for action. He was ready to shoot.

CHAPTER 15

Bang!

Pamela and Jean both let out a yelp as the intensity of the noise assaulted their eardrums. Turning back to see what had just happened, they saw Noel had the revolver firmly in his hands and Abdul had fallen to the floor slain.

Noel was ready, this had all been premeditated in his head. He had planned and planned for this moment. Now it was finally here, he was not going to falter.

At the last second, just as Abdul had been about to shoot Pamela, Noel had wrenched out his revolver, cleanly shooting Abdul in the chest. He had fallen backwards in a heap on to the floor. It had all happened so fast, neither Sajit, Kamal or Babu had time to react.

Noel was lucky Jean had found that scissors on the floor. It had been all he could do to keep his face neutral when she had passed it over and he began severing the cord bit by bit.

Sajit came to attack him next but Noel hit him hard over the head with the gun sending him flying straight into the precious mahogany desk. Springing into action, all fear suddenly deserting her, Pamela hit Kamal over the head with a chair knocking him out. He was so predictable. She had anticipated his next move with ease.

"Jean, go and find Maggie." Noel roared, as he prepared to fight Babu. "Now."

Jean quickly picked the scissors up off the floor, cut her wrists loose and fled the room. Running back down the dark corridor they had come through, she had no idea where she was going. No real agenda. Her head told her Maggie was probably over in the marquee somewhere, so she decided to check there first.

On she went through the warehouse, on high alert for anyone that might have heard all the commotion or anyone that might be on her tail. Thankfully, there didn't seem to be anyone around. Then, seeing a light in the distance in front of her, she sprinted towards it, emerging onto the familiar plain with relative ease.

Across the way, stood the marquee. Quickly forming a plan in her head, Jean thought she would have to approach this carefully. She knew she couldn't just dive in head first. She didn't want to cause a scene.

As predicted, one of Abdul's team was standing directly outside the compound and she would need a reason for getting in. Normally the girls were marched into the marquee with Kamal, Sajit or Babu in tow. It would look suspicious presenting herself.

As she contemplated different ways to get past the tall man with sallow skin and a stocky build, she hoped she would be allowed in. She steadied herself to catch her breath. Dressed down in jeans and casual t-shirt, he was watching everything that was happening around him. He scrutinized the men as they entered, sizing them up and down in search of any trouble.

Finally, walking confidently across the grounds, she approached the man in charge.

"Excuse me, Sir, can I go inside?" she said, doing her best to sweet-talk him. If she weren't in so much danger, she would find this very easy. "I forgot my jacket. It's very cold." she finished with as much charm as she could muster.

"My lady, anything for you." he said as he stepped aside and allowed her to pass.

Peering behind all the curtains and doing her best to block out the sights that greeted her, she searched and searched the whole way through the marquee. Everything from blonde haired beauties to stunning brunettes met her in that marquee, each one of them personified by the drugs they had been force fed. Some of them were semi-naked, others were barely dressed, just lying there on the bed, motionless, waiting for the next piece of their body to be taken. Some were mid-session, the men cupping their breasts like dolls and the girls lacking the capacity to know their bodies were being ravished for the pleasure of foreign men. Jean had to shake her head a few times in despair. That had very nearly been her.

Finally, she came to the last miserable curtain. Wrenching it off the rail, she recoiled in horror, flinging her hands to her mouth.

A young woman sat in the chair beside the bed, dressed in a black mini skirt, red top and a fitted black jacket. A beautiful elegant shawl was wrapped around her neck, embalmed in a haze of colours to offset the black and a shiny pair of black boots complemented the look. Red lipstick dotted her mouth and lashings of black eyeliner defined her eyes. Her brown hair had been neatly brushed back into a wavy ponytail decorated with a little red ribbon. The woman had been carefully tended to and they had obviously dressed her up with the objective of taking her somewhere. She looked gorgeous. But she was very pale, her glassy eyes staring into a vacuous space and she wasn't moving. Or breathing. The woman was obviously dead.

It was Maggie.

CHAPTER 16

"Maggie, no! Please God, no. Please don't be dead." cried Jean as she bolted over to her friend, kneeling beside her. Grabbing hold of her hand, it was ice cold and her skin was clammy. It was then Jean noticed the used syringe and dab of blood on a piece of cotton wool littering the floor. "Maggie, wake up."

Maggie didn't stir.

"Come on Maggie, please wake up." Jean said desperately. "Wake up Maggie, we have to go."

Frantically slapping her on the wrist, checking her pulse, pinching her cheeks, anything that might breed signs of life, Jean tried everything. Still, Maggie didn't stir.

Jean continued to beg her friend to wake up for what seemed like an eternity. As if possessed, some outward compulsion made her keep trying. Jean then made several attempts to lift her up off the chair but her friend's body was limp, lifeless and heavy. It was at that point Jean finally accepted that her best friend, her partner in crime, was gone.

"Maggie." she wailed.

Jean hugged her best friend to her, cradling her in her arms, as heavy sobs came thick and fast. Jean had never had a friend like Maggie. On the surface, Jean appeared to be confident and carefree, but on the inside, she was a vulnerable mess. Only Maggie understood that. Nobody understood her like she did. Sweet, gentle Maggie who had only ever cared more for others than herself.

When Jean had been upset about her lack of contact with her dad, Maggie had been there with a listening ear and a warm hug. After many of her legendary fights with Pamela, she would ring Maggie in a huff and she would always be there to calm her down. When Jean had broken up with her last boyfriend, Maggie had come straight over with pizza, ice-cream and a bottle of wine, and helped herself to the best chick-flick she could find. In Maggie she had found a real friend, true companionship and she knew she would never find that again. What would she ever do without her?

The worst part was, Jean had never really thanked her, never really told her how much she had meant to her. And now she never would. She had taken her for granted, relying on complacency and assuming she would see her every day. Wasn't that normal for someone her age, Jean thought?

The horror of the last few days, of everything they had been through, and now to find her best friend dead, was all just too much for Jean. Anger flashed through her veins. What had she ever done to deserve this? Why had they been forced into this hell-hole? It was supposed to be an epic adventure for them, making loads of happy memories. Instead, it had ended in tragedy. Why did she have to die? It should have been her.

Then it clicked. This was what Abdul had been talking about. News of Maggie's death had already reached him. He had known all along. And she was next in line to be sold to the Sheikh. She needed to get out of here. Fast.

Hearing a loud commotion outside, she heard her father's voice. He had hit the man outside over the head and was jumping through the cubicles, ripping down the curtains as he went. Pamela was hot on his heels.

Eventually, he found Jean cradling whom he could only surmise was her friend in her arms. As he looked on, he could see his daughter's heart breaking. Poor Jean was devastated.

"Jesus, Mary and Joseph." exclaimed Noel as he quickly ground to a halt. Blessing himself now, it was chilling to think how easily that could have been Jean. How easily his daughter might have met the same fate.

"Maggie!" roared Pamela in horror, dashing past Noel to rush over.

Pamela had been far from a perfect mother, but in that moment, she ran over to comfort Jean. As Jean slowly let go of Maggie and placed her gently back on the chair, Pamela could feel her daughter breaking inside.

"We have to go." said Noel softly.

Just then, they heard the sound of sirens approaching. Red and blue lights penetrated the premises and they heard the squeal of tyres as brakes were slammed to the floor.

"The police are here." said Noel.

The marquee was suddenly ablaze with activity. The tension was palpable as all the men screamed and ran, fleeing into the wilderness. Half-naked men were scurrying off pulling up their pants, tying buttons and pulling on their shirts over sloppy vests as they ran as fast as they could out of the marquee. Pulling over the curtain to shield themselves, Noel peered out first to see what was happening outside. He was very aware that Sajit, Kamal and Babu had only been knocked unconscious, they wouldn't be long coming round.

"What are you doing?" asked Jean, as she spotted Noel peering out the curtain.

"I'm trying to hide from the bad guys." he replied.

"But that makes no sense. The police are here. We can go."

"Alright alright, I'm just making sure the coast is clear."

"Dad, what about Maggie?" asked Jean.

"I'll talk to the police for you, they'll look after her and organise for her body to be brought home." he said gently, tears brimming the surface of his eyes again.

"Do we just leave her here?" Jean asked amid an onslaught of sniffles.

"Yes, we do." he said soothingly.

"It just feels so wrong, I should be bringing her with me."

"I know you should." said Noel, pushing her hair off her face and placing it neatly behind her ears. "We're all sad to lose Maggie but the police are here now, they will make sure she is brought home."

"Okay." she sniffed.

After Noel declared the compound a safe space, the three of them emerged from the marquee to scenes of chaos. Police cars, ambulances and fire services had all arrived on the scene. The paramedics had already located Abdul and were carrying him out on a stretcher, vigorously trying to feed him with an oxygen mask. Elsewhere, paramedics, police officers and detectives were tearing through the marquee rescuing all the young women that had been trafficked.

Jean watched, as the girls were brought out of the marquee, big grey blankets wrapped around them. Some of them were shaking, some of them barely able to walk, others a clammy mess, each one of them in various stages of drug infusion. The drugs their persecutors force-fed them to render them defenceless, obedient objects, used to fulfill men's desires. Unwillingly forced into prostitution, how were they ever going to return to real life? How would they ever adapt? Their bodies had been violated to despicable proportions against their will and the psychological repercussions would be enormous. Not only that, they would also have to deal with the aftermath of a drug addiction. Jean wondered how long they had sat in that marquee? Some of them had been held captive for years. Her heart lifted at the part she had played in exposing this dive of a place and bringing these captors to justice. Scarred though they may be, her heart smiled as she thought of the many happy reunions to come for these girls and their families.

Next, Jean spotted paramedics carrying someone out on a stretcher covered in a white sheet. Instantly, she knew it was Maggie and she ran over to them, placing her hand on top of the cold, impersonal white sheet. It was hard to believe her friend had ended up here, so final. After a few moments, the paramedics told her they needed to move on and so she had watched as they catapulted her into the ambulance, bound for the hospital mortuary.

The place was swarming with police officers as they made several arrests. Sajit, Kamal and Babu were being wrestled to the ground, each one of them flanked by two police officers trying to handcuff them. Raoul had been tracked down as well much to Jean's delight. She looked each one of them in the eye with a sense of satisfaction. She was glad to finally see the back of them. Even if it was bittersweet.

Several more officers were attempting to arrest some of the clients that didn't quite manage to escape. They were predominantly big fat men who could never have outrun fit police officers. It was then she saw Detective Rashid and she went straight for him.

"Detective Rashid." she said as she ran over to him.

"Jean…" he said, turning slowly towards her.

"I just wanted to say thank you."

"You're welcome. I'm glad you're safe." he said with a note of sincerity in his voice.

"I'm sorry for giving you a hard time."

"Don't make a habit of it." he quipped, before a look of concern appeared over his face. "I'm sorry about Maggie and for how all this turned out."

"I'm sorry too." she replied, unable to say much more on the subject.

"The paramedics will see to your injuries okay." he said kindly. "Then the police will escort you back to your hotel. If there is anything else you need, just let me know."

Detective Rashid acknowledged Noel and Pamela then before proceeding to assist with other elements of the investigation.

A police officer arrived and put a blanket around her shoulders and she was led to the police car along with her parents. As the car bumped along the road, Jean found herself entering a state of numbness. In the last ninety-six hours she had witnessed both the best and worst of humanity. That was an incredible position to be in. After everything she had seen, she didn't think she was the same person anymore. She wasn't the same person anymore. Gone was the carefree ditz who only cared about make-up and boys. Gone was the self-conceited idiot who only cared about herself. She was far more serious now and it was difficult to fathom how she would make a return to real life. She guessed she was descending into a state of shock which was to be expected. But she was determined to overcome it for Maggie's sake if nothing else. She owed her that.

And she had her dad back in her life now. Obviously, they hadn't chatted about things yet given the circumstances, but they would. Maggie would have been thrilled that they had found each other and were being afforded the opportunity to reconnect. She was looking forward to getting to know him. It wouldn't happen overnight but she felt sure it would happen on a gradual basis. She could almost visualise Maggie's face encouraging her to develop this relationship with him and not to shut him out like she did with most people. Typical! She had always been Miss Bossy Boots.

Life was strange, Jean reflected. It was true what they said, as soon as one door closes, another opens. She had lost her best friend but she had gained a father. She was going to commit to building this relationship wholeheartedly now and put everything on the line. It was never too late. It was what Maggie would have wanted.

'It's over now', said her father now in the car beside her. And it really was.

****

Back in the Gresham Hotel in Dublin, the Tidy Towns competition was going full steam ahead. A number of volunteers with Dublin City Council were up for an award, Ava Adams among them. She hadn't wanted to come due to everything that was happening overseas but she had kind of been under obligation. She was sitting at a table with her fellow volunteers in the function room, the men drenched in a sea of tuxedos and bow ties while the women were a vision in colour. A beautiful crystal chandelier swooped from overhead and the tables were perfectly spaced apart. The stamping of feet signalled hardworking waiting staff who were busy serving drinks after the extravagant meal they had just eaten. At the front of the room was a large stage and a small table of trophies. It was a beautiful, glitzy event but the entire charade was lost on Ava as she was too preoccupied with Maggie. Where was she now? Was she still alive? Any other time she would have gloated over her nomination for such a prestigious award, but tonight she couldn't have been more disinterested if she tried. As they sat listening to representatives from Dublin City Council and Tidy Towns waffle on about nothing, Ava heard her phone ring. She didn't recognise the number. She had better answer it, she thought, it could be news about Maggie. She excused herself as discreetly as she could and left the room.

"Hello?"

"Hello, is that Mrs. Adams?" said a thick foreign accent on the other end of the line.

Ava squinched her eyes shut. After all these years she still flinched whenever she was referred to as a married woman.

"Yes, this is she."

"This is Detective Rashid. I'm calling from the police station in Nepal. I'm the Detective assigned to investigate the disappearance of your daughter Maggie."

"Yes, have you found her?" Ava's heart leapt. "Is she okay?"

A moment's hesitation from Detective Rashid and Ava knew the news wasn't good.

"I'm very sorry Mrs. Adams but we found Maggie's body in the marquee. She had been injected with a lethal dose of heroin."

Ava dropped the phone to the floor letting it crash and break before falling to the floor herself. She heard Detective Rashid's voice saying "Hello? Mrs. Adams? Are you there?" on the phone but she couldn't speak, couldn't function, couldn't do anything right now with the shock. Her entire world had just collapsed.

Inside the function room, she could hear the MC calling out the nominations for the Best Helper.

"And the winner is Mrs. Ava Adams." he announced to thunderous applause.

Her head was spinning. It couldn't be. It just couldn't be her Maggie. They had to have it all wrong or it must be a case of mistaken identity or something. Placing her head in her hands, hot tears spilling down her face, she did everything to tell herself it wasn't true. But of course, it was.

The door of the function room opened and her team of volunteers came out to find her. Almost in slow motion, they filed out of the room, saw the forlorn look on her face and immediately ran over to comfort her. There were probably about four of them in total. With reams of mascara running down her face and smudged lipstick, she must have looked like something out of the joker. She didn't care, her Maggie was never coming home.

"Ava, what's wrong?" her closest friend Sheila asked as she knelt down beside her in her gorgeous turquoise-blue dress. She really did look stunning tonight.

Ava had already briefed her on the Maggie and Jean saga. "It's Maggie." she said and she didn't have to say anymore.

"Oh my God!" said Sheila, as her hands flew to her face, all over her make-up.

"Take me home," Ava cried, and Sheila sprang into action. Sheila was superb. She was so calm and so practical in a crisis. She always knew exactly what to do.

"Paddy, you get the car and bring it around the front. Aine, you'll need to take care of things inside." she said, barking orders at the other volunteers. "Tell the organisers there's been an accident or something and Ava won't be accepting the award tonight. Go."

Thanks to Sheila, they had been able to make a discreet exit, avoiding a scene. Aine had retrieved her bag and coat for her and together Sheila and Paddy bundled her into his car. She had never been more grateful to get out of there and she would always hold Sheila in high regard for that. Once they were securely back in Ava's house, Sheila sat her down on the couch and fixed her a brandy. She was under orders to drink up. It would take the edge off the shock, she said.

"How am I ever going to get over this Sheila?" Ava said in despair, as she took a sip, the soft liquor like a dagger whooshing down her oesophagus. It was more than a stiff brandy she needed. "I can't go through this again."

Sheila put her own glass down on the coffee table and sat down beside her. Putting her arms around her comfortingly and staring her straight in the eye, she said:

"You can and you will. You'll just have to pick yourself up again, like you did before."

"I can't, not this time. My darling girl is gone. She's all I've got Sheila."

The house was a shrine to her little girl, every picture, every piece of furniture, every cup, every glass, all reminders of the person she had lost. She would never see her pretty little face, never hear her voice in the hallway, never get a hug or a kiss goodbye again and the thought was unbearable. Through her blurry vision, she could see pictures of Maggie dominating her sitting room wall and right at that moment Ava resented every single one of them. The book Maggie had been reading before she left lay on the coffee table, all her DVD's lay stacked in a corner, the cushion Maggie had made specially on the couch beside her. She seemed to be trapped in a nightmare of reminders of her only daughter and her mind began to swirl.

"Ava, are you alright?" she heard Sheila saying through the fog in her brain. Sheila had been at a loss to find the right words to comfort her friend.

"I just can't believe she's gone." she replied.

"I know." Sheila replied gently, picking up her drink from the coffee table, and handing Ava a tissue.

"And now all I'm left with are the memories – pictures, videos." Ava said, more to herself than to Sheila.

"You also have the memories in your head. No-one can ever take those away from you."

"I know. But she was only twenty, her life was only beginning. She didn't even get a chance at life. It's not fair. Why her?"

"Why anyone? We'll never have all the answers. We'll never understand." Sheila replied calmly.

"I never imagined it would be the last time I would see her when I dropped her off at the airport that morning." Ava said, through a fresh batch of tears.

"Oh Ava, I don't know what to say. She was some girl. You should be extremely proud of her." replied Sheila, lost in her own thoughts and memories.

Ava sat there shell-shocked staring in to space. Unable to focus her mind, she just could not process the news that her little girl was gone. How much more could she take? She retreated in to her own little world, her mind a whirlpool of thoughts. Spinning. Racing. Seeing this was the way her friend was going to stay, at least temporarily, Sheila went to fetch a blanket and wrapped it carefully around her friend before falling asleep herself.

CHAPTER 17

In a Dublin house, a woman sat waiting anxiously for the doorbell to ring. She was expecting a visitor and it wasn't going to be pleasant. She was wearing her finest black pants and dressy white blouse. She didn't know why, it wasn't like the incoming visitor was a stranger, far from it. She was preparing to expose her deepest vulnerabilities and speak the truth for once in her life.

She glanced over at her kitchen counter and inhaled the smell of her baking. She adored the smell of freshly cooked baking. Half a dozen scones now lay on the rack to cool on her island countertop. Yes, several friends of hers had encouraged her to invest in an island countertop and she could see why. It completely transformed her kitchen, brought her right up to speed with a modern twist and she loved it. For an individual such as her, who loved cooking and baking, it gave her so much space and she knew it wouldn't be lost on her.

Pamela let out a sigh of contentment. Her cafe business had gone from strength to strength ever since she had opened its doors ten years ago. Popular with the locals and offering all day breakfasts that melted in the mouth, it had been a roaring success. Without Jean, it would never have materialised. If she hadn't marched her to the doctor all those years ago to get her the help she needed, none of it would have been possible. Opening that cafe business was the best thing she had ever done. It hadn't been easy of course but with the help of a grant from Entrepreneur Ireland, it had slowly transitioned from pipe dream to her reality. For the first time in years, she had a reason to get up in the morning, she was passionate about her work and she loved every minute. So much so, it didn't feel like work. She felt alive and invigorated, and naturally it had helped her to recover from the dark cloud of depression that was always lingering.

Hearing the doorbell beat the familiar sound into the house, she leapt off her high stool to answer it. It was time.

"Noel!" she said now, opening the front door to greet him. "Come in, come in." she beckoned.

They walked into the kitchen and as soon as Noel got the sniff of baking, he was all over it.

"You were baking." he remarked.

"I was, I made some scones." she said. "Help yourself. I'll get you some tea now."

"You were always such a good baker." he said now as he devoured a scone and Pamela placed a hot mug of tea in front of him.

"So, you said you wanted to talk?" Noel said, after they were fed and watered, and nursing their second cup of tea.

"Yes, I did." Pamela began nervously. She had rehearsed this speech so many times in her head but she wasn't sure what would actually come out. "I'm trying to be a better person and I just want to properly apologise for taking Jean away from you. That wasn't fair."

Noel stopped dead in his tracks midway through his cup of tea, caught completely off guard. He had been expecting a lot of things when Pamela had reached out to him but he hadn't expected to be milling over old ground. What was done was done.

"You really hurt me." he found himself saying now.

"I know I did and I'm sorry."

"You knew how I felt about my mother abandoning us. I wanted to do the opposite and be the best Dad I could be to my children. You knew that and you still took Jean away from me."

"I wasn't thinking straight, my head wasn't in the right place."

"That's a great excuse."

"I swear! Look, I barely even knew what I was doing. I was so tormented because I wasn't bonding with Jean. Do you have any idea what that's like? Not being able to bond with my baby. I thought she hated me."

"Do you think it was easy for me?" Noel spat back. "How many times did I come home from work to find her soiled or wondering if she had been fed all day? I was patient, I asked you to get help Pamela."

"I'm sorry."

"It's no good telling me you're sorry now, it's too late." he said. "I would have supported you. I would have been there for you but you shut me out. And you cut me out of Jean's life too."

"Can you ever forgive me?" she pleaded.

"I don't know." sighed Noel. This was a heavy topic of discussion that he really hadn't been expecting. "It kills me that I wasn't part of her life. I can't pretend any different." he said honestly. He had no intention of sugar-coating it.

"I told her you abandoned her." Pamela said quickly. There. She had said it, she had told him.

"What?" Noel exploded.

"I told her you abandoned her." she repeated, cowering in her seat. "That's why she never came looking for you."

"Ah for goodness' sake, Pamela." Noel said.

"I'm sorry, I couldn't bring myself to tell her."

"So you decided to paint me as the villain and save yourself, is that it?" he was almost roaring now as he stood up.

"What was I supposed to do?"

"Tell her the truth." he said, edging closer to her now until their faces were mere inches apart. "You have totally confused her now."

"I have, haven't I?"

"She's grown up believing I wanted nothing to do with her. Now she's just supposed to accept that I never stopped caring? What is that going to do to her?"

"I'm sorry, I don't know what to say."

"This is a bloody mess." said Noel, sitting back down in his high stool and struggling to make sense of it all.

As they both retreated into their individual turmoil for a moment, Pamela went over to the kitchen counter and picked up the item she had left out earlier. Bringing it over to the high stool, she handed it to Noel.

"Here, I wanted you to have this." she said.

"What's this?" he asked, as he glanced at the heavy book-like item that was now in his hands. He felt the familiar plastic texture, relished the flower image that littered the front cover. It was thick too.

"It's a photo album. I had it made for you. It's pictures of Jean from when she was a little girl and growing up."

"Really?"

"Yes, really."

"You did this for me?"

"Yes, I figured it was the least I could do." she replied. "It won't make up for all the years you've missed, but it's a start."

"Thank you."

Together, they spent the next hour pouring over pictures of their little girl as Pamela filled him in on all of her adventures.

In spite of his earlier frustration and resentment, he was touched. It didn't make up for everything but it was a nice gesture and he appreciated the thought. It helped Noel begin the process of reacquainting himself with his estranged daughter.

EPILOGUE

Mr. Barreton, Maggie's boss, sat in his big office. He was nervous. It was so out of character for him, it almost blindsided him. Strewn all over his desk were different bits of paper - minutes of meetings, unfinished articles, and more notes than he knew what to do with. Gathering the loose parchments and collating them into a neat pile, he tucked them away in his drawer. Glancing at his watch, he saw that it was just approaching 11 o' clock. She'd be here any minute. Maggie's best friend Jean had practically harassed him to secure a meeting. After several attempts, he eventually relented. He knew a discussion about Maggie would be foremost on her mind and he was dreading it.

News had reached his ears of the turn of events in Nepal and the office had been awash with sadness since Maggie's passing. Everyone had been shocked to the core in the days that followed, finishing their work with a heavy heart. The lively banter and chat that normally permeated the office had been replaced with a stony silence. Staff had decorated her regular sitting place in the kitchenette with pictures and notes as they planned to put a scrapbook together and present it to Maggie's mother shortly. Mr. Barreton only knew her a short time in a work capacity, but already he had recognised in her a woman of exceptional quality. She was a remarkable journalist and a very talented writer with a glittering career ahead. It was an utter tragedy that her life had been so cruelly cut short.

He was just signing off on his latest article, a piece on the pros and cons of a democracy, when his assistant stuck her head in through the door.

"Jean's here to see you." she said.

"Great, send her in." he replied.

Straightening his tie and combing his fingers through his hair, Mr. Barreton prepared to meet his guest. Moments later, Jean came bounding through the door, hand outstretched. Dressed down in a matching peach capri pants and t-shirt combo, her choice of fashion reflected the roasting hot summer outside. They were in the middle of a heatwave, or should that be Indian summer, Jean wasn't sure which, and temperatures outside were scorching. A dressy pair of sandals added some much-needed glamour to the whole ensemble.

"Mr. Barreton, thanks for meeting me." she began confidently as she went to shake his hand. "I've heard lots about you."

"Why, thank you." he replied, indicating the seat in front of him. "What can I do for you?"

Observing the young woman before him, it was easy to see how she had become one of Maggie's staunchest friends. She had a presence about her that commanded your attention, a kind of inner vulnerability that was offset by a strong determined personality. Mr. Bareton found himself intrigued.

"As you know, I'm one of Maggie's closest friends." she started, getting straight down to business. She had never had much time for small-talk. "In the aftermath of everything that happened, I wrote a piece about her and I would like you to publish it for me. As a mark of respect. A eulogy of sorts I guess." she finished.

It was now early August, almost three weeks to the day since Jean had set foot back on Irish soil. Returning home had been tough. Feelings of failure at not being able to save her friend began to bubble over and she struggled to sleep. Nightmares plagued her. Each day she felt more wretched than the last becoming a vicious cycle she could not break.

The funeral had been bleak but facing Maggie's mother in the aftermath had ripped her heart clean out of her chest. Arriving in her house, they both just stared at each other for a long minute, as the weight of everything that had gone before lay between them. Both in need of moral support, they rushed to embrace each other. As they hugged, laughed and cried at various memories of their mutual hero, no words were needed. Together, they realised they would always have the memories and nothing could ever take that away from them. Importantly for Jean, Maggie's mother had given her a form of forgiveness.

"You can't blame yourself Jean." she had said kindly as they sat down at her kitchen table over a cup of tea. "It was not your fault. You did everything you could."

"I just hate it so much. I hate that I lived and she didn't." confided Jean. "I feel so guilty all the time."

"Don't be so hard on yourself, you're too young to be living with that kind of guilt." she said gently.

"I should have brought Maggie with me the first time I escaped." she protested.

"You did the right thing Jean, you really did." Ava had persuaded her.

"Did I? Maybe I *was* selfish." she said now. "How could I leave without her, my best friend?"

"Jean, you have to let this go. You can't keep blaming yourself forever."

"I just wish I hadn't left her there. But there was a man chasing me so I couldn't…" she finished, her voice trailing off as she succumbed to yet more tears.

"You couldn't have done anything more and for that I will always say, thank you." Ava said with sincerity.

"I really thought I was doing the right thing, you know." Jean said, through her sniffles. "Going to find the police. I thought they would help me. I knew I'd never be able to save her on my own."

"Of course you did. Anyone would."

"We were just two girls by ourselves, we wouldn't have stood a chance in that place. They had guns and everything."

"There was no way you could have fought them and you know that."

"Yeah." she cried, as the tears started to come again. "It was too late for Maggie. And the worst part is, she was alive when I was brought back in. But I couldn't get to her."

"It's okay, it's okay." said Maggie's mother, hugging her again.

"By the time I got to her she had been sold to the Sheikh and given a lethal dose of heroin."

"Jean." said Maggie's mother, looking her directly in the eye. "You need to forgive yourself. You did nothing wrong. It's those buggers who did this to her need to feel guilty, not you."

The empathy and forgiveness that Maggie's mother expressed had helped her enormously. Although in one way, Jean would have preferred her to be furious with lashings of curse words ricocheting off the rooftop, she needed to hear that she didn't blame her in any way. She had been ravished with such inner turmoil and guilt, she hadn't been able to let go of it until she heard those words. It had been very therapeutic for both of them.

She had also had the stress of establishing a relationship with her father to contend with. She had lived her whole life believing her father wanted nothing to do with her, believing he had abandoned her. Now she was supposed to form some kind of relationship with him from the ashes? Did she call him Dad? It didn't work like that. To find out the whole thing had been a lie forged on her mother's deceit had been very painful. She had felt robbed of her childhood and she was angry with her mother. She was angry at her father too for not trying harder. She hadn't been on speaking terms with either of them for days as she tried to figure out which one was worse. She was so confused. She missed Maggie now more than ever as she tried to rectify the torn mess her life had become. She would have known what to do. Typical of her to disappear in a crisis.

Eventually, satisfied that she had at least subjected Noel to a few days of torture she relented and agreed to meet him. For their first official meeting, they arranged to meet in a local coffee shop. As she waited for him, she couldn't stop the nerves flowing. Would they get on? Would he like her? Obviously, they had chatted away amicably over in Nepal, but that wasn't reality. They had been blown up into a bubble of tragedy and disaster and were holding each other together. She was glad to have him back in her life though, even if it was a case of too little, too late.

The door opened as Noel walked in and she waved over at him to signal her position. He looked every bit as apprehensive as she felt. As he walked over and took a seat, she found herself responding to him. Regardless of the anger she felt, he would always be the man that travelled halfway across the world to rescue her in her hour of need. She could never stay angry at him for too long.

"How are you?" Noel said now, unsure of what kind of reception he might get.

"I'm alright." she replied. "You?"

"I'm okay." Noel smiled.

It was a little stiff and awkward for them now. Coming back to face reality threw them a fresh curveball and a new set of challenges. How were they going to make this relationship work?

'Noel, look I'm sorry. It's just really hard for me. Mam always said you walked out on us and I believed her,' she said eventually, cutting to the chase. They had exchanged enough pleasantries to last them a lifetime.

"I know." he replied with a sigh.

"As far as I'm concerned, I grew up without a father."

"Of course. And I'm sorry." he said with a heavy heart and he meant it.

He had been expecting this. It was inevitable they would have to have this conversation. Like the elephant in the room parading around them, it needed to be addressed. They couldn't move forward until they discussed the issues of the past and it was only fair to Jean.

"Mom told me the truth." ventured Jean. "You never left?"

"No, I didn't." he said, more vehemently than he had intended. "I came home one day to find you and your mother were gone. You were only a toddler."

"Why do you think she left?"

"I don't know. It wasn't easy on your mother either. She did have a terrible time with postnatal depression. And I should have tried harder to get her the help she needed. But she refused point blank to admit there was anything wrong." he said.

"It's alright, I know what she's like." Jean replied calmly, before pausing for a few moments. "Only, I don't think it was postnatal depression Dad. She suffered from full-blown-depression. I was just the catalyst that brought it on. I finally made her seek professional help when I was twelve."

"Really, she never told me that. What happened then? What did they say to her?"

"She was diagnosed with Clinical Depression and started on anti-depressants."

"I can't believe she never told me that." he said, slightly annoyed now. "All the time I've spent with her in the last few days."

"She probably will tell you in her own time. I think she just wanted us to have a proper chat first."

"And she never told you exactly what happened that time?"

"No." replied Jean.

"Okay, what you've got to understand is, I'd been trying to contact Pamela every day for two years. Two years." he repeated. "She kept ignoring my calls, texts, everything. Eventually, I had to give up and realise she wasn't going to relent."

"I know." said Jean. She could see he was getting flustered now as they talked this over. Pamela could really have saved a lot of heartache on both sides if she had just told the truth.

"I could have gone to social services I suppose but what courtroom would side with the father?" he continued.

Reaching across the table she put her hand on his.

"Noel, really, it's alright. You don't have to explain."

"I loved her." he said, tears brimming the surface of his eyes. "I really wanted us to be a family. It's the greatest regret of my life not being a father to you. You have no idea how badly I wanted to be there. It nearly killed me."

"It's okay. I understand why you did what you did."

"I can't believe she never told you what really happened. She led you to believe that you weren't wanted, that I abandoned you. What must that have done to you?" he said in despair.

"I can't pretend it was easy. But I was loved, I had a good life. And Maggie was like a sister to me. I did okay."

"All I can say is, I'm sorry."

"Look, it's just going to take some time to get used to this, that's all. But I'm looking forward to getting to know you Mr. Brady." she said more cheerfully now. "Get ready, because you're in for one hell of a bumpy ride."

"Do you not think I've learned that already?" he said with a cheeky smirk and a smile.

They had left the coffee shop with promises to meet again amidst a flurry of hugs and kisses. Noel had of course told her about his wife Michelle, his two children and Jean had been delighted to learn that she had gained two half siblings. She was looking forward to meeting them when the time was right.

It was funny, she had vowed she would never speak to her father ever again and if the circumstances had been any different, she probably wouldn't have. Exposed in all her vulnerability on that miserable terrain of land, she had needed him and her resolve had waned. It was going to be a long process to bridge the gap of all the years missed but they had each other now. They had the present and she was confident they would get there in time.

Now, as she sat in the chair facing Mr. Barreton, she knew exactly what she needed to do. She handed the article to Mr. Barreton. It felt like a fitting tribute to publish Maggie's eulogy with the newspaper that she had worked for, that she loved and with staff that had shown her such kindness. It felt right. Taking a sip of water from the desk, she sat back in her chair as she waited.

Of course, this wasn't the only achievement since coming home. Jean had been so consumed with guilt over not being able to save Maggie, something she was really struggling with. But when she researched support charities for trafficked women, all she found were supports for women trafficked in to Ireland, not women who had been trafficked abroad. Their case was so unique it seemed it didn't merit support and Jean had never felt more alone. It really stung. So, in her typical proactive style she decided to do something about it. Writing Maggie's eulogy was the easy part.

First, Jean wrote a detailed account of her experiences and posted it on facebook, naming and shaming the Volunteer Camp that had organised their trip. She knew it would likely bring them into disrepute but Jean had no qualms about that. The Volunteer Camp had taken their money and hadn't bothered to vet their workers ultimately costing Maggie her life. Next, she contacted every single Irish newspaper that she could think of. Naturally, they refused to name the Volunteer Camp but all the details of her ordeal were there in print.

The response to her article was overwhelming. Not only did she receive thousands of messages of support and condolences, but also Irish women were reaching out to her to share their experiences. In response to this, Jean, together with Maggie's mother had decided to establish the Maggie Adams Foundation in honour of a beloved daughter and best friend. This would mean that Irish women trafficked abroad would get the specific support they needed. They were still in the throes of officially registering the foundation, putting a board together and enlisting their patrons. But the good news was because Jean had gone public with her story, there was plenty of support forthcoming. It was Jean's dearest hope that they could lobby for Volunteer Organisations like theirs to employ more stringent safeguarding procedures so events like this could never happen again. If only Raoul had been properly investigated, Maggie might still be alive.

Dearest Maggie,

Many years ago, a friendship was born between you and I. Inseparable almost from birth, we guided each other through childhood into our teens. As we blossomed into two teenage girls both going through our share of pain, we bonded doing the regular things that teenagers do and grew into bosom buddies.

When your father died, I could see you were so sad. I could see that you were in dire need of a compassionate friend and so I tried to be there for you. I know what you're thinking – who would have thought shallow Jean, who lives in her own cocoon of make-up, fashion and boys would ever have concern for anyone else? You probably wondered why I stuck around after your father died. To all intents and purposes, I wasn't that kind of friend. But the truth is, I saw a lot of myself in you. You were grieving the loss of your father. I was grieving the loss of a father I thought had abandoned me years before. But the difference was you weren't afraid to show your pain. You never shied away from confronting it head on. I did. Oh, I wore my mask every single day but inside I was just that hurt little girl. I admire you Maggie because you were brave. I wasn't confident. I was just a scheming little coward.

Which is why it is so difficult for me to write this article in your place. It should have been you that lived Maggie, the world was a much better place with you in it. When we decided to travel to Nepal, or when you bullied me into it rather, it was to be the ultimate adventure of a lifetime. I can still remember those jitters of excitement as the plane took off from Dublin airport that morning. We thought it was to be the best six weeks of our young lives. Unfortunately, it didn't quite turn out that way.

Discovering your lifeless body will forever be the most harrowing ordeal of my existence. It was impossible to believe it was the face of death. Death! So young! I just couldn't understand it. You had so much living to do, so much you were going to achieve, such ambition. The greatest tragedy of all is that you were robbed of all that for some careless infusion of heroin.

Why did they do this to you Maggie? Why! Why! Why! I keep asking myself the same question and reconstructing the chain of events until my head hurts. It's so unfair.

I grieve now, not only for your death but for all the things left unsaid. I should have constantly told you how much you were appreciated, how much I valued our friendship and more. Hindsight is a wonderful thing, given only in retrospect.

But I can't grieve forever Maggie and I know that you wouldn't want me to. I know you would demand that I keep living my life without you. It's so hard but I know I must.

As I close the chapter on this book of memories, please know that you were like a sister to me. Your kind caring ways were infectious and your zest for life infiltrated all those around you. You embodied what it really means to be a friend and I know that my life will forever be marked with a huge void. A void that should be filled by you.

My friend, my comrade, it pains me that you will not walk with me through life. Every memory I make from here on in will be stained with your absence. But I know you will be with me every step of the way.

I will never forget you, never forget the memories we shared or the achievements won.

Miss you now and always.

Rest in Peace Sweet Girl,

Jean.

When Mr. Barreton did eventually speak, he choked on his words.

"We'll definitely be publishing it. That would be a privilege. It's beautiful." he said as he reached for a tissue. It was then she knew it was a powerful read. It was testament to the impact Maggie had had on Mr. Barreton. The impact she had on everyone around her. Maggie would be so proud. As she walked out of the office, Jean had a smile on her face. Maggie hadn't left her. She was still around, still protecting her. She could sense it. Even in her death, she couldn't get rid of her. She should have known.

Life would be okay as long as she stuck around, Jean thought, as she got into the lift and the doors closed after her.

THE END

AUTHOR'S NOTE

- Sexual exploitation continues to be the main reason for human trafficking in Nepal with three out of every four women trafficked for this purpose.
- In most cases, parents or relatives are involved, directly or indirectly.
- Up to 10,000 women and children are trafficked between Nepal and India every year.
- After the 2015 Earthquake, incidences of trafficking and prostitution went up.
- Sometimes, victims are hidden right in front of us, disguised in places such as construction sites, restaurants, elder care centres, nail salons, agricultural fields and hotels.
- According to recent reports, the Nepali government is still not doing enough to prevent human trafficking.
- Nepal has inconsistently implemented 'anti-trafficking' laws, the Trafficking in Persons Report 2016 found, and continues to have a narrow definition of human trafficking.
- The Governments laws do not criminalise all forms of labour trafficking and sex trafficking.
- Prosecutions and convictions of traffickers remains low. Only a few hundred cases make it to the courts every year.
- According to the Human Rights Commission, China and South Korea have emerged as new

trafficking destinations in addition to India and the Middle East.
- EU Statistics: More than 14,000 trafficking victims registered for 2017/2018.
- Half were from outside the EU

If you have been affected by any of the stories featured in this book, please know that help is available.

Ruhama https://www.ruhama.ie/

Doras https://doras.org/

National Women's Council of Ireland https://www.nwci.ie/

The Immigrant Council of Ireland https://www.immigrantcouncil.ie/

The events relating to Maggie Adams are loosely based on Aer Lingus Flight EI164 in 1981. This flight took off from Dublin Airport bound for London. However, five minutes before the plane was due to land, the hijacker, Lawrence James Downey doused himself in petrol, stormed the cockpit and demanded that the plane carry on to Le Touquet – Cote d'Opale airport in France. There were 113 passengers and crew on board. They all survived.

ABOUT THE AUTHOR

While I have been writing for many years, this is my first completed novel. My other work includes a number of short stories, poems, and feature articles. Alternatively, I can be found singing in a gospel choir or participating in amateur dramatics. I find my inspiration from all walks of life, from the old man sitting alone in the pub, large gatherings of people in Croke Park on match day to families spending time together in the park. I currently live in Dublin with my husband.

ACKNOWLEDGEMENTS

To my family and friends for all your continued love and support. You know who you are.

To those who have believed in my writing for a number of years now, thank you.

To Orla Kelly, for encouraging me to escape out of my cage and emerge on the outside. This was one risk so worth taking.

To my beloved parents…..the three musketeers will forever remain intact!

Finally, to my long-suffering husband who supports me through the highs and lows of life. You're my forever and I love you to bits!

If you are reading this, thank you for taking the time to read my work.

PLEASE REVIEW

Dear Reader,

Thank you for taking the time to read my book. If you enjoyed it, I'd really appreciate if you'd tell others about it, and if you could leave a review in Goodreads or anywhere online – that would be great.

Thank you,

Triona

9 781915 502490